What did I really expect? To say goodbye with a little dignity, to close a chapter in my fantasy life. This is what I would have told my sometime lover, Em, if she had cared, but the truth was I hadn't decided. I wanted everything and nothing. I wanted to go back in time for a little while, to meet Rosey again for the first time knowing what I knew now. I wanted to know what it would have been like if I'd said yes to her that night ten years before.

I looked at myself in the mirror in the faded dirty hall on the way to her rented room, making sure my face was perfect even though my throat felt like I'd been drinking stomach acid. It didn't help my digestion when Rosey answered the door without a robe like she was expecting someone else. She was wearing black cotton bikini panties with the name of a men's brief manufacturer stitched around the waistband. Her breasts were still full and high and the nipples were pushing against the lace of her thin black brassiere while I was looking down stupidly at the floor, at the walls, anywhere but at her body.

My face was burning up. "I don't have any clothes on," I said when I meant to say nothing. "I mean you don't have any clothes on," I said.

"Jesus, Virginia." Rosalee laughed.

LONG GOODBYES

A VIRGINIA KELLY MYSTERY

NIKKI BAKER

The Naiad Press, Inc.
1993

Printed in the United States of America on acid-free paper
First Edition

Edited by Katherine V. Forrest
Cover design by Pat Tong and Bonnie Liss
   (Phoenix Graphics)
Typeset by Sandi Stancil

Library of Congress Cataloging-in-Publication Data

Baker, Nikki, 1962–
   Long goodbyes : A Virginia Kelly mystery / by Nikki Baker.
      p.   cm.
   ISBN 1-56280-042-6 (paper)
   1. Kelly, Virginia (Fictitious character)—Fiction.   2. Women
detectives—United States—Fiction.   3. Lesbians—United
States—Fiction.   I. Title.
PS3552.A4327L65   1993
813'.54—dc20
                                                    93-24908
                                                        CIP

*For Lynn S., Jackie D., and a
small offering in memory of M. R. H.*

Acknowledgments

Thanks to V. A. Brownworth, J. Redding and K. V. Forrest.

Disclaimer

When I grew up, I put away childish things. Now I begin to see through a glass darkly; but one day I shall see face to face. Now, I only know in part, but then shall I know even as I am known.

I Corinthians.

In the end it came down to damage control, you understand. Her or me. It came down to her vision of me as some kind of predatory monster opposed to my sense of humanity.

Afterwards, I held my hands up to my face and turned them over. They were the same, of course — human hands, but I looked at them for a long time, standing over her with my legs set apart and her body on the floor between them. My hands looked to me as if they belonged to someone else. Someone capable of violence and I hadn't really meant to hurt her — at least not much, but the scarf was twisted around her neck and then it was all knotted up in my hands. She was really the one who had meant to hurt me for something that was, just like her body *lying there on the floor by the sofa, so much dirty water under the bridge. The scarf was caught around her neck and I was pulling it and pressing her windpipe with my thumbs. Her eyes were wide and open and her tongue was reaching out from between her teeth as if it were a fat red snail sending its foot from inside its shell and I could smell the cologne rising up from her neck like dark sweet smoke.*

She seemed to drop slowly when I opened my hands as if she were floating and then suddenly there was a dull thud like the sound of a dampened drum when her head hit the floor. The light from the lamp by the couch, made a halo shadow of some dark angel around her head and as I looked at my hands, the skin of my knuckles was chapped and cracked from holding on to the wool.

When I took the scarf away, I could still see the marks it had left around her neck. The friction from the wool scarf had made a ring around her throat like a red choker necklace and there were two thumb marks at the center of her throat coming up into ugly bruises. Her body looked smaller, standing where I was, above it, and more fragile, less threatening. The blood vessels in her eyes were broken and the color had drained out of her face but her skin could have still passed for seventeen years old, no lines, no marks except of course at the neck. Her face was smooth and sweet as cream. Her hair was still as blonde as when she was a girl.

I drew the front curtains and put the scarf in the pocket of her coat, took her hands and pulled her across the carpet towards the front door. I could have tried to carry her. I did try, but her body was heavy and awkward like a big sack of potatoes, flopping over my shoulder. Her arms and legs hung limp against my back and I couldn't bear to feel her dead body cooling, next to mine. So, I pulled her by the wrists across the entry hall. Then out the front door to her car. The heels of her shoes made a grating sound against the wood and rumpled up the rugs and she shed her hair in a trail out to the porch as she went. Every few feet her head and neck buckled up, then gave, buckled up then gave as I dragged her along. The chain of her necklace must have broken then. I put it all in the trunk: her body, her coat, her gloves, her purse, her airline ticket and drove the car out into the woods. I didn't expect anyone would miss her for a week — maybe two, and with any luck no one would find the car until spring. All that was left after that was to vacuum, and rest and reflect on her passing over a nice glass of red wine.

I

I remembered it in the vaguely disjointed way you recall the events of a bad dream, in grainy pictures and symbols that meant nothing at the time and everything in retrospect. Rosalee's room was close and dark. It held the faintly sweet smell of shut up places and the gritty pile carpet was a color that had effectively crossed fresh baby puke with old rust. Through the space between the drapes, a stream of light lit up the month-old, year-old dust that was suspended in the stagnant air.

My sense of the place was that its cleaning ran to perfunctory, squeezed in between tenancies so as not to dampen the fortunes of a room that rented by the hour, a room badly in need of a paint job, whose walls had been changed from white to dingy grey over the years by cigarettes shared in the countless moments of animal afterglow such a room must have seen.

The Johnny Appleseed was the only motel within twenty-five miles of the town of Blue River, making it a popular favorite on high school prom nights. I was there ten years later, living out my own little high school fantasy, ten years too late with my face in Rosalee Paschen's hips. She was the closest thing I had to a high school sweetheart. I was there in that seedy room listening to her husky breath and the way it caught when I hit the right place with my tongue. She would gasp then as if she'd had a single lonely hiccup. But if I hadn't known better, when her breath was even, I might have thought that she was asleep on my face. What was worse, the minimum of sound and movement left me with the sinking feeling that she might not be having a very good time for all of my efforts. That was hard to take when I had been dreaming for years now of how I would lay in her arms after such an event and listen to her tell me that she always loved me. Of course, by then I was beginning to accept my situation for what it was.

Years before, when I was passing for something approximating straight, I'd fucked my neighbor Jake Holmes on a kind of a lark. Some girl I had recently thought I'd loved, hadn't thought to love me back and Jake had been nursing a well-timed, long-lived crush on me. So, I'd taken out my frustrations in the messy Chicago studio apartment he rented down the hall from mine. Not that Jake had been an unwilling whipping boy, shouting pornographic words of encouragement as I'd straddled him on the floor near his Soloflex weight machine. Not that the sex hadn't been very pleasant, but I would rather have had a little happily-ever-after to go along with it. I would rather have had the girl. And as nice as Jake was, it wasn't something that I could easily get past. So, I'd felt like shit, if somewhat more relaxed, when I went off to clean myself up in his tiny mildewed bathroom. I chalked that afternoon up to experience, put it in the book as an impromptu matter of convenience for me who couldn't keep a girlfriend, and for Jake who didn't have a girlfriend, a small accommodation in a more footloose era before AIDS could be imagined as a heterosexual disease. Given this, the fight Jake started when I came back into the living room seemed to come from nowhere.

Jake was pulling up his boxers and he kept his

back to me while he asked if I'd ever made love to a really beautiful woman. "I mean a girl that looked like a model," he said.

The girl who'd recently broken my heart was five-foot nine inches tall, and played women's lacrosse, but Jake hadn't specified exactly what kind of model he meant. So, I told him I had and he shook his head in a silence I chose then to construe as speechless admiration, but recognize now as something more akin to disgust. Then he faced me and buttoned up his shirt.

"So, why do you ask?" I was waiting for the compliment I thought I deserved because, after the lacrosse player, my ego needed it.

I watched Jake fluff up his hair where our roll on the floor had flattened it down, and waited some more while he put his shirt back in his pants as kind of an afterthought. "No reason," he said. "It's just that I never have. That's all, and I guess I'm jealous."

"Thanks." His answer made me angry. "So what do you call me, then?"

He was angry too. He said, "So, what, do you call that, Virginia? Making *love*?"

What I would later call this remark was: the end of our friendship. There were hard feelings after that though I couldn't say from what exactly as it was my understanding, given to me as advice from my father, that men were unemotional about sex and neckties among other things. It took years, until that afternoon at the Johnny Appleseed for me to figure out that the slight Jake had given my looks was tit for tat.

That afternoon while Rosalee rocked back and

forth against my face, I was getting to know payback; and it was a bitch that she could look past the grand significance of this fantasy event for me in search of nothing more intimate than the proper rhythm, the most effective speed. Her legs were splayed and twitching around my ears and the shadows on the ceiling made old spent ghosts. They seemed to whisper their suggestions in the rattling of the wind against the window panes, things that I imagined they themselves might have liked. And I could hear myself whispering above their jumbled voices, "Please tell me what you want," promising sadly, "Just tell me and I'll do anything."

But for as much as I would have liked to move mountains, I couldn't give Rosey whatever it was that she was looking for that afternoon. I kept trying anyway until all the light had spilled through the hole between the drapes, and the room had faded out to black and into heavy echoes of long past lovers.

Half-awake in the quiet I was sure I could hear her laughing at me from someplace far away. It had, all of it, been something short of my imagined champagne and roses, and afterwards the best Rosalee had been able to manage was a look of absent, sleepy pity. It raised the goose bumps on my arms like a cold October rain and I couldn't get warm again. So, I shook myself to sleep watching Rosey's back on the opposite side of the lumpy double bed and fighting tears.

When I woke up a couple of hours later, my contact lenses were stuck in my eyes and the crust on my corneas was so thick I could barely read the digital clock in the TV. But I thought it said 8:00

pm. Rosey was gone and if it weren't for the cheap room I hadn't rented and the key she'd left on the short scarred dresser by the television set, I'd have written off our afternoon as just another nostalgic little fantasy about first love and missed opportunity. But the institutional-style white cotton sheets still smelled like her cologne; and under them, the tired old mattress was sagging in the place where she'd slept. Outside the cars rolled past on a wet road and I could hear the sleet beginning to beat against the window.

My jeans were on the floor where I'd dropped them hours earlier. So, I pulled them up over my hips and put my dirty underwear in the pocket of my coat. If I'd had a million dollars in that pocket, I would have given it all for a shower anywhere but in that seedy little room. It didn't help that on my way out the front desk clerk leered at me as if I were some kind of low-budget working girl. He told me that my "friend" had paid the bill; and I wondered how much of our afternoon he had managed to overhear through the tissue paper walls or to watch through the crack in the filthy curtains.

II

Before that visit to the Johnny Appleseed — about a week before I was due home for my ten-year high school reunion — I'd gotten a letter, which I could tell was from my mother. I recognized the postmark and the handwriting on the front. My mother claimed she was keeping alive the old-fashioned habit of written correspondence. What I suspected really was an aversion to the telephone. A phone call required dialogue. Questions and answers about lovers and friends and weekend activities when neither my mother nor my father wanted confirmation as to the particulars of my life. My sister Adeline who was straight got the phone calls, but my mother wrote to me, sometimes as much as once a week, newsy cheerful letters that asked nothing and didn't really require answers. Inside this one was a recipe for molasses cookies, the address and phone number of a young man who'd recently moved to Chicago, and a clipping from the *Blue River Reporter* with a yellow post-it note stuck to the headline. Beside the young man's address and phone number my mother had written: "In case you need some new friends." On the post-it were the words: "Thought you'd like to know . . ." in black felt-tipped pen and perfect, looping script. Above the headline, the date of the article was August 14, 1992 and the clipping said:

LOCAL WOMAN DROWNED AT SUMMER HOME

The body of Margaret Arkin, longtime Blue River resident, was found Sunday by local officials at Cedar Lake. Authorities speculate that she may have developed a muscle cramp while attempting to swim the width of the lake late Saturday.

The deceased's husband, Harry Hobart, contacted local police Saturday night when he became alarmed that his wife had not returned to their cabin after several hours. Police dragged the lake early the following morning. Mrs. Arkin is survived by her husband, Hobart, daughter Sarah, and sister Lola Wing of Indianapolis . . .

The story went on like that for a number of paragraphs describing Marge Arkin's long tenure in the community, her activity in the PTA, and her son Emery's "extended illness" some years ago, but I knew all about that, so I skimmed to the end which said, *"A memorial service will be held on October 1 . . . In lieu of flowers, the family asks that donations be made to . . ."*

There was a long list of charitable organizations that Marge must have thought were important, but I didn't finish reading them all. Instead, I folded the clipping and filed it with Emery's yellowed obituary which I kept in a dresser drawer under my bras, close to my heart.

Emery Arkin had been a soft-spoken, smooth-faced boy who wore his hair just a little too long and walked with a little too much of a swivel to be very popular in a small-town, midwestern high school. We'd grown up together casually, but had gotten tighter than a new pair of panty hose in that I'm-queer-and-so-are-you sort of way, long distance during college; and Emery had replaced Sandra Crab as my best girlfriend. He'd listened to me ramble when I was in love; and when I was dumped and pathetic I could call him up day or night to have him tell me that he'd always care.

I couldn't remember not knowing Emery. But when he died, it was weeks before I could cry for

11

him. His passing, at twenty-five, seemed to me as inconceivable as my own. I didn't have much more than a speaking acquaintance with his mother, Marge, but her death seemed almost as sad because it made me grieve for Emery all over again.

Marge Arkin had been a red-headed pillar of a woman with a ballsy social demeanor and a two-pack-a-day habit she wasn't too interested in breaking. Emery seemed to have taken after his father except in his fondness for good-looking men — that I was sure he'd gotten from Marge.

His father had run off years ago when Emery and I were about fourteen and his sister Sarah was only months old. Emery didn't like to say much about it. So, I didn't ask. But Emery and his mother got along all right. Marge worked long hours as a paralegal for a Columbus law firm. She had her boyfriends, he had his, and Emery kept the house for his mother and little sister after school.

As much as I knew of it, Marge's life seemed perfectly self-contained and ordered, so it was surprising when my mother's weekly clipping service announced Marge had married Harry Hobart, our old English teacher, shortly after Emery died. Attraction between them seemed at best improbable except that they were both objectively attractive people. I thought, now, maybe Emery's mortality had shaken Marge too, and maybe I wasn't the only one who didn't relish the prospect of growing old alone. When I was sixteen, Harry Hobart had been a brand new twenty-something-year-old teacher. That made him about fifteen years Marge Arkin's junior; and at the time their marriage seemed to me like a refreshing twist on the old cliche.

I hadn't sent a card, but Harry Hobart was the kind of good-guy teacher who could be depended upon to show up at ten-year reunions all ready to say how well everyone had turned out. I imagined I would have a chance there to tell Hobart how sorry I was about Marge.

And I expected, of course, that the list of reunion attendees would also include Rosalee Paschen. She was the subject to which my mind wandered when I was depressed about Em and examining my what-ifs: what would my life be like if we'd tried a little harder; if I'd loved Em a little more; if I'd had the guts to have said yes to Rosey Paschen. I didn't know the answers but I was counting with all of my fingers and toes on seeing Rosalee again.

I knew for a fact Rosey would be at the reunion because she'd called out of the blue to tell me about it one evening months back at the beginning of September. I was pretty well toasted and there was a party going on in the other room. More correctly, there was a party going on in all the rooms of my apartment except for my bedroom where I'd hidden the phone so I wouldn't end up with calls to Tahiti courtesy of my drunken guests. Had the phone not rung, there might have been a kind of a party in my bedroom as well. But as it was, the phone call was auspicious; it saved me from myself.

I sent some woman whose name I've forgotten back out into the crowd, shut the door and sat down in the pile of coats on my bed trying to make heads or tails of the voice inside the phone. It was saying: "Ginny, I need to talk to you about that night at Johnson's farm." The popping and crackling on the line made figuring out who it was on the other end kind of a challenge.

That night I wasn't much up for challenges, but the connection sounded like long distance — that or a public pay phone. And I thought for sure it was a woman's voice, the husky kind that could have made a good living selling fantasy sex on 1-900 numbers. That meant it was either for real, or it was a prank courtesy of my gal pal Naomi Wolf who was out of town and liked those kinds of jokes.

The thing was, I remembered the night at Johnson's farm and maybe the voice — although less vividly. It was the night I'd almost been seduced for the first time and I concluded that whoever belonged to the voice was somehow connected. That meant the connection had to be pretty ancient romantic history. That also meant the voice had to be Rosalee Paschen's. But it had been a pretty good party and that train of logic took some time to pull together — too long.

"Don't you remember me, Virginia?" she'd asked as if she might have been hurt if I hadn't.

"Sure," I said. "Of course, I do."

That made her laugh. It was a short little snorting sound. "Well, it's nice to know you're still the same consummate bullshitter you always were. That's good because consistency is what I need in my life right now. It's Rosey," she said, "in case you really didn't know."

She didn't give a last name; but then, she didn't have to. If it was really the Rosalee Paschen I knew, then the butterflies flapping at the sides of my gut were right on time. I swallowed some more of my beer to see if I could drown them.

The Rosalee Paschen I remembered was big, blonde and athletic with the emphasis on athletic. She'd had a sweetly wicked smile she'd show me sometimes from across the desk in three o'clock study hall; and underneath her layers of sweat pants and crew socks, when I watched her in the showers after gym, she'd had soft curves and full breasts and a general quality that suggested she might just break my heart. It was a combination I've always found particularly engaging, the way that moths are so especially fond of porch lights.

A call from Rosey was a pleasant surprise. "Where exactly are you?" I said. "There's a party here, but I could leave."

"No, but I need to talk to you." She was breathing husky breaths into my ear over the phone.

I was kind of enjoying it; and I put my beer down on the dresser so I could give her my undivided attention. "Fine," I said. "Let's talk. Where are you?"

"Not here. But we'll talk at the reunion in December, okay?" She sounded as if her request was urgent which I thought was strange coming from a woman I hadn't spoken to in ten years. She meant our ten-year high school reunion — the one I'd been hoping to miss even though it was scheduled the weekend before Christmas which fell on a Tuesday that year. High school was a time I wanted to forget, a dark tunnel beginning in puberty and ending in young adulthood, a long ugly hormonal tantrum. But I was wondering what could be hot enough to make Rosey Paschen call me up after so many years, and cool enough that it could keep for another couple of months. No good answers came to mind.

"We're talking now," I said.

"This isn't something to discuss over the phone." She was breathing hard again and I hoped she would continue. "Look, are you coming, Virginia, because it's important. If you ever cared about me you'll come."

Her voice broke slightly and it gave the invitation a special kind of charm I would have liked to explore further. But someone was banging on my bedroom door.

I said, "Why don't you give me your number, and I'll call you back. We can talk about it then, all right?" I cupped my hand over the receiver, shouting that this wasn't the bathroom. Then the pounding stopped and footsteps trotted down the hall.

Rosey said, "Listen, Virginia, why don't you just make it easy and be there." Her voice had developed a pushy edge that wasn't doing much for me at all. "I need you to be there."

"Wait," I said. But she'd already hung up on me. I was put off enough to forget the whole thing, until I remembered that the last time I'd ignored a request like that, it was something I'd lived to regret.

Five years before, in the spring when I thought Emery Arkin was still in sunny California, he had called me to tell me he wasn't.

"I'm living at home with Marge." He had quit his job as a landscape architect, given up his house in Irvine and was working for the State Park Service back in Blue River at minimum wage. He had traded in his two-seater sports car for a Japanese-made truck and he'd bought a dog. He was going to get a motorcycle to go with the leather jacket he liked to wear. He was growing his hair. He was changing his life. "Come back and see me, okay?" Emery said. "I've missed you, Ginny."

I'd missed him too. But I'd had a lot of things going then. I still had fantasies of a partnership at Whytebread and Greese. I was buying my condo. They were things that seemed important at the time. Going home was always difficult and I tried not to do it more than once a year.

It was several months later when Emery called again saying, "Look, I haven't seen you in ages, Virginia, and we need to talk."

But I had met my then-girlfriend, Emily, the previous week and thought I was building myself a life. I thought Emery was something that could wait. Except he didn't call again and in a couple more months my mother sent one of her clippings from the *Blue River Reporter* announcing his memorial service.

I couldn't attend. I'd used up all my vacation time and I was way too far back in the corporate closet to explain to the human resources department why I ought to get personal leave because a gay white man felt as close to me as blood relations. So, I sent a note to Marge instead, a short one because it didn't seem like there was very much to say; and what there was, I didn't know that I could put into words.

Time passes and I hadn't thought of Emery for much longer than it took to get misty-eyed, and then to put him out of my mind. Remembering was just too sad and I felt too sorry and selfish for not making the time to see him before he died. Wherever he was, I didn't think he'd forgiven me for it. Sometimes in Chicago when my phone would ring, I'd expect to hear his voice bawling me out, and Emery seemed to haunt the streets of Blue River when I went back home. I found myself looking for him around every corner, ready to buy me a drink just like old times at the White Horse Saloon, his new red truck parked out front and his big yellow dog locked up in the cab.

Only twenty minutes down the Indiana Toll Road out of Illinois, tears were already budding up in the corners of my eyes. On a Thursday evening the week before Christmas, the stretch of asphalt was dead as downtown Toledo, Ohio, and all the way to I-80 there was nothing to look at for miles but a hunk of Gary, Indiana steel decay, bleeding smoke and rust at the horizon.

My father had come up in a town like that, made by big steel before the dirty work had been replaced by low-paying, hopeless jobs at 7-Eleven Stores and fast food restaurants. Jobs that didn't build or produce anything. They were, when I thought about it, disturbingly similar to the one I currently held in the great expanse of the financial services economy.

"The eighties are over," Andre Rutherford was saying to me from the front seat of the car. He had married my friend from high school, Sandra Crab, the ex-cheerleader, two years ago. Sandra had grown up into a suburban matron with clear pecan-colored skin, very good cheekbones, and a lot of thick brown processed hair whose maintenance must have taken up hours of her Saturday at some Michigan Avenue salon. Marriage and pregnancy had seemed to agree with her and Sandra was happier than I'd ever remembered; that made me happy too.

As for her husband, Andre — he was another matter. He and I were still dancing around each other awkwardly in conversation that was forced at best and punctuated with nervous laughter, but with Sandra, friendship was still like an easy walk. It went along for a while, stopped to rest, and started up again without losing any charm or direction. She lived just outside of Chicago, less than fifteen miles from me, but when I'd called begging a ride home to our reunion, I hadn't really talked to Sandra for a year and a half, since before things had fallen apart with my ex-girlfriend, Emily.

My car was in the shop again. My Italian car which was a work of art not made to be driven. Naomi Wolf liked to say that the car was at its best standing still in the garage as a lead-in for a joke whose punch-line described hell as a place where all the mechanics are Italian, the cooks are English, and the waiters are French.

Sandra had offered the ride and it was easy enough to fall back into old familiarities as if my car trouble was just a convenient excuse to renew our friendship. But it still hung between us that I hadn't made the effort I should have to get to know her husband and that I'd exited their wedding reception before the open bar had closed on the excuse that Em was waiting at home. As it was, my first impressions of Andre had to do with the bladder infection he'd given Sandra early in their

19

relationship. It didn't help things that Sandra, who knew I was gay, and Sandra had given me some unmemorable last-minute excuse as to why I wasn't asked to be a bridesmaid.

So, Sandra and I had made a tacit agreement for this long car ride to keep the conversation polite and bland with emphasis on subjects where we shared complete agreement. This eliminated topics of greatest interest—namely my queerness and Sandra's decision to quit her job in computer sales in order to raise some as yet undetermined number of Andre's offspring. Not that I was anti-family. It was just that Andre's impending daddyhood seemed so unencumbered compared with Sandra's mommyhood (time elapsed 7½ months) which had been life-changing, Sandra confided, filled with morning sickness and nap attacks.

When she'd quit her job to raise babies, I had suspected his chauvinism was at the root of it, but I had to admit that at first glance Andre Rutherford didn't seem very much like a pig, even if I was reserving my own judgment. He was the model of a 90's man, a good catch, and Sandra bragged that he cooked dinner every other night when she was working. Andre was the sort of guy who wasn't hard to like. His looks were pleasantly sexy in a clean fingernails kind of way without being either effeminate or intimidating, and he could always manage a deep, easy laugh that sounded as if he'd never heard your joke before. When he laughed his big laugh, Andre's pencil moustache spread across his face and his little tiny ears rode up on his head as if he were trying to wiggle them.

"The good times are gone for good," Andre told

me as if it were a revelation, looking straight ahead through the windshield with his eyes on the snowy road. But he seemed well-fed enough himself. At thirty-three, a businessman's gut had already started over his belt and a beefy roll of chestnut skin was sitting up on his shirt collar like a log. From the back seat, I watched it crease and buckle when he moved his head as if the back of his neck were smiling. His wiry black hair was standing out from his head like the bristles on an expensive brush.

"Yep, the game is over." Andre's law firm, Richman and Redding, did mergers and acquisitions. Times were tough and it was news in *Crain's Chicago Business* how Richman had rescinded the offers to their summer associates. They'd canned twelve partners, and Andy, as Sandra called him, had found himself on a newly created limited-partner track that curtailed the probability of his ever becoming obscenely rich. This development alone seemed to me like a perfect reason for Sandra to continue her career, but I kept my mouth shut and agreed with Andre that things were not what they had been. In fact, Whytebread & Greese, the investment firm where I myself worked, was due for a shake-up and the stress wasn't doing anything to help what I thought might be the beginnings of an ulcer.

Andre shifted to scratch the small of his back. "The game is over. And you know, the only difference between you and me, Virginia, is that you came in at the top of the eighth inning and played right field and I got in at the bottom of the seventh, playing left." It was the kind of sports analogy I'd grown to dislike from working at Whytebread, but Andre managed to make it sound unaffected and even vaguely thoughtful. He spread his legs a little wider in the car seat and leaned his head back so the meat on his neck pressed up against the headrest. Andre said, "Well, in a couple of months the shit is really going to hit the fan and all those white boys are going to be fucked just as sure as me."

"Don't curse," Sandra said. "Not in front of the kid." She rubbed her belly and Andre looked across the seat at her as if they were on their very first date, smiling the way I'd have liked someone to be smiling at me. In love. The way I would have smiled back.

"Keep your eyes on the road, Daddy," Sandra said.

Andre laughed and I laughed too, sucked into that dopey bubble of wonder that surrounds first love and the birth of children. Somewhere along the line I'd lost track of that rush of emotional free fall in my life and I wanted it back.

Wanting to see Rosey Paschen again was the simple pedestrian logic of looking to find your keys in the last place where you'd left them. I thought maybe she was looking for something too since she'd taken the trouble to send me a follow-up note after her phone call about the reunion. I was still flattered, and flushed when I thought about it as if I'd had a little too much wine and a rich dinner.

Ten years ago Rosalee was the first in a series of blondes who had marched through my love life, the rest of them following her like a chain reaction. I'd been through eight in the past seven years — nine if you counted Joan DiMaio, but Joan was dead and that was another story, one I was trying to forget.

Rosey Paschen was the first woman to move me in ways that had now become familiar. I remembered at a slumber party once she whispered not to tell anyone while she held my sweaty hand all night in the dark. For weeks after that I couldn't think of anything else and my chest was heavy all the time.

When I'd read the little note she sent after her phone call in September, it was clear Rosey hadn't lost a bit of charm in the interim. She had written simply: "I'm still coming. Are you?" The note was signed "R" and had arrived from I didn't know where, with no return address. But somehow Mary Ellen McMann from the ten-year reunion committee had found Rosey to send an invitation. And somehow Rosey had managed to find me again with what I took to be an invitation of her own.

I still thought of her sometimes when I was alone, in the warm fuzzy way you think of nice things that have happened long ago. I'd read her short note over several times the day it came and then hidden it with Emery's clipping at the bottom of my underwear drawer as if it were a school girl's secret.

My ex-girlfriend, Emily, and I made love again for the first time in weeks one afternoon when she stopped by for her visitation with the cat, Em with off-handed surprise — and I with the tingling anticipation of being with someone else.

When we'd finished, Em lay back spread-eagle on the bed we used to share and stretched her legs. She had moved out after my affair with a crazy lawyer named Susan Coogan, but we'd arrived at an understanding, fallen into an on-again-off-again routine that served her needs as well as mine. I thought of it as progress, but Em's therapist referred to our arrangement as "co-dependency."

Em groaned, and rolled over on her side to the far edge of my futon mattress. Then she looked discreetly at the alarm clock beside the bed and must have decided she owed me conversation.

"Do you want to talk?" she asked as if it were a chore. "A penny for your thoughts."

But I was thinking of Rosalee and didn't want to share. "I'm too tired," I said.

Two years ago, Em would have cared that I could do without her company, but both of us had gone past caring. She put her tongue in my ear for old-time's sake, and rolled over again presenting me with her pale, freckled back. In a few minutes, I could hear her breathing gently through her mouth.

I listened for a while to her sleeping. Then, I put on the robe she'd given me three Christmases ago, when she said we'd always stay together, and went to sit in the living room with my cat, Sweet Potato, on my lap. Sweet Potato and I had a beer and I scratched between his ears the way he especially liked until morning came. It was gratifying to know that at least one of us was satisfied with our existence.

Out of Andre's car window, Indiana was nothing but open frozen fields and run-off ditches dividing a four-lane stretch of highway. He was singing tunelessly along with the radio while he drove, a song whose melody I knew from what seemed like a million years ago. But I'd forgotten the words; it felt like a requiem for a time in my life that was all used up. The car rolled past the gravel turnarounds where state troopers were waiting to make their ticket quotas, and Andre kept singing in his rumbling baritone like white noise. In the back seat, I was pretending to sleep, leaning my cheek on the frozen window glass, as a defense against human contact. In front of me, Sandra slept genuinely, with her head falling first onto the padded shoulder of Andre's tweed jacket and then rolling across her neck to rest against the passenger door, lolling back and forth. The car bumped along through the endless highway road construction; and I watched Sandra sleep, filled up with the loose-shoed well-being that pregnant women seem to have cornered. Her life was full of the hope that comes with: "Plant a tree. Write a book. Have a child," and I couldn't help wondering if there was a way that I could bottle that feeling and sell it. I would have bought some and wrapped myself in it so I could live like Sandra without worry, in the present and the future. But I was on my way back to Rosey Paschen in a kind of a family-sized Volvo time machine, back into my own past, not as it was, but colorized by all of the experiences that had come since I'd left it.

I imagined many pasts in my hometown, as many as there are individuals, as many as there are points of view. If they took up space, in the air over Blue River there would have been a huge traffic jam of individual perspectives returning, making it hard to avoid unfortunate accidents of colliding perception. As it was, I could never really say how I felt about seeing the little sign at the side of the road announcing the town limits.

III

It was eleven o'clock at night and through the big bay windows off the front porch I could see my father waiting up for me in his favorite reading chair. He looked greyer than I remembered him even six months before when he'd come through Chicago on business. His hair sat close to his head like the tight, short nap of institutional carpeting. I stared at that same hair every day in the mirror and the grey coming in at my temples, the imprint of his genes on my head. His hair, now a good deal more salt than pepper, had once been as black as my own.

In the living room window, my mother was waving in big open-handed circles, knocking on the window glass and laughing. She had kept her long thin figure through two children and menopause. But my mother's face had aged from pretty into the collection of character lines that could cause a woman to be described as "handsome." She had high yellow skin, and a full wide mouth that she liked to keep in nearly constant motion. I had inherited her mouth with maybe a little less of a tendency to run it, but people used to say most everything else about me had come from my father's side. Although as I'd gotten older I'd begun to favor my mother more and she promised that it meant I would age well. My

Mom was always happy to see company because my father was a man of short sentences.

"How's it going kid?" He walked out to the driveway to meet us in his house slippers and robe, smiling widely. My father hugged me hard and shook Andre's hand, then Sandra's. He had been a nice specimen of a man himself when he was younger, but he was dark-skinned and his courtship of my mother in the 1950s had raised some hackles on her side of the family. The intervening years had hollowed my father out like an old tree and he'd never lost the weight he'd put on twenty years ago when he quit smoking. Now, his chest caved into the paunch above his belt and his figure looked less like a Y and more like a pear.

He laid a thick black hand on my shoulder, blue at the nails, wrinkled and midwestern-winter-chapped at the knuckles. "You kids come on in and get warm. Come in and have a drink. All right?" he said.

"A short one though." Andre turned his wrist over and checked his watch, a gold and stainless number that suggested his billable hours at Richman were considerable. Then, when he thought no one was watching, he glanced over to ask for Sandra's permission with a look so sweet it almost made my teeth hurt.

She stretched, with her hands on the small of her back and an expression of self-satisfaction spread over her face that was one part baby and about three parts man. "All right. Let's have a short one."

He took her hand and squeezed it. Their pervasive coupledom made my nerves feel itchy like a bad case of poison ivy. Not that I would ever begrudge a friend any measure of happiness, but I just couldn't see how being straight, pregnant, and married to a man of the appropriate color was a license to hog it all. If somebody had been ready to pin a medal on me for staying with Em, I thought, my own unsanctioned marriage might have turned out differently.

"We'll have a short one," Sandra said. "None for me though." She made a cutting gesture in the air with her wrist and open palm. "We want this child to grow up with his full complement of brain cells."

"That's right, honey," Andre said. "Any child we make is going to be a black Einstein."

I laughed. My father laughed too, but for different reasons. "All right," he said. "Then none for her." He clapped Andre on the back like they were college chums. When he turned to me, his smile faded slowly as if he'd thought of something sad. Andre was still grinning stupidly under his big blue cashmere coat, his cream-colored scarf hanging off his beefy neck. The few minutes in the cold had turned his cheeks a cheery brick red by the time my mother came out on the porch in her house shoes.

My mother held the door open with her back while she spread her arms to hug me in the doorway. "You kids come on in." She hugged Sandra too, quickly, as Sandra passed by. "You girls look so good. You look good too, Andy. Merry Christmas." My mother had taken to wearing her coarse wiry hair short and wild. It was streaked with grey since she'd stopped trying to color it. The kinky mane stood out from her face and made her look regal and rather fierce.

My parents still lived in the split-level, brick and

siding affair where I'd grown up. For Christmas the front porch and the two-car garage were strung with blinking green and red lights and there were electric candles with yellow filament flames in the windows. Ours was a suburban neighborhood where the houses looked a lot alike except that their porches and steps might be different, or the fronts and backs might be turned around on their manicured lots. But the yards were big, and by the way most people measured success, my father was a poor boy who'd done pretty well for himself.

That night he was looking out from his porch at the enormous, plastic, negro Santa Claus he'd put in the yard like he thought so too. All down the street the houses and trees were outlined in all-weather Christmas lights flashing red and green and blue and yellow like some strange suburban landing strip.

My father held the screen door for my mother. Then he picked up my bags from the porch and dropped them in the hall by the entrance to the living room, an L-shaped space that flowed into a connected dining room and out through french doors onto a wide brick patio at the back of the house.

Our house was what might politely be described as "lived-in," and my parents' furniture was a hodgepodge of styles my mother had liked individually, but which no interior designer would ever have thought to put together in the same room. So, a walk through the place was a survey of the last thirty years of furnishing fads in twenty-two hundred square feet.

Along with the furniture she'd specifically purchased, my mother had recently taken to adopting old battered negro heirlooms from her well-remembered Kentucky childhood: orphaned end tables, cane sewing rockers, and oak plant stands whose owners had passed away. Uniformly bruised from misuse and age, they were scattered throughout the house haphazardly, a pine rocker in the entryway, a set of oak plant stands in the living room.

It seemed that, in the time it took for me to look away and back again, the house had been transformed from the house where I'd grown up (which used to be full of modern art nudes, noise, and children's finger paintings held up by refrigerator magnets in the kitchen), into a sprawling receptacle for faded memories and bad kitsch, my grandparents' house as it was when I was a child of ten. Sometime in the last few years the wall in the living room by the upright piano had grown pictures of me and my sister, my father, his parents, my mother, her aunts, and assorted other relatives (some dead), looking out through the glass with flat stern faces, in picture frames the way your lawn could be covered with mushrooms overnight when none were there the afternoon before. The room had taken on the smell of furniture polish, and almost by magic a candy dish full of salted nuts had appeared on the coffee table by the couch. A little patchwork crochet blanket I'd never seen before lay folded on the seat of my father's favorite reading chair as if two old people had gotten cold waiting up for me past their usual bedtimes.

When my folks were gone, I imagined now, I wouldn't have the heart to throw the junk out either. It was, all of it, pieces of my collective family history; and in my advancing age I was starting to believe my mother that the worn old wood and yellowed pictures could make a house feel "homey." Closing in on thirty, I was starting to notice all kinds of little bits of my parents' foibles in myself. Lately, I had started to want the term homey applied to my own living situation. I felt myself succumbing to my middle-class suburban programming: co-habitation, commitment ceremonies, slab houses, and screaming babies were looking better and better all the time.

"You know, this is the first artificial tree we've ever had," my mother was saying as she took Andre's coat. Downstairs in the rec room the frost-colored six-foot pine substitute was blinking on and off over an embarrassingly large collection of presents, and someone whose name I couldn't remember was crooning: *"Christmas is for children,"* from a badly scratched record my mother had owned for probably thirty years. She was of the opinion that there was a right and a wrong way to celebrate Christmas. The right way had to do with consistency, live trees, homecomings, bad music, and tins on tins of homemade Christmas cookies; and as my mother talked to Andre about the fake tree she sounded as if, more than anyone else, she was trying to convince herself she hadn't let her family fall afoul of the proper traditions.

"We've never had anything artificial before, but Addie isn't with us this Christmas. And besides," my mother caught Sandra by the arm and whispered, "I'm just plain sick of vacuuming up those damn needles every year." She closed the hall closet on the coats and ushered us into the living room. "I made some crudités in case you're hungry."

"What can I get for you kids?" My father rubbed his hands together gamely, but his eyes were tired.

Andre said he was having scotch.

"What you and that baby need is some cranberry juice," my mother told Sandra. Her face lit up at the word baby. "And you shouldn't let yourself get cold, honey." She squeezed Sandra's arm again and put the blanket from my father's reading chair around her shoulders.

My mother took a seat in one of the side chairs that faced the bay windows, and Sandra and Andre sat down on the couch. It was an overstuffed Bauhaus thing that my mother kept having re-upholstered as fabrics went in and out of style. Last Christmas and the one before it had been a kind of heavy green-brown tweed, but the fabric of the year was apparently a red and brown Navajo blanket-looking weave. Andre took Sandra's hand again as she laid her head on his shoulder, and I thought I might be sick. It was just a little more wholesomeness than I could stand. Either that or the couch pattern in combination with Sandra's dress was making me dizzy. She was wearing pearls and a kind of a muu muu with a baby doll waist that started just below her breasts. Its Christmasy green and gold pattern was at war with the couch.

"I need a drink," I said.

"Have some wine. It's good wine." My mother turned to me. "And go help your father put out the vegetables, Ginny."

"I need a real drink," I said.

My father rolled his eyes and shrugged. "Well, you know where we keep it," he said. "There's tonic in the refrigerator." I knew from experience that the hard stuff was on the top shelf of the hall pantry, and when I came home I liked to drink my father's Bombay Sapphire with just enough orange juice to give it some color or just enough tonic to carbonate it. Gin could generally take the sharp edges off a visit with my parents; and since Sandra and Andre had decided to pose there on the couch for a negro Norman Rockwell Christmas card, I thought I ought to have a double.

"You could make me one too, Virginia," my mother shouted from the living room, "and bring that vegetable plate," she told me. "There's dip in the refrigerator." Then, she was onto something else about babies and diapering shortcuts to Sandra in a kind of a party voice as if she were talking over loud music. Through the kitchen window I could see a skyline of suburban tract homes all across the neighborhood. Their outlines were like a child's stick drawings done in dots of red and green crayon, line pictures blinking on and off in a neon advertisement for Christmas in the Heartland.

"Have you seen what we did to the kitchen, Sandra?" my mother was saying. "I've waited twenty years for my new kitchen and I finally made him get it done for me. You've got to get men trained early. That's one mistake I made."

My father could hear her too and he stiffened up for a minute the way he always did when she made him angry. He said, "Oh, Jesus Christ, Elaine." Then he sighed, "Well, that's your mother." He opened the refrigerator, found the ice trays and put them down on the counter to break.

My father was generally an easy-going man. If he

got mad he didn't stay mad for long, and when my sister and I were kids, he never hit us. That was my mom's job. My dad believed hitting was a serious business; the only thing I'd ever seen him sweat for more than an hour was politics and my sexual orientation.

I had a feeling he'd known for a long time that I was gay, ever since he'd watched me mooning around over Rosey Paschen. Even though I'd never specifically talked to him about it, I knew from the way his jaw stiffened when family friends asked me who I was seeing that my father was smart enough to add one to itself and come up with two. It was a comfort to me that the knowledge hadn't killed him the way my mother promised me it would, but he didn't like the concept much and ignoring it was probably contributing to his grey hairs.

"Your mother's glad you came home for Christmas. So am I." He stopped breaking the ice into the trays long enough to squeeze my collarbone the way you'd scratch around a puppy's neck. His hands were cold. What he meant was: we love you, but we wish you could be someone else. We wish you could be Sandra in there with that nice black man.

"Now, I had Ginny naturally." I could hear my mom still talking in the living room like the droning sound of a fan on a hot summer night. "Black folks had natural childbirth way before all that stuff was popular."

As he listened to her, my dad's face registered a mixture of exasperation and genuine amusement that made me miss him, made me miss the time we'd spent disassociated from each other's lives over nothing, over who I chose to love.

My mother was saying, "Now Adeline was a C-section. She was a preemie." It was her canned explanation for anything my sister did, which lately was spending Christmas in Jamaica instead of here.

Months ago Addie had called to say she wouldn't be home for Christmas and it hurt my folks.

"I have that light-deprivation, winter-depression-thing. I think they call it SAD," she'd told me. "Or something like that. I've been diagnosed. So, I've just got to go to Jamaica. My doctor prescribed sun."

"So, who is he?" I asked. It was a good bet that Addie wasn't going to Jamaica alone. She ran through men just a little faster than I went through women; and I wasn't sure my parents worried any less.

"A medical doctor, Virginia," Adeline said. "A member of the AMA prescribed this treatment for my health. I wish you'd loosen up." Addie danced semi-professionally with a small jazz company in New York. But her day job was waiting tables for the business lunch crowd at a trendy leather and wood pub in Manhattan; Addie was always making friends. She was three years younger than me, four inches taller, and ten pounds lighter. But I liked her anyway.

"What are you going to tell them about not coming home?" I asked her.

"Whatever." I could imagine her raising her bony shoulders at the other end of the line. "But I've got to do what's best for me and you know, I need my sun. I'll tell you something else, too. You'd better start taking care of what's best for you. Because nobody else is going to do it." New York had made Adeline pretty tough. "Live a little. Life's short, girlfriend. And if you hadn't noticed, Ginny, you're not getting any younger." Addie talked as if time were standing still for her.

I said I didn't need to be reminded of my age and she laughed. We left it at that because Adeline wasn't one to hang on the phone especially when the call was on her dime.

My father told me, "You know this is the first Christmas we've had without both our girls." Nobody had wanted wine, and he was mixing the drinks on the butcher block island counter beside me. I was setting out the glasses, and he was pouring them.

"We know you're grown," my father said, "but your mother still worries about you and Addie when you're not with us." He put the ice cube trays back in the freezer and made a sleepy sentimental smile I wasn't used to seeing. "You know, you never stop being a father," he told me. "I miss my girls."

I could have asked him what there was to miss, since he didn't know me anymore. Hadn't tried to know me. Didn't know what and who was important in my life and couldn't find the courage to ask about anything more intimate than the weather in Chicago or my prospects for advancement at Whytebread and Greese. But I didn't. My dad looked worn out by the dissonance between his love for me and his disappointment in the life he believed I had chosen out of obstinacy. It made me sorry for him. It made me even sorrier that I thought he would rather have had me be Sandra, that he'd rather have been talking to Sandra about Andre, about the house they'd just bought in a quiet bedroom-community outside of Chicago, about the baby they were expecting that would be his first grandchild. If I were Sandra, my daddy and I would have sat on the couch together with his arm around my shoulders like he used to do and he would have counseled me to work again after my children had gone to school, because it had been such a good thing for my mother.

Instead he asked me blankly, "Are you happy, Virginia?" The stubble on his face was as grey as gun metal and his small black eyes were cloudy. "You know, your mother and I just want you to be happy."

"Sure," I lied. "Of course, I'm happy." It was what he wanted to hear. I thought my happiness was the least that I could give my father after all he'd given me; and he smiled an old man's smile as if my happiness was all he'd ever wanted.

Then, I helped him carry the drinks and a plate full of raw vegetables and dip back to the living room where the dog, Scout, was rooting cheerfully in the crotch of Andre's pants. My mom was still holding forth on the subject of kitchen contractors and my father shouted at the dog until he slunk away. Then he passed out the drinks and sat down again in his reclining chair by the door with his eyes half closed and a sleepy expression on his face. I was amazed my parents had grown so used to each other that my father could pass out to the sound of my mother's voice the way some people could fall asleep with the television on. It seemed like a very nice thing indeed to have been happily married for so long that your lover could bore you comatose.

I put the vegetable plate down on the oak coffee table in front of Sandra, on the glass part in the center, and took a seat next to my mother, in an upholstered side chair with a winged back and dark wood armrests. My mother said she'd had the pair re-done last May to match the Navajo print on the couch.

"Now this is healthful isn't it?" my mother lifted the edge of the vegetable tray slightly by way of an invitation to eat and went back to telling Sandra about the importance of finding a good baby sitter early. Andre was nodding and Sandra was stuffing her mouth with vegetable dip for two.

"We didn't go out for nearly six months," my mother confided in her party voice, "and let me tell you it nearly ruined our marriage."

Andre nodded some more. My father reclined his chair and began to breathe heavily through his mouth while my mother prattled on and on about diaper services and day care. In a little while, the dog came and sat down under my father's feet.

The dog had been mine when I was a child, but now belonged completely to my parents. When he was a puppy, Adeline and I had dragged him home by the scruff of his neck, swearing the dog had followed us. My mom named him Scout after a character in that novel by Harper Lee and let us keep him. Scout was a big black labrador mix, old now and moving painfully with arthritis, but I remembered when he was young he could catch a tennis ball, thrown as far as I could make it go, on the first bounce.

Now, every night my grey-headed father carried his greyer dog up the stairs so the beast could fall asleep in the hall outside my parents' bedroom. Every morning my father carried Scout downstairs so that he wouldn't pee on my mother's Belgian-made Oriental rug. I imagined someday I would take care of my father and mother like two tired old dogs, the way they cared for the slobbering bullheaded animal lying underneath the footrest of my father's chair. But lately, I'd been wondering who was going to take care of me when I got old.

I had nearly fallen asleep on that cheery thought when my mother paused in her rambling to ask how things were going at Whytebread. It was her way of including me in the conversation, which I both appreciated and resented. Appreciated, because she'd made the effort. Resented, because it never occurred to her to ask if there was anything besides work in my life.

"Same stuff, different day," I said. That done, my mother went on to subjects of greater interest, and I addressed myself to my Bombay Sapphire which I was finding to be very pleasant company.

"I'll bet you girls are excited about your reunion?" my mother said. "Jack Ward is going to be there, Ginny. I ran into his father at the grocery store last week. He's getting his PhD at Stanford. I'm sure he'd like to see you."

When I looked up from my drink Sandra was

mouthing the words, "What a geek. I'd stick with girls," at me from in between bites of celery and it was everything I could do not to laugh.

In high school, Jack Ward had been a thin, myopic boy with a persistent stutter. He was two years younger than me and half an inch shorter but he fit my mother's desperation criterion these days: black and educated with a factory-installed penis.

"Well, it wouldn't hurt you to be friendly, Virginia," she frowned. "He might have some friends."

I said, "With friends like that, who needs enemies."

Sandra laughed but she was the only one. My father was snoring and Andre was rattling the ice in his empty glass. My mom stood up, still frowning at me, to refill it for him.

"I got a note from Rosey," I told her just to be hateful. Rosey Paschen was persona non grata in my family. When I'd introduced her after a softball game ten years ago in her letter jacket with the leather sleeves, my mother looked like she wanted to take me off the team. Rosey was my mother's worst nightmare: big, white, sports-playing and dykey-looking.

My mother took Andre's empty glass and went off to the kitchen as if she hadn't heard me. When she came back she asked Sandra, "How many children are you planning? I hope you don't have a preemie. You know, once you have a preemie, they just keep getting earlier." She handed Andre his drink. He looked down into the glass and tasted it gratefully.

"We would have liked more children, but we had

to stop. Ginny's dad would have liked a boy," my mother said.

My father grunted from his sleep. The dog was snoring too.

"Yeah, I'd like a son." Andre took another sip of his scotch and brightened up. "You know, someone to carry on my name and all. But as long as it's healthy. Knock on wood." He hit his knuckles on the side of the coffee table. "We'll take what we get." He and Sandra looked across the couch at each other and nearly cooed. Andre related how Sandra had asked the doctor not to tell them the sex of the child from her prenatal tests as a matter of principle. "But I agreed with Sandra completely." Andre tinkled the ice in his glass around. "We've made all of these decisions together.

"We think it's important for professional blacks to make a commitment to children," Sandra said. "The under-class is breeding us out of existence and we, Andy and I, want to do our part to stop it." She looked at me significantly, as if I were Onan spilling my seed on the ground. "All educated African-American people ought to think about having children."

Andre uncrossed his legs and swished his drink around some more before he raised the glass again and said, "You realize, of course, as a race, our gene pool is going straight to hell."

Sandra inclined her head gravely as if the production of babies by inferior classes was a serious matter indeed.

My mother nodded too and managed just the weakest, barest little smile at her guests. She had grown up in the stiff-backed tradition of black middle-class etiquette, a precursor to the Walt Disney school ala Thumper: If you can't say nothing nice, don't say nothing at all. Of course, my mother applied this only to non-family members.

What she did say was, "Maybe you'd like some more crudités, Sandra?" She lifted the crystal serving tray and tilted it politely towards the couch as if she hoped Sandra and Andre would take the opportunity to fill up their mouths. They didn't and the tray looked like it had begun to feel heavy before she put it back down on the coffee table. My mother folded her hands in her lap with a kind of pained resignation.

"Drugs is what it is," Sandra was saying happily and Andre was bobbing his head in agreement. "It's crack cocaine and junkies. You know, sterilization is the best thing for them."

I put some onion dip and cauliflower in my mouth so I wouldn't feel obliged to open it. Then, I washed it all down with a slug of gin. That worked nicely so I had another. Pretty soon, I couldn't feel my fingers and the whole conversation sounded very far away.

"The solution is sterilization. It's cheaper than prison and it's cheaper than welfare." I kept eating and Sandra went on until my father woke up. His family had come north looking for the promised land in the steel migration, for jobs that were all gone now. Sandra's politics had brought him up short and he was glowering at her with an attitude that would have frozen river water in July.

"A whole lot of things are cheaper than welfare." My dad's eyes were little black points in his stiff brown face. "Some people think education's one thing that could go a long way."

"Come on now." Andre's smile spread his thin careful moustache dimple to dimple when he saw that he had offended my father. He spread out his hands and held his palms up. "We're not talking about educable groups here, Mr. Kelly. Now, you know, she's absolutely right. We're talking about third and fourth generation professional welfare mothers here. They don't even want to do any better for themselves. They've got no pride. They've got no sense of our struggle in this country." Andre shook his head slowly. "And nits make lice, if you know what I'm saying, Mr. Kelly. Those little street corner hoodlums aren't kids that want to learn to read and get a job. All they want to do is hang out in their hightops, make bastards and live off the system. But, of course it's worse in the city." He hunched his shoulders and spread his palms out again to indicate he was not including in his social recriminations the little piece of suburban heaven where my parents resided. "Out here I guess it's different."

My father narrowed his eyes some more. "I wouldn't count on it. It's not so different." He had another sip of his drink and smacked his lips before he opened them again. "I don't think things are so different here at all."

My mother and I helped ourselves to a little more winter vegetable crudités.

"You kids can't forget we have our share of tragedy out here too," said my mother as if she were proud of it. "We have unwed mothers and drugs; and some absolutely terrible things have happened here

43

in Blue River. You know, this past spring and summer, they found those girls from Ohio State sliced up in the woods near the Johnson's place and the police thought it had to be somebody local who did it, and of course, Marge Arkin just died, your friend Emery's mother. Drowned in September."

"August," I said.

"Whatever," said my mother, "at that house up in Cedar Lake she bought after her father died. Marge had quit that secretarial job, too."

I said, "Paralegal," and my mother shrugged.

"Well, I heard her father left her enough money from somewhere that she didn't have to work any more. Of course, Harry was still driving that old beater of his." She was shaking her head with something in between pity and relish. "You know Marge got married recently to one of the teachers up at the high school," my mother explained, "four years ago maybe. Harry Hobart. Did you girls have Hobart? Remember I sent you the clipping, Ginny. Harry's overwrought, you know. We didn't have time to get anybody so he was nice enough to stay on for this semester, but he's not coming back next year. Poor guy. He's taking a leave of absence after Christmas. They've had to hire a substitute to teach some of his classes and that little Crawford girl he tutors is beside herself with the SATs coming up." She laid a finger across her lips as if she were thinking hard. "Now, didn't you used to baby-sit that Crawford girl?"

"Addie did," I said. "It was Addie that used to baby-sit Page Crawford."

My mother shrugged "Well, it just goes to show you anything can happen, just when you think you

44

have everything." She put another piece of celery in her mouth and blinked at me pleasantly. "You can get hit by a bus just crossing the street. You know, Marge's girl went to live with her aunt in Indianapolis. She was younger than you kids." Her conversation had idled down to a seamless stream of garden variety small-town gossip. "Maybe fourteen now. And you know Mary Ellen McMann is back in town. She opened up a little nouvelle cuisine restaurant. Well, it's nice some young people like it here," my mother sighed. "You girls should really keep up your subscription to the *Blue River Reporter*."

I slept soundly that night on those magic pacifiers of good gin and clean flannel sheets and dreamed that I woke up the next morning as someone else, someplace else — someone straight, married, and pregnant, in a big house smiling to myself like the Mona Lisa, but I was married to William F. Buckley, Jr. and that hadn't made my parents happy either.

It was a surprise and a relief the next morning when the room and I were the same as we'd always been. Still the room where I'd had my first period and hung on the phone all night while Sandra told me about some boy to whom she'd given her all. My bookshelves were still there against the walls with the cheap little wooden dresser and a painted chest my grandfather had made for me. The room was the same way I'd left it the night before and ten years earlier, except this morning it was spinning.

The walls were tilted on their sides going around and around, and faster and slower and faster and slower with the wicked angular momentum of a gin and tonic hangover. My head hurt and my mouth felt like the outside of a peach. Every time I opened my eyes, the ceiling and walls took dizzying turns around my head. In another of its subtle ways my body was replaying Adeline's reminder that I wasn't getting any younger — and I wasn't even getting what I thought I wanted.

Since the time I'd lived with my parents in this suburban tract house, what I'd gotten was way too old to drink in the style to which I'd become accustomed, too old to have to lie about my lovers, and too old not to worry about growing older all by myself. The week before I had discovered still more of my mother's heredity in the new collection of varicose veins that spread along my upper thighs. It was a discouraging revelation that the alternative to dying young and suddenly like Emery Arkin was to die in bits and pieces through the nasty erosion of age.

My Blue River High School yearbooks with pictures of me when I still straightened my hair, and my face didn't even have laugh lines, spun around on my shelves, spun all around my bed making me feel like every one of my parents' failed hopes for me was stored up in that room, making me sick. When I'd pulled it together enough to put my feet on the floor I decided what I needed was some air.

IV

Outside, the street was empty and cold enough for me to notice my sweat pants were developing holes in the knees; and I ran along for a while to get myself warm but my lungs filled up with frost and then, I couldn't breathe. It wasn't a very comfortable feeling. So, I put aside vanity and walked instead. There was no one around to impress. Besides, walking always helped me think. What with Emery, Rosey, Sandra and Andre, I figured I had a lot of thinking to do; and I'd nearly made it all the way to downtown before it occurred to me to change directions.

When I'd grown up there, Blue River was the kind of place where you could walk on the streets at midnight with nothing to fear but drunken drivers. People only locked their houses when they went on really long vacations. Neighbors looked out for each other, and you left your windows and screen doors open on hot summer nights. Since I'd left, things had changed, but even in the worst part of town, a stroll on some deserted street at seven o'clock in the morning wasn't taking your life into your hands. Solitude was one of the few things from my childhood that was still safe and still the same. That morning it was exactly what I was looking for.

I'd let my feet take me down by the old dance pavilion along the path of the railroad. A few years ago the town made a project of paving it. When I was a kid, it was two iron rods with gravel and grass between them that could take you all the way to Columbus if you had the time and the inclination to go.

I wandered down the path south out of the subdivisions, half knowing where I was going. Still it was almost a surprise when I turned down Dean, the street where Rosalee Paschen used to live. The house her family rented was on the opposite end of town from my parents', a neat white frame on the old side of Blue River where the lots were smaller but the trees were bigger and the bungalow houses had more character to them than thirty-year-old brick and siding. As I passed Rosey's house towards the end of the long narrow street where it crossed Whitehall Way with its overhang of gnarled and beaten oak trees, I wondered if her family still lived there.

That morning the oak leaves were gone and the limbs of the big trees stretched out above me like someone had drawn twisting black lines with a charcoal pencil against the pale grey sky. As I walked through the arch they made over the street, I could hear loud voices down the block. An old white-haired woman in pink sponge rollers was chasing a younger blonde, shouting angry words that I couldn't make out.

The old woman's broken little body seemed to fly along, her arms stretched out and her hands bent into claws. She was screaming like some aged harpy and she caught the younger woman by the sleeve of her long tan coat. Then there was the sound of the slap in the still morning air.

The old woman seemed to grow in size until her hand met the cheek, and then she shrank back again into something small and weak-looking. The young woman's face snapped hard to the side and the old woman knotted her fists and brought her arm up swinging again, but the younger one caught her hand this time and I watched the old woman fall to the ground. I was running before she hit the pavement, waving my arms and shouting, "Hey!" and "Wait!"

The younger woman saw me and turned and ran with her long camel coat flowing out behind her to a red car parked further down the street. When I finally reached the old woman, the car had already turned away down Sutton Street and all that was left was a black stain of oil on the snow. The white-haired woman was nearly on her feet, but I caught hold of her arm to steady her.

"Are you okay, ma'am," I said. "Do you want me to call the police?"

"Whatever for?" the old woman said. "I'm fine." But she was still panting. "I just slipped on the ice here, that's all." She pointed at the sidewalk to a patch of bumpy frozen snow as she shook my hand off her arm.

"But I saw that woman knock you down," I said. The street was quiet and empty again and the tracks the red car had left in the snow were now indistinguishable from the tires of all the cars that had come before it. "Did she hurt you?" I asked.

But the old woman had begun to walk away. I followed her anxiously, caught her arm again, and she whirled around at me looking small and fierce. Her fist came up again as if she might have hit me too, but I let my hand drop from her arm and she stopped herself in mid-swing blinking at me as if for a moment she'd mistaken me for someone else.

"I'm sorry," I said, "but I was only trying to help."

Her eyes were as pale as a watercolor sky and she looked at me as if I were crazy. "I don't know what you're talking about," she said. "I don't need your help."

And I watched her walk away slowly down the street, limping slightly on the side where she'd fallen, her runny blue eyes aimed at the sidewalk, on the lookout, I guessed, for more ice. Her figure got smaller and fainter until I couldn't be sure I wasn't seeing ghosts the way I seemed to see Emery Arkin every time I turned around. After a while I walked in the opposite direction, down the arch of naked trees towards Sutton Street.

It took another half an hour to wind my way through the side-streets downtown to Ewing's Drugs & Sundries on the main drag. I stopped in there and bought my father a *New York Times* with some money I'd found in the pocket of the beat-up old green ski vest along with a wad of Kleenex and an old wind-up Timex watch.

Ewing's was the only place left on Main Street that sold anything of use. The other storefronts had been filled up with fancy bakeries and cappuccino joints, the trim on the wood facades painted over in cheery pastel colors. By the Crown Movie Theater, I found the little nook where Mary Ellen McMann had opened up the restaurant my mother was talking about, Spike's New-Style Main Street Cafe. The menu was posted in a white wooden box out front; and I would have wondered longer about how bok choi was going over with the natives, but my fingers were getting cold. So, I rolled the paper under my arm, stuffed my hands in my pockets, and kept on walking down Main back north towards Linden.

There were greens and holly wrapped around the poles of the street lights, and childish depictions of pine trees, Santas, and reindeer had been finger-painted on the store windows by artsy adults. The clock on the Blue River Deposit Bank read eight o'clock. That Friday morning, I was searching the faces of the few people on the street diligently for someone I knew well enough to ask for a ride home, but none of the early morning coffee junkies looked even vaguely familiar. When I spotted Harry Hobart coming out of the automatic teller at the Blue River Deposit Bank, the ends of my fingers were pretty well numb.

"Hey," I shouted, "Mr. Hobart," and waved the paper over my head wondering if there was anything mildly ridiculous about a twenty-nine-year-old calling a thirty-eight-year-old Mister.

Even if time had made us peers, I still didn't feel right using his first name. Maybe it was because Mr. Hobart still looked pretty much the same as when he'd taught me English. He turned around slowly, and smiled over his nerdy black glasses like he was expecting a pleasant surprise. I had learned years ago that large mass is encumbered by the law of inertia, and Harry Hobart was huge in an ungainly, almost boyish way. He had a square jaw and a clear pink complexion, a dimple in his chin and a lot of dark hair which he combed straight back without a part. I had almost forgotten his size until he crossed the street and I got a better look at him.

A huge black wool coat that made him look even wider at the shoulders hung open over a burgundy cardigan and black plastic rubbers covered his size twelve shoes. Years ago Harry Hobart seemed too large for the room, too close to the ceiling lights, and always vaguely bent at the neck when he'd filled the doorways before and after his classes. He used to pace up and down the rows of students, as big as Gulliver, reciting things like, "I celebrate myself," and "I am nobody who are you," with the book left open on his desk while he talked so you'd know he knew the poems by heart. To a seventeen-year-old girl, Hobart seemed like everything your father wasn't, not tired, not old, not bald, or black and on the offensive, waiting to bristle over the kind of service he got in some department store. Hobart wore crisp white shirts, hip ties under oversized sweaters — and sideburns which were back in style. He was romantic by association with the poetry he liked to teach, giving hope to straight white girls that they might not have to wake up one day in the lives of their mothers. Giving hope to queer black girls that the world would be a fair grader as well. Ten years had left little creases in his forehead, but Harry Hobart had still somehow managed to hold on to the timeless fairy tale charm of a matinee idol.

He had crossed the street before I could tell if he'd recognized me after so many years. Then he said, "Well, Virginia Kelly, fancy meeting you here," and I put out my hand for him to shake. Instead, Hobart pulled me into his coat for an unexpected hug. "What have you been doing with yourself, little girl?"

"Lately freezing my yin yang off, Mr. Hobart," I said, and laughed. Tiny snow flakes were beginning to fall. I could feel them melting on my face as I waited for him to take the hint.

"I have my car parked on Maple. Can I drop you somewhere?" he asked after what seemed, in the cold, like a good long time. I told him he could.

It was three blocks from the corner of Main and Linden back down to Maple and I passed the time by rubbing my chapped hands together and watching my breath make smoke while we walked to his car. Hobart used to drive an old green Karmann Ghia convertible, winter and summer, but this winter I noticed it was sporting a brand new candy-apple-red paint job and a For Sale sign in the back window. I was less than confident about the heater, but any ride at all seemed better than walking.

"Is there a new car in your future, Mr. Hobart?" I asked.

Hobart unlocked his side of the car, and grunted, "Uh huh," as he stretched across the stick shift knob to open the passenger door for me. Glossy travel brochures advertising places in Italy and Greece were piled on the front seat and he tossed them into the back so I could sit down. "I was thinking about something more dependable. I think it's a sign I'm getting old," he said. "So, you're home for Christmas? Happy holidays. Are you enjoying them?"

The new car and the European vacations seemed like bad form from a man too bereaved to hold down a job, but who was I to judge the ways that Hobart consoled himself? I left that kind of dogma to my mother and to the Catholic Church.

I said, "Coming home is always tough, you know?" and he looked at me as if he did know.

"It's nice you've got a family to come home to,

though." Hobart's size would barely allow him to shift the gears of the little car if he were alone, and a passenger seemed to make it harder. "I'm on my own this Christmas." He was working the stick around his leg and frowning as if driving took as much thought as brain surgery.

I wanted to ask why he wasn't spending his Christmas with Emery's sister, Sarah, his stepdaughter, but good manners got the better of curiosity and instead I mumbled, "Just drop me here." We were coming up to the sign for my street, Osage, on the left.

"You're sure?" Hobart stopped the car. My house was about a block up at the end of the cul de sac off the main road. It was a small enough town for Hobart to know where I lived, but I was surprised and flattered that he remembered. "I can take you all the way, Virginia."

"Here is fine," I said. "I'm sure." Even inside the car it was cold enough that I could see my breath, but Hobart lived about six miles out past the opposite end of town and it didn't seem polite to take him any more out of his way. "I'm sorry about Marge."

He dropped his head slightly and was quiet for a while. Then he squeezed my hand in his over the emergency brake. "Thanks, Virginia."

His hand would have made three of mine. "Thanks for the ride." I squeezed back, and was so sorry for him that before I'd thought about it very hard I was inviting him home the following Tuesday for Christmas dinner. Extra people were another of my mother's Christmas traditions. She always said company made her feel more Christian.

Hobart thanked me before he laid his hand back in his lap and I thought I knew what my mother meant. Our little human interchange filled me up with that Jesus-y, Christmasy feeling that I hadn't been able to get from the colored lights.

After we were through smiling at each other, Hobart asked me, "Do you still hear from your friend, Rose Paschen?"

It wasn't such a strange question. Hobart had his own special interest in Rosey. He'd been her tutor when she moved to Blue River from Hogansville. Hogansville wasn't much of a school district. On top of that Rosey played varsity women's sports all four seasons, and worked part-time at Ewing's sweeping up after school. Hobart had volunteered to help her keep her grades up. It was a favor he did for some other kids too — Buddy Williams, the star quarterback, and Jane Wallick who was trying to get into Yale. Rosey had seen Hobart for English and history every Wednesday for two years in the evenings at his house. After graduation she'd gone to one of the Seven Sisters on a basketball scholarship.

He asked about Rosey as if he'd been giving the question some consideration. Even though I'd lost track of her, I didn't want to admit that to him. Maybe I didn't want to admit it to myself.

Sure, I told him. "Rosey's coming back for the reunion." I figured since she'd written me in the past six months, the intimacy I was implying was really only a white lie. "She wrote me about it a month ago." I stood by the car while I talked. The window was cracked to keep his windshield from fogging up in the cold and I talked to him through the space under the canvas top. "I'm sure she'll be at the party tonight. She says she's really looking forward to this."

"That's what I hear, Virginia. So I guess I'll see you both tonight." Hobart put the car in gear and it pulled away with the sputtering sound of a muffler held on by old rust. I watched his cloud of grey exhaust until he turned the corner onto Park, but I couldn't lose the feeling that Rosalee Paschen had been writing to him as well.

That morning I took a long bath, soaping my breasts with the hands of an imagined lover until my mother knocked hard on the bathroom door. I was thinking of a perfect lover — not Rosalee exactly. But then, I'd learned perfection was awfully hard to find.

V

I believe there is only one rule of returns: always come back looking better than when you left and even if perfection is hard to find, there's still a percentage in striving for it. The night of the reunion I was working to death my rayon palazzo pants and my little suede shoes with the velcro buckles and cutouts on the sides. My skin was clear. I had a forty-dollar haircut and nearly a full carat of brilliant white diamonds in my ears. With regard to the rule of returns, I was pretty sure I had it covered.

In high school, I had been a loser with

Coke-bottle glasses and a shy kind of awkwardness that came from knowing my crushes were on members of the wrong sex. I had never been pretty in any obvious way and if nothing had changed much on that score, at least I had learned to work with what I had.

As bad as things had been for me, they were as good for Sandra Crab, but I was at peace with that too. Sandra had always considered me her special geek. She took care of me, made sure I got invited to the best parties, even if I just held up the wall when I got there. She'd twisted a lot of arms to make sure I had a respectable date to our senior prom and I felt vaguely like I owed her something for that, loyalty, friendship, something better than the petty jealousy I'd been feeling earlier about her heterosexual privilege. But then, I was feeling like life owed me something too, for my adolescent pain, a little upside, a little happiness and love. I figured life owed me Rosey Paschen now that I had an idea of what to do with her, and I had a feeling in my gut that life was finally going to pay up.

Andre dropped Sandra and me off at the curb front of the Blue River High School gym while he went around the back of the building to park the car. The gym seemed smaller somehow even though the only inches I'd added in ten years were around my waist. For the reunion party, the basketball hoops were locked up against the walls and covered with red and white streamers, our school colors. The gym was filled with faces I used to know, changed slightly by hair loss and the beginnings of age, but still familiar and I found myself saying names I hadn't thought I would remember. At a table by the

57

entrance, Brooke Nadler, the homecoming queen, was checking off attendance and handing out a home-made, stapled booklet titled, *What Ever Happened to the Class of '81.*

Brooke had never been a rocket scientist, but I was surprised that a little survey of the room hadn't clued her in. Previously blonde bombshells were looking brown at the roots and wide in the hips. All-state athletes had turned into world class couch potatoes. Big men on campus and pretty boys were generally busing tables at the Sizzler Steakhouse and sending away for information on Monoxidil. Brooke herself had developed some nasty bags under her eyes and a premature set of wrinkles I imagined were from too much sun, since the reunion booklet said she was selling Mary Kay cosmetics out of a pink car in Fort Lauderdale.

There was the scattering of doctors, lawyers and Indian chiefs. It wouldn't have been fair to say that success in high school was in complete inverse proportion to success in life, but the relationship was close enough to restore my belief in God and Justice. That is until I ran smack into Emery Arkin's picture. That pretty much stopped the warm fuzzies dead in their tracks.

He was smiling out from our senior yearbook in one of those folded-hands shots with the smokey blue background, his head half-turned to show off the side without the cowlick. The yearbook patter below the picture read: *Track 1, 2, 3, 4. Talks to the trees.*

Someone had decided to use Emery as Blue River's own AIDS poster boy. Along with the yearbook was a donation box and a stack of pamphlets about HIV on a little card table in the corner at the end of the bleachers.

Beside the picture, there were some words to Lane Hennessey, the only boy in our class to take home economics all four years. Rumors that he was queer had forced Lane to import his senior prom date from another high school and the joke that followed was that he'd probably sewn her formal. I could see him across the room, overdressed in a dinner jacket and tuxedo pumps, on the arm of some blond curly-headed Euro-stud who looked like he'd stepped out of *Gentlemen's Quarterly*. *What Ever Happened to the Class of '81* said Lane was designing men's wear in New York. I didn't doubt it.

"Isn't it great Lane's taking up donations for AIDS research," someone said. I turned around and Beth Sturdevant was standing behind me wearing a blue and white plaid jumper with a white lace collar, navy blue woolen stockings, flat-heeled navy shoes with buckles, all of this accessorized by a velvet headband and little brown bag with blue accents that matched her hose as if she'd been outfitted by a personal shopper at Laura Ashley. It was a shock. Especially since the last time I'd seen Beth, she was sporting dirty-looking shoulder-length hair, and that junior Dead-Head look with a homemade tie-dyed T-shirt and faded-out jeans under her cap and gown. "It's so sad," she said as if her politics hadn't changed as much as her wardrobe. "You know, you never think it could be anybody you know and then there's something like this."

After I agreed, there wasn't much left to be said. So, Beth rocked on the heels of her flats and repeated the obvious. "People just can't do enough."

I nodded, but I was all out of words and my eyes were wet. For all the lip-service I'd given myself over Emery's death, for all of the rhetoric about love and friendship, the only things I'd managed to actually do were to cry and write out a few AIDS donation checks that were always smaller than they ought to have been.

"It's okay to cry." The color of Beth's hair reminded me of a pair of brown suede pumps I'd once had. In the background, that Michael Jackson song, "Thriller," was coming over the loudspeakers on the stage.

"I cried too. You know, it's very sad." Beth patted at her eyes with a paisley accent scarf.

"I'm okay," I said. "I'll be all right in a minute." But my chest was heaving. I knew I was puffy-eyed and paint-streaked and I couldn't seem to catch my breath, listening to Michael Jackson singing "Thriller" in a voice I would have bet dollars to donuts had been produced by estrogen. Across the gym Sandra and Andre were waving me over to say hello to Buddy Williams, yesterday's big-time football jock, today's divorcé with a beer gut and thinning hair. Ten years ago he wouldn't have stopped to kick me in the hall, but times had changed and, if I hadn't been so busy hyperventilating, it might have even given me some satisfaction.

"Why don't you come on with me." Beth took me by the elbow the way people try to help little old ladies across the street, and hustled me down the hall so we could fix our make-up together in the bathroom.

"That's better." She was smiling into the long warped mirror on the wall and readjusted the headband, smoothing down her mouse-brown hair with both hands. "Now, isn't that better?"

"Sure." My nose was running and I wiped it with the back of my hand. "Sure thing."

"You're okay?" She put her face close to mine and squinted. Her eyes were green against her heavy black eyeliner.

My nose kept running and I blew it hard on a paper hand towel that felt like it had been made from unprocessed tree bark. "I'm fine," I said. "I'm all right now." But the sandpaper towel had scraped every bit of skin from underneath my nose which started to bleed.

Beth opened her purse and rummaged for what I thought was going to be a tissue but instead turned out to be her brown lizard skin wallet. "You want to see my kids?" Beth asked me and the thought of them made her smile in spite of herself. Then she dropped the ends of her mouth politely so that I wouldn't see what a nice life she was having. "Are you all right?" she said again.

"What about your kids?" I said. "I'd love to hear about your kids, if you want to tell me." I kept wiping my nose on my fist and my fist on the towel. Pretty soon the nosebleed stopped.

She took a plastic book out of her wallet and gave me a running narrative as she flipped the pages. The boy was named Edward; the girl was Tara. They were five and seven, respectively, and belonged to her husband from his first marriage, but she loved them as if she'd had them herself. "At first Tom wanted another child that would be ours," she said, "but these are ours now. Now Eddie and Tara are mine." They were clean white children and she seemed to me like a character from a film. Her voice and her life seemed very far away. "They're good kids, but I guess I'm partial."

"Children are amazing. They're a miracle." I didn't know myself exactly what I was talking about, but Beth was nodding as if I'd managed to communicate it. "When they're born, they're so small," I said, "you know, but everything they need is there."

"And they grow so fast." She shook her head and smiled down at the pictures. "It makes you wonder where the time has gone. You know, Ginny, we're getting older. There's no mistaking it."

"I'm sure feeling older," I groaned.

Beth said, "Sandra told me about your friend." I watched her lips move. She was choosing her words carefully. Meaning well was a trait of Beth Sturdevant's that I'd always appreciated. "Sandra told me you were happy and I just want you to know I'm glad for you."

Emily and I had been officially broken up, despite our occasional sleeping arrangements, since my trip to Provincetown in July with Naomi, which made Beth's information a little outdated. But I thought the sentiment was nice.

Beth put her billfold away. "It's good to have someone, you know?" She smiled and there was lipstick on her teeth.

"Sure," I said. "I know what you're saying." There

was no point in going into how things had fallen apart for me, because it wasn't her fault and I didn't feel like crying anymore.

She squeezed my arm and pulled me down the hall. "Come on, if we don't get back, Virginia, people are going to talk." When we got to the door of the gym she gave me a hug and said, "Stay right here while I go get Tom."

But instead, I wandered over and got a beer from the keg by the stage; and when I looked up from my glass Beth was showing her husband and her snapshots to Leslie Howe, the prom queen runner-up, and Joey Crawford, whose Dad had a car dealership. The husband was a thin, wispy looking man with hips starting under the waistband of his trousers, and a paisley tie in a neat little windsor knot at his neck. The *What Ever Happened* book said he had a business in Columbus selling life insurance.

I stuck close to Sandra and the beer keg, air-kissing people whose names hadn't entered my consciousness in ten years, waiting for Rosalee Paschen to show up, and re-reading the photocopied handout from the reunion committee. It was the general alumni news litany of engagements, marriages, births and dead-end jobs. The blurb about Emery said simply that he'd died of AIDS-related complications in October, 1986. It seemed a diminution. A life that had meant something, at least to me, summed up in one short sentence. But what was written under my own name didn't say much more: "Virginia Kelly is a security analyst at the investment firm of Whytebread and Greese in Chicago, Illinois. She is single and lives in a North

Side condo on the lake front with her cat, Sweet Potato." The space for Rosalee Paschen was empty.

"So what are you doing still single?" Buddy Williams was smiling at me with the big brown bedroom eyes that used to get him everywhere. But some things change and apparently that was one of them. Reading between the lines in the alumni booklet suggested that Buddy had just been kicked out by wife number two and the threadbare jacket he was wearing looked to me like a side-effect of child support payments. He was working through his commitment issues, he said, in a twelve-step serial divorce recovery group and by getting active in the Men's Movement. I was looking over Buddy's shoulder at the door and covering my mouth politely as I yawned.

"No children either?" Buddy asked and I shook my head.

"Well, that's a shame because you'd make some pretty babies," Buddy said. "Shit, I bet you'd like being married." He winked.

I told him I didn't know about that but I guessed he did because he'd done it enough and he thought I was flirting.

"So, it's funny how we all ended up in Chicago." He meant me, Sandra and himself. Then he leaned in closer as if he was going to share a secret. "If I'd known you were this much fun, Virginia, I would have asked you out in high school. A fine-looking lady like you ought to have a man." Buddy dug around in the inside pocket of his jacket until he found a calling card, which he put in my hand very carefully as if it were a special gift. His name, address and home phone were printed on the card in raised black letters. "Now, that's my new number after the divorce. Chicago can get lonely." He winked again and if I hadn't known better I would have credited a nervous tic. "You ever need the company of a gentleman, baby, give me a call."

I was about to tell him exactly what I needed when I spotted the blonde from that morning on Dean Street in the doorway of the gym. She wore the same long camel-hair coat over a short black skirt and suit jacket that looked like she'd walked out of some Wall Street board room. Her hair was cut short at the nape of her neck, teased up big in the front and the ends were frosted in that late-eighties career dyke chic.

Buddy Williams wet his lips and let out a long low whistle.

"Who is that?" I thought Buddy and I had found some common ground.

He smoothed down the little net of hair on the top of his head and grinned. "Well, I'll be damned,' he said, "if that's not Rosalee Paschen."

Her lips were uncompromisingly red against a smooth cover-girl mask of pale makeup and highlighted cheekbones. But when I looked at her heart-shaped face more closely, there were the same pale blue eyes, same Roman nose, same U-shaped dimple between her lower lip and chin. I couldn't say what Rosalee Paschen could have been doing knocking little old ladies off the sidewalk on Dean street, but one thing was clear. I wasn't the only one who lived by the "rule of returns." The last time I'd seen her, Rosalee was given to oversized men's cotton shirts, dirty old blue jeans, and white high-top Chuck Taylor basketball shoes. Ten years ago, tinted

Clearasil acne medication was the nearest thing she'd had to foundation base, but still, when I looked beyond the window-dressing and the new coat of paint, her face hadn't changed much in ten years. Neither had Mary Ellen McMann's; she was blocking my view.

"Mary Ellen McMann," I started to say. "You look just the same," but I stopped myself when I realized it wasn't much of a compliment.

Mary Ellen had grown up into a plain, compact woman, short but solid, an older version of her younger self. Even in the dead of winter she still had the splatter of little brown freckles scattered over the bridge of her pug nose and her hair was so red that when the light caught it you would swear it was purple. She'd cut her hair all off except on the top and had moussed what was left up into little points. "Mary Ellen," I said, "I recognized you right away."

She said, "Call me Spike, okay?"

"Sure, Spike," I said, but it was hard not to think, Mary Ellen. "Whatever you want."

"I've changed my name — legally." She confided, "I never really felt like a Mary Ellen."

"Didn't you really?" I was looking past her to Rosalee who was beginning to break away from her group at the door and walk in my direction; and I was working my way as fast as I could across the gym towards the keg, and the door, to meet her, in what I imagined would be the kind of reunion of which romance novels are made.

The only problem was that Spike/Mary Ellen was walking along in lock-step beside me chattering about her name change, and I couldn't shake her.

"You know, inside I always felt like a Spike," said Spike.

"It was good you went with it, then." I told her I was still called "Ginny."

"You always looked like a Ginny, though." She touched her hair fondly and batted her eyes over the rim of her plastic cup as if she thought more of her looks than the rest of the world and she was waiting for popular opinion to catch up. "You look good," she said. "Really good. Did I tell you that?"

I said, "No, but flattery will get you everywhere." I had meant it to be witty, but her tone was making me a little nervous.

"That's something I'll be sure always to remember," Spike said, as if she were storing the information in some special part of her brain even then. I could have sworn she was looking down my blouse.

"I think I see Rosalee," I told her. "Rosey Paschen." We had nearly made it to the door. There was a crowd of Rosey's softball playing buddies around her, big-shouldered girls with good arms. She didn't seem to quite fit in with them anymore. The short black skirt and the sheer hose were much more Gianni Versace than I would have expected, much more than I would have ever guessed she could afford. "So, I think I'll go see what's going on with Rosalee," I said to Spike by way of an exit line.

"Oh, right, Rosey." Spike saluted me with her plastic cup. "I'd forgotten all about Rosey Paschen." She said it as if she were surprised I hadn't.

But I hadn't and it still gave me the chills when Rosalee squeezed my shoulder on her way to the opposite end of the gym, past me right over to where Sandra was standing with Andre. All I could do was to follow her with Spike at my elbow as if I'd been planning to go that way all along.

I tried to pick my jaw up off the floor when the first thing out of Rosey's mouth was, "Andy Rutherford, fancy meeting you here."

If Rosey had meant the remark to sound off-handed, it didn't. She could barely hold her cool, thin-lipped blonde face together while she got the words out.

"Hi, Rosey." Andre managed to shake her hand out of something that looked akin to Pavlovian conditioning. His face had turned the color of stale chocolate. Rosey's was red from her forehead down the neck of her silk blouse; and I didn't need a mirror to know how my own face looked because I could see Sandra's.

"Nice to see you again," Andre said.

"Yes. Well, I guess it is." Sandra planted both hands near her hips and stuck her pregnant belly out like a bumper.

"Sandy." Rosey's teeth were clenched together. "You look good. Are you expecting?"

Sandra's head was starting to weave back and forth on her neck. "*We're* expecting." She took a sideways step closer to Andre and looked at him significantly.

"Well, pregnancy suits you," Rosey said. "I don't think I could ever carry off the weight."

Nobody said much of anything else for quite a while and Andre made his voice several octaves deeper as he tried to explain, "Rosalee was on the other side of the Wedgewood deal two and a half years ago in Atlanta." His baritone was pleading.

"You remember I told you about Wedgewood, before we were married."

"Of course." Sandra meant of course he hadn't. "Nice seeing you again Rosey." She leaned forward and kissed the air near Rosey's cheek, then she turned on her heel and left us with a back view of her houndstooth-pattern maternity knit. Andre lagged behind her by about three steps with his shoulders hunched and his hands in his pockets up to the elbows.

"Well. There goes one hurting brother." Buddy Williams straightened his tie and looked off in Andre's direction, shaking his head. "Whipped," Buddy pronounced. "The man is just plain whipped and baby I know from where I speak. Bitch reminds me of my first wife." He cocked his thumb and index finger at me like he was pointing a pistol and winked his big brown eyes some more. "Don't be a stranger, now." He went away chuckling to himself.

I was hoping Spike would go with him, but instead she turned to Rosey and started talking. "Wedgewood. My, that sounds exciting." Spike was glaring at Rosey as if we were three on a date. In my book we were, and the trouble was, Spike didn't show any signs of leaving.

The foam from her beer had left a froth moustache on her upper lip and she licked it off. Spike proceeded to tell us what I already knew from reading the reunion handout about how she'd left Arthur Anderson three years ago, gone to cooking school and come back home to open a local cafe this year. Spike was the Spike of Spike's New Style Cafe. The place was getting good reviews in the Columbus papers which she seemed prepared to go on about at

69

length and I was afraid she might have brought the clippings with her. Spike asked, "What exactly do you do for a living these days, Rosey?"

"I'm a transactions lawyer," Rosey said as if she thought it was a big deal although she neglected to mention the name of her firm and I figured that meant it was second tier. I knew the drill myself from working at Whytebread, the dregs of investment banks. At the bottom of the barrel, the rule was: mention the field and not the firm. "I met Andy on a case two and a half years ago. Small world," said Rosey as if she wished it weren't.

"That's nice." Spike nodded absently as if only half listening. "So, are your folks still in town? Maybe you'd all like to try the Cafe one evening. I could get you in."

"I'm at the Johnny Appleseed on Winthrop Road." Rosey's voice was clipped and suddenly angry. "My family and I don't get on so well. We don't spend too much time together."

"Really? I'm so sorry." Spike wrinkled up her nose and her freckles congealed on the bridge in a solid brown mass.

"Don't be," said Rosey. "I'm over it." Then she smiled at me. "You know, I've got to say, Virginia Kelly, you've turned out pretty well."

It was a left-handed compliment, but not enough so that I didn't like it. I assured her that regular haircuts and a standing appointment with the dermatologist could do wonders. "But that's awfully nice of you to say. You're not looking so bad yourself." We went along like that for some time, her complimenting me, and me complimenting her back until Spike began to look as if she would rather have been someplace else.

"Oh you two." Spike's face was pink and it clashed with her hair. What she meant was stop, and she changed the subject back to food again where she seemed most comfortable. The monologue was uninteresting enough that I let my mind and my eyes wander down what little there was of Rosey's black crepe skirt, down the sheer black hose on her long white legs and back up again. It was nothing I hadn't seen before but somehow she was managing to make it look new and especially interesting. The other interesting thing I noticed was the spat Andre and Sandra were having, the two of them tucked away in a quiet corner of the gym by the lighted exit sign. I couldn't say for sure, but I didn't think it was a discussion on child rearing since the conversation ended with "Fuck you," from my reading of Sandra's lips. When she shut them Andre walked away looking so pathetically hangdog that if I hadn't been hating him so much for upstaging me with Rosalee, I would almost have been sorry.

"The real trick to a souffle," Spike was saying brightly, "is to start with your eggs at room temperature, otherwise you don't get the height you need." She pressed a finger to her lips. "Oh, and always use a very clean pan."

Andre took the long way around the gym, past the buffet table and the little pile of AIDS information beside Emery's yearbook picture. By the time he made his way through the crowd, back to where we were standing, Spike was in the middle of an involved discussion of lobster bisque.

"Sandy's tired and I'm taking her home." Andre looked quickly back across the room to where Sandra stood frowning by the door with her arms across her chest. "I'll be back." He squeezed my arm. "All right? I'll come pick you up in a little while. I won't forget you, Virginia."

"What a promise," Rosey said.

Andre opened his mouth and then closed it again without finishing what he'd started, but I got the feeling it would have been ugly if he had. "Virginia, I'll be back, all right?" he said to me. Then he stalked away with his scarf at his neck and his coat over his arm. I watched Rosalee watching him until he'd crossed the gym and had followed Sandra out the door.

"You know, transactions were going great guns when I met Andy," Rosey said rather sadly. "It was nice. The billables paid for therapy."

I didn't know exactly what she was getting at, but I had a feeling when I sorted it out I wouldn't like it much at all. So, I didn't even try. Avoidance is one of my special gifts and I wasn't especially interested in any past that Rosalee Paschen didn't share with me.

"Anyway, I change the entire menu at the Cafe every week. That's how I spend most of my days now." Spike kept talking to fill the space that was left when Andre walked away. "With my nose in a cookbook or trying out something new in my kitchen. You have no idea of the muscles it takes to cook." Spike rolled up the sleeve of her peasant blouse and made a fist that showed off her bicep. "Go ahead and feel it," she said like she was letting me in on something good. "I go to the YWCA three times a week too."

I poked her arm with my index finger.

"No, really feel it. You can't tell anything that way." She took my hand and closed hers on top of it above her elbow. Then she held it there a little too long to be anything but flirting. "Lifting Calphalon cookware will do that for you." Spike asked Rosey if she wanted to feel her muscle too.

"No thank you," Rosey said. "I have my own." She turned to me as if Spike weren't there and asked, "Why don't you go with me to the ladies room." It was the invitation I'd been waiting for all my life. Behind us, Spike was still standing in the middle of the gym with her sleeve rolled up and a flat-looking beer in her hand. I felt bad for her but not bad enough to stick around.

"Did you get my letter?" Rosalee asked after she closed the door to the washroom. Her voice made my palms feel sweaty.

"What letter?" I lied, trying very hard to be distant, but I could smell her cologne as she sat on the sink and it was melting my resolve.

"I wrote you a letter." She was swinging her legs and the heels of her pumps clicked against the tile on the walls. "It was very mysterious. So you'd have to come. I didn't know if I'd get to see you again."

I was slouched against the paper towel dispenser. "I got your phone call, so here I am," I said. "Anyway, it seems like we've had our reunion already."

Rosey looked at me dimly, blinking her cool blue

eyes, and I went on, "I saw you on Dean Street this morning."

"You did?" Her feet kept beating the same even sound against the tile. "I think you must be mistaken about that, Virginia."

I said, "I was jogging and you were fighting in the street with an older woman." It was both a question and a statement, because I was pretty sure of the facts. What I wanted to know was the whys. "A little old woman with white hair in curlers was chasing you. You both stopped. Then she slapped you and you knocked her down."

"What?" Rosalee's face had the faintly stupid expression of an unvarnished two-by-four. "I don't know what you're talking about," she said, and the clicking stopped against the tile. "What did you see?" she asked me again, and I couldn't bear to tell her how I hadn't recognized her at first. I knew what I'd seen on Dean Street but I just didn't have any way to prove it. Besides, when I thought of the words I'd said, they seemed pretty implausible even to me.

"What did you see, Virginia?" she asked.

"I don't know," I said, "I guess you must have a twin somewhere, either that or I'm just going crazy."

Rosey hopped down from the sink and smiled at me in a closed-mouthed way as if she were inclined to believe the latter. Then, she went into the bathroom stall to pee and I talked through the door while I waited, little bursts of words that didn't quite fit what I'd wanted to say. "I think of you sometimes. You haven't changed." When what I meant was I haven't changed, and please don't have changed how you feel about me. I said, "You look just the same only with shorter hair," and meant I

74

hope you're the same inside, and I promised myself for her, "I can tell you really haven't changed at all," telling lies to the outside of the steel bathroom stall partition.

When she came out, Rosalee hooked her arm in mine and took me on an aimless walk from the ladies room, to the coat check and around the parking lot, a long slow walk. The wind was blowing up my back and I could smell the smoke of fireplaces in the air, that and the vaguely sweet smell of dope burning somewhere close by. I could feel her arm against my breast even through my thick wool coat, and I hoped that she hadn't brought me all the way out in the cold for nothing but a chat.

I remembered sitting close to her like this during softball practice in the late spring when the sun was just warm enough to go out in shirtsleeves. It was the year we won some games, a good year for a single-A Division school with a particularly small enrollment, partly thanks to Rosey who played shortstop. I watched her all season from the bench, kicking the dust with the toe of my barely used cleats and cheering. I wasn't much of an athlete, but she was and I admired her for it; I wanted to be good at sports too, mostly so she would admire me. So that she would dream about me the way I dreamed about her. My ambitions were modest and so were my dreams, about rubbing the back of her neck when she came off the infield wet and dusty, about kissing her neck and running my hands down the sides of her thick jock waist. But mostly I'd just smile stupidly and pass her the water jug when she sat down next to me on the bench, after they'd called in her relief. Standing next to her tonight, I found myself nostalgic for exertion and sweat.

"I've really missed you," I said.

Rosey looked at me sideways and gave me back my arm. "You don't even know me. You miss the person I used to be."

"All right," I said. "That too."

"There's nobody like that around anymore." She frowned. "Get over it." Then she smiled again, but I couldn't say for sure that it was at me.

The moon looked like a big grey balloon and we walked along under it not talking. "What was it you had to tell me," I asked after a while.

"It has to do with how I was to you and what I meant by it. I didn't even know who I was," Rosey had started to answer when Spike came up behind us wearing a short little blue pea coat and a tasseled middle eastern scarf wrapped around her face, up to her eyes.

Spike said, "You two can't have a tryst in the parking lot, people will talk." Which I took to mean that she would talk. Her hair stuck out in orange points over the scarf so she looked like either the top of a pineapple or a bandit out of some bad spaghetti western depending on which half of her face you were considering.

"We weren't trysting," said Rosey. "It's too fucking cold out here for that."

Spike looked disappointed. Not as disappointed as I was.

I said, "We were talking," and meant for Spike to leave. But she didn't.

"Talking about what," said Spike.

"Old times. Talking shit." The wind seemed colder suddenly and I pulled my coat around me. "Just old times," I said.

"You can't change them." Rosey smiled a bitter smile that was there and gone so fast I wasn't sure I'd seen it, but I knew somehow the conversation I'd come out in the cold to have was over.

"What's the point? You can't relive them and you can't get them back." Rosey looked up at the ghost grey moon and made a circle in the gravel with the toe of her pump. "Somebody told me Buddy has some pot," she said. "He's got it over by the gym. Come on." She turned and walked back towards the building, talking to me over her shoulder, moving further and further away. "Are you coming, Gin? Let's get high. We can talk later," she was promising. "Let's get high."

"Then," I said, "I'll see you later." I was already high. I wanted to say, "You make me high." I said, "I'll see you later."

Rosey shrugged and kept walking. The wind lifted the top of her sprayed hair in sheets. I watched her join the circle by the door of the gym. "Quit hogging it, you bastards," I could hear her saying. Then there was laughing. I turned up the collar of my coat, stuck my hands in my pockets, and listened to it.

"Are you gay," Spike asked me like she already knew.

And when I told her I was, she tried to hold my hand. I thought maybe Spike had seasoned into a woman somebody would have found attractive. She was working on a kind of artsy-craftsy look and she'd gotten pretty good at flirting. But while there was nothing really wrong with eggplant, I didn't much care for that either.

It was mystery to me that people who left you cold could carry such a big torch for you and vice versa, when it seemed that romantic attraction ought to work like the pull from the poles of a magnet — opposite, equal, and blissfully predictable. It was certainly the way I would have preferred things, but that night Spike wanted me and I wanted Rosey and Rosey wanted dope; so, not much of anything was going my way.

Spike and I walked. All I could see of Spike were her sad little eyes and the points of her hair and even in the streetlights the night was too thick to tell the color of either.

"When did you know you were queer?" she asked.

"When I saw Rosey for the first time after she transferred here. I was sure the first time she spoke to me." It was embarrassing the way the words came out and I looked at the ground for a long time. When I looked up again, Spike was smiling an odd tilted smile as if she'd thought of something sweetly funny.

"That's nice. It's so romantic." She put her hands way down in the pockets of her coat, slouching, and smiled at me some more. She said, "You know, Ginny, I've had a crush on you for years."

I am convinced that the things that you remember most clearly are the things you have remembered most. That's the way it is with me at least. What I've replayed in my mind, I can sometimes call up again with perfect clarity, the way you can hear a song in your head all orchestrated just by thinking about the lyrics or even what you were doing when you heard it last.

I liked to remember the party for our high school graduation. It was held at Brad Johnson's family farm, party lights all strung in a square along the house, out to the barn, along the barn and back again. The beer was in old metal drums filled up with ice set far away from the bonfire. People parked their cars up and down Jekell Road, so many of them that we had to park mine at the bottom of the hill and walk up to the house waving our arms and hoping no one was so drunk they couldn't see us coming.

When Rosey caught me looking over the shoulder of that evening's fixed-up date, looking at her, she grinned at my indifference to him and I thought my socks would melt.

"I'm watching you," she whispered, and she walked with her beer back into the shadows. Later I wandered away from my date and went to find her there.

"What did you mean, you're watching me."

"I'm watching you," she said. "That's all."

We were standing in the shadows by the side of the barn and the voices from the party sounded faint, almost like a memory. I wanted her to kiss me and, of course, she did. I felt her tongue with a new imagination in all the places I would have liked it to be. Even while she rolled it in my mouth, I felt her hips and thighs grinding pleasantly against my own. She took back her tongue and kissed me again softly in the dim light from the paper lanterns strung up beside the barn. The evening air felt cool and clammy around us.

"We should stop," I said. "Someone might see."

Rosey laughed into the neck of my blouse and whispered that she didn't care who saw. "I don't care about anything," she said. "Just watch," and she kissed me again, deeper. Her bravado took my breath away, and at the same time I felt like she was giving me a kind of gift. It was the feeling that I belonged somewhere with someone, that there was someone in the world who wanted to love me. But I got scared. I made her stop and then she was angry.

"All right, do what you want then, Virginia," she said, "but just don't be sorry for it. There's nothing I despise more than regret."

I phoned the next day wanting to apologize for having had too much to drink, but she wouldn't take my call.

I told myself all summer that I didn't really know what I wanted from that night, and I contemplated my sexuality in clinical kinds of Freudian terms from the textbooks with yellowed, breaking pages I'd checked out at the Blue River Public Library. But of course I had known. I had known it all along and she had started with her kiss the slow painful process of my accepting my attraction to Rosey Paschen as general to women and not specific to her. That realization had been everything to me, pain, pleasure, rejection, embrace; it had allowed me to become who I was. Even now it was hard for me to believe Rosalee Paschen wasn't somehow the special one among all the other women I'd known. All my other lovers had contained a little bit of her.

First love can be like that sometimes, living forever in the question: "what if," in pieces of all your subsequent lovers, the shape of a leg, the set of a chin, making you believe that if you find the right combination, you can get it back. And what is it? Lost innocence. The way that old friends will sometimes haunt you from the faces of grocery clerks and bank tellers so that in bed or in the check-out line you may catch yourself remembering. Remembering what? Your past.

It was Rosalee who first let me feel proud, but it was Emery Arkin who took me to my first Gay Pride Parade, the last week in June, on a Sunday during one cold summer I spent working outside of San Francisco. I rode a bus and then the BART for two hours from the hinterlands and stayed the night before at his apartment. In the morning we had cookies and cocaine for breakfast and went to the Civic Center with a cooler full of beer to wait for the Parade. Emery knew everyone and we came home with more beer than we'd brought. I remember when the people with AIDS walked by looking thin and holding their banner, and the line of bodies cheering the parade stepped back three feet. I stepped back with them because it was 1984 and AIDS was a disease that happened to people I didn't know.

I saw my second Gay Pride Parade by accident in Chicago two years later, riding my bicycle through

Lincoln Park. I ran into the Parade without knowing it was there. So I asked a cop directing traffic what was going on.

"Fags," he said. "Gay Parade." And I wheeled my bike to Fullerton and Broadway for a better view.

It wasn't so bad to be alone in the friendly crowd. A man I didn't know, wearing buckskin chaps with fringe on the legs, gave me a beer from his six-pack. Free beer and a drag show like the first time with Emery. But the People With AIDS contingent had gotten bigger and their lives not so far removed from my own. Eight years later my own life couldn't have felt any further away from me and Emery, coked-up and drunk on Market Street in San Francisco in 1984.

"I've had a crush on you for years," Spike said again. She put her hand on the arm of my coat and it died there limp and red-looking in the cold.

"That's flattering." It was all I could think of. "It really is."

"So, how about it, then?" Spike said.

I thought I could make out Rosey smoking dope in a crowd of figures outside the floodlights on the side of the gym.

"You and me," said Spike.

Rosey was laughing. A man I thought was Harry Hobart came out and took a hit of the joint they were passing around the circle. He put an arm around Rosey's waist and she stiffened for a second. Then she laughed.

The night was cold and very still.

"You fucker, Hobart," I could hear her saying.

Everybody laughed.

The red tip of the roach moved around the crowd and Spike took my hand. "Let's go for a walk. Come on."

"I don't know you anymore," I said, "and you can't get it back, Spike, once it's gone."

"Maybe." Spike's small, crooked teeth were shining at me in the dark. "Maybe not. But you can always give it a try."

She was right and I walked with her back to her car, my gloves holding hands with her gloves, and remembering my first blind date with a woman.

Emery had set me up with a nurse practitioner at his clinic in San Francisco, whom he'd met when he and his boyfriend, Stash, had come in to get rid of their anal warts. The nurse had quit because the men at her clinic kept dying of AIDS and it was bringing her down. So, she was selling real estate instead. She was nearly forty years old and filled up with a middle-aged female horniness that frightened me. She said "Clit" all the time. "Clit" like you'd say "ice cream," and it embarrassed me. But Emery had romantic company planned for that night; so, high on some more free cocaine and beer, I asked the real estate nurse if I could stay with her at her apartment. In the morning, she took me to breakfast.

Now, in Spike's car, I had that awkward mismatch of intentions again. Kissing in the dark, I wasn't sure where anything was, and she was everywhere with her hands. Behind us by the door to the gym, I thought I could hear Andre's drunken baritone rising above Rosey Paschen's throaty laughter.

It was late when Spike finally drove me home, so late that people had turned off their Christmas lights. The street was cold and dead and dark, and it felt like we were the only two people left on earth. In front of my house, Spike turned on the dome light in her car and rummaged through the glove compartment until she found a pad to write down her phone number and address.

"Call me soon." Spike slipped the paper into the pocket of my jacket, took hold of my coat lapels and kissed me like she meant what she said.

As her car pulled off down the street I could see my parents' bedroom light go off.

The front door was unlocked. Upstairs, I stepped over the dog's broad sleeping back in the hall without waking him, and got ready for bed on tiptoes, too tired to sleep and much too cold. So I told myself stories, remembering old times fondly until my brain idled down enough for me to pass out.

The summer I spent with Emery in San Francisco, a woman was pursuing him anonymously, by mail. She wrote him letters, enclosing pictures of her breasts, big brown ones with dark wide aureoles, and Emery joked that the letters were from me. He said he hoped they were from me because her passion frightened him.

One night late, we heard stones on the window

glass above his dining table and were sure that she was coming for him, a scorned angry woman, perhaps with a weapon. The Berkeley police didn't take us very seriously or make us feel any safer. So, we slept together on Emery's waterbed, reasoning that if I slept alone in his bed, the woman might mistake me for him when she raised her ten-inch blade in the dark, but if I slept out in the living room, I'd have the bad luck to be the first thing she would encounter in her jealous frenzy.

I was so afraid that I held Emery's hand all night. In the morning, he cooked breakfast for me, joking that we were, both of us, still alive; and he made me take off my shirt to prove I hadn't sent the notes. He wanted it to have been me, I think for his peace of mind, and, of course, as a small victory for his gay man's vanity. In the end, though, he told me he didn't think I'd sent the notes because my breasts were much too small.

Years later when I'd visited that apartment, the side streets in Berkeley were still closed off to auto traffic with grey round cement barriers, and tall weeds still grew in the spaces left for flowers. The new owners of Emery's apartment had gentrified it, had painted it white and teal and cut the grass. And there were no chickens in the back yard anymore. No bicycle chains left soaking in oil on the porch. And I stared so long at the building a woman came out and asked me what I wanted.

"Can I help you?" She wore loose Guatemalan clothes, had red nails and tired middle-aged, ex-hippy bags under her eyes from working to pay the mortgage.

"I must have the wrong address," I told her.

But the first time I'd seen it eight years before, Emery Arkin had been sweeping out the bottom apartment. He did his cleaning once a week starting in the bathroom and sweeping through his bedroom, down the hall to the kitchen, into the living room/dining room where his boyfriend, Stash, kept wild rattlesnakes he'd found in the desert, and out to the front porch, down those steps straight into the yard. One day I remembered he'd dropped his broom in the grass and ran to hug me with both arms as I'd come up the stairs.

The night of the reunion party I dreamed about Emery and his old Berkeley apartment. Of me standing in the middle of his living room while Stash's snakes coiled around and around me until I was all covered up. At the end, all you could see was my shape wrapped up under their bodies like the coil pots I'd made from modeling clay in school art classes as a child.

VI

The next morning, I woke up to the smell of chocolate, and there were baking sheets and shiny, metal cooling racks all over the kitchen counters, with cookies set out by the dozens like widgets on a vast production line. It was a Christmas tradition that later my mother would put them between layers of wax paper in metal tins with a broken piece of white bread on top and give them to people with whom we didn't exchange formal presents.

When I'd come downstairs into the kitchen, she was pressing down on a big knife with both hands, chopping walnuts for more cookies on a wooden cutting board. I reached over her shoulder, made a circle around the glass mixing bowl with my index finger, and licked it. My mother stopped chopping nuts only long enough to scowl at me.

"Can I help?" I palmed two cookies from the racks and put them in my mouth too. The assistance was a token offer, filial duty, because we both knew I was all thumbs in the kitchen and absent-minded. Time got away from me and I burned things.

"No thanks." My mother wiped her hands on a dish towel she had hung over shoulder. "And don't eat any more cookies, Virginia, or I won't have enough." She scraped the nuts off the board into the batter in her mixing bowl, then dropped the knife into a sink full of soapy water, washing up as she went along, the way she always insisted I did whenever I used her kitchen.

The heat from the stove took the morning chill out of the room and my mother was surrounded by Christmas cookies, hemmed in with batter and the bowls and pans sticking out of her steaming dishwater. "How could you not have enough cookies?" I said. "Are you sure you don't need any help?"

She looked up, still dropping lumps of batter off a teaspoon onto her cookie sheets. "You can clean up the bathroom for me later, Virginia," she said as if

87

she were offering me a chance at the Publisher's Clearinghouse Sweepstakes. "Go talk to your father now, he misses you."

During the holidays, my father spent his mornings in the living room, reclined in his usual chair and reading his papers.

"Anything happening in the world?" I tossed a peanut in the air and caught it in my mouth. It was a trick that used to make my father laugh when I was younger.

"You got in a little late last night. We were worried." He barely looked up. "Sandra called at midnight to make sure you'd gotten home okay. When you weren't here, your mother and I didn't know what to think."

"Mary Ellen McMann gave me a ride." I told him that Sandra and Andre seemed like they needed a little privacy. "So, I just found another way home," I said. "No biggie."

"Uh huh." My father frowned into a day-old copy of the *Washington Post*. "You think you could get that hair any shorter, Virginia?" From my childhood, I recognized my full name as code for parental displeasure the way a dog can read intonation in its master's voice. I had been trained from an early age to my father's subtext.

My hair was very short that season, so short in fact that it lay down on my head like a coarse black carpet. My hairdresser, Pierre, at "We Do You" said it looked elegant. When I'd first cut my hair at eighteen my mother had cried for the years of care that were lying on the floor all around the beautician's chair, the wasted hours she had spent with a hot pressing comb heating up on the stove so that the wild black mane could hang down my back like a white girl's hair for fifteen minutes before the summer humidity kinked it up again. For me the short hair meant freedom from hot curlers and straightening perms, but my father's reference to its length had come to be a kind of shorthand for my lesbianism.

When I was seventeen, he'd talked to me seriously about it for the first time, sitting on the hood of his tan Camaro. We seldom talked, except about my future, what courses I would take at school, how I would make a success of myself. That day, I talked about Rosalee, her championship fielding, her jump shot, her letter jacket. I had more enthusiasm for Rosey than for my future, and it made my father so nervous that the skin on his forehead was buckling up in furrows.

"You know, if that girl tries to kiss you, you hit her." Rosey Paschen was always "that girl" to my dad, a category he expanded in later years to include all of my female lovers as if naming them would make his suspicions about the nature of our relationships come true. Before I could even imagine female lovers as a reality, I wondered if Rosalee's parents had a name for me, and it had made me anxious to think that she might not have even spoken enough about me at home for them to worry.

"Hit her. You hear?" My dad had made a fist and held it low under his chin like he was ready to punch her out himself. But, of course, defense from Rosey had been the last thing I was thinking of.

I touched the stubble that was left above my ears. "Pierre couldn't get it any shorter." I helped myself to another handful of nuts. "My scalp would show."

"Figures," said my father, "with a name like Pierre." His reading glasses were shaped like almonds in thick tortoise shell frames, and he was eyeing me over the top of them sternly. "You still like that neighborhood of yours, Virginia. Not enough black folks up there for my taste," he told me. "You know, Jack Robinson's boy is in Chicago too. South Side. He just passed the Bar. You could give him a call. He's younger than you but he might know somebody." This meaning he might know some nice black men.

"I'm not looking for anybody, Dad," I said meaning I was not looking for a man.

It was not what my father wanted to hear. He shook out his paper and shrugged back into the headlines. "Well, you're grown, Virginia." The paper came up like a screen between us. "It's a free country so far." He didn't seem to notice after a while when I got up and went back into the kitchen.

My mother was drying her cutting board and filling the dishwasher. "Isn't this nice being home." She pulled another dish towel off the handle of the refrigerator and tossed it to me. "Help me dry," she said. "You and me and Addie used to do the dishes together all the time when you were a girl, remember?"

I told her I did. Those were happy times.

She dried the mixing bowl and put it back on its metal stand. "You know, you ought to bring that friend of yours, Emily, back home with you sometime, Virginia. We don't see her anymore since she decided to get a place of her own."

I chalked this new nostalgia for my ex-lover up to whatever my mother had guessed about my ride home last night with Spike McMann. "You never invited her home when she lived with me. I didn't even think you liked Em," I said.

My mother frowned. "Well, I don't know where you got that idea, Virginia." She put the silverware in the dishwasher and pressed the rinse cycle. The machine began to grind and roar. "Your dad and I like all your friends."

My mother saw the world very differently from my father. For my dad, there were friends and enemies, good and bad. But my mother believed that she could mold reality into what she wanted it to be by force of will like the Amazing Kreskin. She'd told me, when I'd come out to her, that I was arrested in this particular stage of my sexual development. She'd said. "You'll get over this gay thing." She'd promised, "You'll see. People grow up at different rates," and she'd threatened, "You'd better get over it soon, because you know it's going to kill your father," and promised again, "Well you're young, Virginia."

I was twenty-two back then. But my mother hated to be wrong and she didn't feel the need to rethink her theory now that I was pushing thirty. My mom could overlook the fact that she knew Emily and I slept together because she believed my sexual orientation was a correctable blip on the curve of my life. She had the inner faith to say the names of my girlfriends aloud the way storefront preachers can confront the devil.

"I don't see Em much anymore," I told her.

"Oh, I don't believe that, Virginia." She hung a dish towel over her shoulder again and took the butter out of the refrigerator to soften for another batch of cookies. "If you girls had a fight just forget it. Friends are friends. They'll forgive."

"We broke up, Mom." Which wasn't exactly true, but the truth of our arrangement had to do with sex and my mother didn't believe that I had sex. "We broke up two years ago," I said.

"I don't know why you'd think I would want to hear about that, Virginia." She made a face like she'd swallowed something sour. "You know, it would really help me out if you'd get the bathroom straightened up before anybody drops by."

These encounters with my mother made me wonder if I had spared her the details of my life because she was unable to hear them, or because I was unable to tell them to her because I was too ashamed to share them.

Emery's mother, Marge Arkin, told me it was AIDS that killed Emery. But I knew better.

I'd phoned a week after I had heard the news and it had taken all of my courage to call Marge Arkin. They say that to speak of the dead is to whisper your own mortality. I was only twenty-four years old then and I thought I wanted to live forever.

When I called her after he had died, she picked up the phone on the second ring. "This is Virginia Kelly. How's it going?" I said, "Do you remember me?"

It was filler and Marge Arkin was worn down by bad breaks to a smooth hard surface; small talk couldn't scratch her. She was calm, but I was crying.

"I didn't know he was sick," I wailed and couldn't

help myself. My grief seemed noisy and excessive even over the phone.

She was smoking quietly into the receiver. "Neither did I." She said, "I didn't know anything until we took him to the hospital. That was the first time, in March. Emery just blew it." Her breath was hard and fast. "He knew he'd blown everything and he was too ashamed to tell me."

I had nearly finished scrubbing out the tub when the phone rang. My mother told me it was Mary Ellen McMann. "I hope you're not planning to run out of here, Virginia, before you do that bathroom." I took this to mean that she wanted me to keep my conversation short. I did. Spike told me she had had a good time the night before the way you thank a prospective lover for a first date.

"Me too." I was lying again. It was a nasty habit, but when I came home to Blue River, I couldn't seem to help myself. I didn't want to see her anymore. Not that there was anything particularly wrong with Spike. It was just that there was nothing particularly right. "I had a good time too." But it hadn't been good enough to do it again, so I lied some more. "My folks are complaining they never see me though, and I think it's going to be hard for us to get together."

"Well, be sure to take my address." She recited it to me again, talking slowly so I could write it down without mistakes. I put the scrap of paper in the pocket of my jeans meaning to let it die in the wash the following week. "I have yours from the reunion committee and if I ever get to Chicago, I'll look you up," said Spike. "In the meantime, maybe we could get together at my place later on tonight when your parents are asleep. I have a fireplace."

There was gritty green cleanser lining the bottom of the porcelain tub. I said, "I don't think that's a good idea. I'm sorry, Spike." In the pause, I could hear her breathing before I put the phone down gently in its cradle and went back to my cleaning.

I hadn't finished getting the soap scum off the sides when the phone rang again and my mother just handed me the cordless, stone-faced. I sat down on the toilet to talk, as she walked out of the bathroom mumbling something about her new career as my receptionist.

It was Sandra on the phone and she started our conversation with an apology. "I'm sorry to be calling you like this, Ginny, but I think Andy's sleeping around on me . . . and I don't know what to do." Her voice was thick and it broke in the middle of her sentence. "I don't have anyone else to call." She took a deep breath and barreled on so quickly that her words ran together. But the gist of it was she suspected Andre of having an affair with Rosalee Paschen. From what I'd seen at the reunion, I had to admit they were certainly having something, but I was trying out the old adage: ignorance is bliss. And it was working for me.

"As if sleeping with my husband isn't bad enough," Sandra whined, "did you hear what she said last night about my weight?"

"Hold on," I said. "Relax."

"Relax? Did you hear me, Virginia?" Sandra took

94

a deeper breath and pronounced more slowly, "I think Andre is fucking around on me. Running into that woman has made him nervous as a cat, and I *know* him. The other thing is she works in New York for a law firm. Andre has been to New York six times this month alone. Sometimes he spends the weekends there working. Working, my ass, Virginia. I know what Andy is capable of."

I wondered what she meant, but it didn't seem like the time to ask.

I could hear her breathing hard again and sniffling. "Well, I don't want you to think he's a bad man; he's not. He loves me, but between us two, Virginia, he's easily distracted. Men," she said, "well they all are, aren't they, and this shortage of good ones has just made it worse."

"I wouldn't know." The tile above the tub was streaking badly and I didn't want to be having this conversation.

"No, you wouldn't, would you?" said Sandra. "But I do, and so do men. They know there's two fine black women for every one of them and then, these cheap little white girls come sniffing up after anything that's out there, wiggling their flat little behinds around. Men notice that for a while until it's time to get serious." Sandra breathed her contempt out hard through her nose. "Yeah, and once they think they've got something steady at home, their noses are open for all kinds of side trips."

"If you're talking Rosey, there's a lot to notice," I said. It was an objective observation.

"Shut up," said Sandra. "If I wasn't all blown up like this, let me tell you, that bitch would be no competition. You just find out for me if she's got anything going on with my husband. Andre's been in New York so much over the last six months, they'll have him paying resident taxes pretty soon." I could hear her eating, crunching something that sounded like potato chips. She swallowed hard and began to cry again. "We stopped having sex since I got so big and now he says he's got to do a closing in New York over Christmas."

It was the first I had heard of Andre working on Christmas, but things were tough and a closing was a closing. I said so; and I told the story of Rosey's letter and her phone call, more to settle my mind than Sandra's. "I think Rosey's a dyke," I said, but the truth was her orientation seemed ambiguous in light of what I'd seen recently.

"So maybe she got confused." Sandra's mouth was full again and she was chewing. "Frankly, I don't care what it is that Rosalee Paschen *prefers* just as long as she keeps her paws off Andre. You're her friend, Virginia, or I guess you want to be. So, why don't you just find out what's up with her. It's in your best interest too, and besides, don't you still owe me for something — all those dates I got for you so you didn't have to look like such a freak?" Sandra laughed but not too convincingly. It was a hard slap in the face. My social indebtedness to her was something she'd never thrown up at me before.

There was a long silence after she figured out how far down her throat she had managed to wedge her foot and then she laughed some more, weakly, as if that might make things okay again. It didn't. I tucked the cordless phone up under my chin and started in on the tub again.

I believe in this life there are some things we really don't want to know about our friends, or families, or lovers. If Rosey was sleeping with Andre, that was one of them, and Sandra was asking me to maybe break my own heart. But she was right. I didn't think I owed her for the bad double dates that kept me from sitting home reading Emily Bronte on Saturday nights, not for anything so specific. But she was right about the debt, or rather the connection. What I owed her was loyalty, because we were the same: two small-town black girls wanting a little happily-ever-after out of life. I owed it to Sandra to let her know if anyone was dealing her shit. That included Rosalee, no matter how I felt about her, and no matter how it was going to make me feel. That included Andre, even if, standing in her shoes, I would rather not have known.

"So okay, we're even about the dates," Sandra was begging. "Just do this one thing for me, all right, because you love me? Sister? You do still love me, don't you, Virginia?" she said.

"Sure." Sandra and I went back a long way and however much she put her foot in it, that counted for something. "All right," I promised, because Sandra was my friend and besides there was no other way to get her off the phone.

When Andre called later, I'd finished cleaning the bathroom and my mother was nicer about giving me the message, but I didn't care much for Andre's tone.

"Listen," he said. "You know, my wife's stopped speaking to me over this thing with Rosalee Paschen. You're Sandy's friend, Virginia. You've got to help me out."

I wasn't sure I remembered signing up with him for those particular obligations, but I agreed we could meet at the White Horse Saloon on Main Street in an hour. When I was in high school, we'd called it "The Whore" and were delighted with our sophistication.

I was late and at thirty-five minutes past one o'clock Andre was waiting under the Whore's faded red awning with the rearing white stallion painted on the front of it. He was looking only slightly less hangdog than he had the night before. He held the door open for me before he stomped the snow off his slip-on rubbers and followed me inside.

The Whore was a dark kind of one-room Midwestern bar with some broken-down wooden tables and chairs in the center, and about eight high-back booths with old black vinyl upholstery lined up along the walls and in front of the windows. The hamburgers came with extra grease and the pizza was so thin and limp the cheese slid right off when you picked it up.

Bob Callen from my American Government class, junior year, was working the bar, looking just like 1980-something with a flannel shirt hanging out from his jeans and a ponytail under his John Deere cap. The place still kept Bud and Old Milwaukee beer on tap and Bob remembered my face if not my name, enough to give us a free round of the Bud for old times' sake along with a basket of stale-looking potato chips from the bar.

Andre put the beers down on the table, slid into the opposite side of the booth and began to take a frowning inventory of the jukebox. Melissa Etheridge was singing some B-side cut about long dead love and old familiar bars. I remembered that Emery and I used to sit in the Whore all day Saturday when we were home for Christmas, because in Blue River there wasn't a drink to be bought on Sunday. Emery would smoke Camels from a beat-up pack, trying to look tough while I watched. The habit was new and he needed to practice it. "Why did you start," I'd ask him.

And he would laugh and say, "To look older for the bars."

His voice had gotten low and raspy since he'd started and I'd liked it better before. I'd say, "Why don't you stop."

He'd laugh. "Can't stop." He'd shake his head and laugh some more and inhale wrong and start in coughing. I thought now, "Can't stop" was the way with a lot of things.

Somebody had spent his quarter to buy Roy Orbison and k.d. lang singing "Crying," sounding just like some winsome brother and sister, and Andre looked thankful for the book of alternate jukebox selections chained to the wall. But after he'd flipped through the music book twice, he gave up and went back to his beer, frowning some more at the window glass.

We had the prime booth by the open storefront, with a view that featured Main Street from Ewing's

Drugs all the way down to the clock on the top of the Blue River Deposit Bank and a gutter full of dirty snow. The window frame was warped away from the glass, and last season's flies were rotting into dust on the battered wood sill.

Andre put his beer down. "Good tunes. Great ambiance, Virginia." He shook his head miserably. "Well, shit, I didn't come here for the entertainment, but it would be nice if there were some." And he laughed his big laugh and drank his beer, sprawling his legs out in the booth.

The sun was coming through our window, warming up the right side of my face and neck, the first sun in two grey overcast days, and I realized that against my better judgment, I was starting to like Andre, his five o'clock shadow at two in the afternoon, his big butch black man laugh, and the whole hard-bodied, Y-chromosome ethos of male otherness which I'd been missing since Emery died. It was a little vacation from the cast of women who populated my social interaction, and if I squinted I could almost see its appeal through Sandra's eyes — or maybe even Rosey's. I was hoping Andre wouldn't spoil the moment by telling me anything I didn't want to have to repeat.

He put a potato chip in his mouth and I watched him lick the salt off his fingers, grinning a bad boy grin that he pulled from somewhere out of his depression. "Well, I've been in worse dives than this," he said. "Not much worse, though." He was still wearing his cream-colored cashmere scarf like some Noel Coward character on the way to a formal cocktail party, but he'd balled his expensive coat up in the corner of the booth like regular folks.

There was a long jagged knife scar in the upholstery behind his head, and in the background the jukebox had slipped off into "Love Me Tender." I told him I frequented the Whore exclusively for the food.

Andre said, "I'm from Missouri; show me."

So, we ordered a double sausage pizza with extra cheese. It had just come to our table on a greasy piece of cardboard and a bed of cornmeal when I saw Rosalee come out of the dime store on the corner of Main and Birch. She put a little bag in the trunk of a red Ford with rental plates and an Avis sticker. Even if she hadn't been with the car, it surely looked like the one I'd seen on Dean Street Friday morning.

"There's Rosey," I said. She was wearing the camel hair coat and jeans and a designer-looking wool scarf tied around her neck in no special arrangement. I'd watched her walk half a block past the Whore, and Elaine's Bakery, towards Ewing's when I noticed my mouth was dry and I'd lost my appetite. "It's Rosey," I said again as if there wasn't a single other thought in my head and I squeezed Andre's arm across the table like he was my teenaged slumber-party confidant. "Will you look."

Andre grunted and turned slowly toward the dirty window as if he would rather not. "Trust me, Virginia, that and a quarter'll get you a cup of coffee." He tapped the window glass with his index finger and scowled. "Listen to somebody who knows."

I said, "I thought that was what we were here for — your confessions." But Andre only had about half of my attention. My eyes were still following Rosey's camel hair coat down the street. After a block the coat got lost in the doorway of Spike's Cafe.

"My confessions." Andre laughed as if nothing were particularly funny. "But that's the point — I don't have any sins, nothing venial anyway." He knocked on wood. "Nothing God doesn't know about," he said. "But fuck that — what worries me is Sandra."

Andre turned towards the back of our booth and took a deep breath. Behind us, a man I didn't know was smoking. "There's not a thing I'd love more right now than a cigarette." He had just quit, he told me. Both he and Sandra quit because of the baby. "I used to only smoke at work. And then I said well, why do it halfway. But, you know, I do miss them with a drink." Andre showed me his dimples, all three, including one in his chin that I hadn't noticed before. "Aw hell," he said. "See? I've given up all my vices. And where does it get me?"

The neon sign in the window was blinking on and off in the shape of a dog with a shiner, advertising Budweiser Beer. The bar was warm and close inside from cooking and body heat and I could smell him across the table from me, his soap and his skin and the sweat that was beading up where his moustache ended on his upper lip. Outside the wind blew the tree branches around, blew open coats and pulled at scarves and hats. He put his beer down and stared out at the street.

"I don't know," I said. "Where does virtue get you?"

Andre said, "Exactly nowhere. Like the law, like everything else." He rolled his thick shoulders, and hunched down over his beer again.

I asked him, "So, counselor, why are we here?"

Andre was staring down at the table. A shadow fell across his eyes so dark that I thought for a second there were tears in them. "Because I love my wife." He looked up and the tears were gone. "Rosalee and I had a kind of a flirtation. Dumb stuff. And she must have decided it was something more — or she wanted it to be. I don't know. We went out a few times while Sandra and I were engaged, before we were married. But Rosey knew I was engaged. Is it so strange that a man and a woman can hit it off and be just friends? Two people being human, like this, like you and me, Virginia?" He took my hand across the table and screwed up his eyes as if he thought he could tell whether I believed him by staring at me hard enough. When he couldn't, he shrugged. "Anyway, it was all before I was married, right?"

And I felt the odd complicated attraction that I sometimes had to men. I was enjoying the feeling. It de-personalized whatever had gone on between him and Rosey, the sense of rejection I might have felt became not rejection but a kind of shared intimacy that Rosey and I could feel this same attraction. It felt like drinking out of the same dirty glass. And his blackness made me believe if she had loved him, then, surely, she could love me too.

"Can't you believe that a man and a woman can be just friends?" Andre asked me, taking my hand.

"Sure." I pulled my hand back and cupped it around my beer glass. His was left there by itself in the middle of the table. After a while he took his back too. "So, then, you'll talk to Sandy," he asked me.

"Sure. Maybe." I shrugged, "Did you sleep with Rosalee?"

I was sorry to see the sexiness go out of Andre's eyes. He raised his broad shoulders up around his ears, shrugging back. "It doesn't matter, does it? If Sandy thinks I did, then I'm completely fucked. Why shouldn't she? I was with my first wife, Jocelyn, when I met Sandra." Andre sighed. "And I'm pretty fucked with her already because I have to work over Christmas."

"Really?" I was talking about the business with his first wife, because I already knew about his Christmas plans, but he answered, "Yeah really," to the wrong question, and followup seemed to be in poor taste.

Andre looked down at the table top and traced the carving of some amateur woodcut artist with his finger. "My flight leaves Columbus at two o'clock. We're going to have Christmas dinner late in the morning so we can eat together and her dad's coming home to be with her tomorrow. So, I guess it's all right."

The knife-work on the table top said, *Troy and Allison forever.* Andre took my hand again and squeezed it hard as if he might have hurt me, or as if he might have wanted to. The veins in his wrist stood out and his skin had the dull warm gloss of polished wood. "I'm swearing to you, Virginia, Rosey and I just went to the movies a couple of times, usually with other people, other lawyers. And if she's made it into something else, I don't think I should have to pay for that. I didn't even know she and Sandy knew each other. I didn't think about it. It was way before I was married and I didn't have anything to hide."

Andre's eyes were almost black like my father's, large and opaque as two deep holes, and I couldn't be sure of what was at the bottom. Their surface was calming though, like the quiet nights, deep sleep and pleasant dreams I wanted to believe in. He said, "I swear she's blown the whole thing all out of proportion."

When he let my hand go, I felt it sort of pulse from where the blood came back into it again, and I was sorry for him.

Andre closed his black eyes and sighed. "It all seems like such a long time ago, now Sandra and I are going to have this kid."

"So," I told him, "just let it go." It was advice I should have given myself, but then again I wasn't looking for advice.

Andre rubbed his forehead. "I thought I had. And then Rosalee Paschen shows up from nowhere and makes this scene." He looked me hard in the eyes again and he spoke with the persuasive soft-voiced intimacy of promises made in the dark: "Now, what I need from you, Virginia, is to get Sandra to let it go. I need for you to talk to her." He took another gulp of his beer and belched. "Excuse me," he said, and then, "I wish to hell I knew what it is that women want, you know?"

I didn't.

"You know what men want?" He put his glass down again on the table, hard.

I thought, Men want sex. My father explained this over a very expensive lunch at the Oak Club

Restaurant when I was maybe sixteen or seventeen, by way of a cautionary word.

"From the age of about fourteen to sixty-five, men want sex," my father had said, expressing in this bit of wisdom he was doing right by his daughter. "Myself included," said my dad. His world was black and white for the sake of simplicity, peace and order. "No exceptions, men are pigs."

I've since learned that in one respect my father was right, that everyone is capable of pigginess. Women too, with few exceptions — myself included.

Andre rolled a piece of pizza into a log and bit it. "Do you know what men want?" He answered himself with his mouth full. "Men want everything, Virginia. We're just like kids. We just want everything and sometimes we can't decide."

Through the window I could see Main Street all decorated with holly and tinsel on the street lights, promising Santa Claus and presents. I said, "That's what women want too. Too many people chasing too little happiness. Everybody wants a little more than they've got and the world keeps spinning around."

Andre looked at me blankly as if I were speaking a language he didn't understand. Then he said to me in very plain English, "You know, I didn't appreciate it at first when Sandra told me you were a dyke." He leaned on the word as if it might explain any number of flaws in my character. "I thought you might be carrying a torch for my wife. I couldn't blame you because Sandy's very, very special. And hell, it seems to me like kind of a waste, you're a nice looking woman yourself. But live and let live is what I say, you know?" He took another bite of his pizza and showed me his dimples. "I don't think you could get Sandra, though."

"No." I smiled too because I liked Andre in spite of his nasty politics, for giving me something easy to tell my friend, and because men are so very simple sometimes. "No. I don't think so; she loves you very much," I said.

"Well, I've got what she needs." Andre raised his hand for Bob Callen to bring us over another couple of beers.

Two rounds later Rosey Paschen came back for her car.

"There she is again." I gathered up my coat and purse from the booth beside me, and told Andre I had to go. I had heard his version; however much I wanted to let things go at that, a promise was a promise. I said, "Look, I've got to talk to Rosey. I'll come by the house and have that chat with Sandra later, all right?"

"Whatever you want. Just get Sandra to relax, will you?" Andre looked down into his glass and I left him there to pick up the tab. From outside I could see him still scowling over his beer. He looked up and waved goodbye with an open hand and crossed fingers. My cheeks were burning with a cheerful kind of optimism that made me believe everyone would get exactly what they wanted this Christmas. I could barely feel the cold as I ran down the street to catch up with Rosey.

VII

Rosalee Paschen's rental car pulled away from the curb before I could reach her. So, I made an illegal U-turn in my father's beater. She'd crossed Cherry, Birch and Pine Streets downtown and was heading north towards Maple when a dirty blue Toyota cut me off and I was stuck behind one of the five stoplights in town after she'd turned left on Center Street. It was a long light with a left-turn arrow. But it changed in time for me to see Rosey stick a note card in the front door of Mary Cornish's little bungalow at the corner of Center and Walnut, then march double-time in her tennis shoes and sweats down the snowy walk back to her car, hunching her shoulders and rubbing her hands together in the cold.

Miss Mary Cornish was both the algebra teacher and the high school guidance counselor, because Blue River was a small district and she'd had to double up. The most interesting thing about Miss Cornish was that in retrospect I thought she was a dyke. She'd lived with the social studies teacher, Miss Cahill, for years. They'd bought the place on Walnut Street God knows how long ago and if two spinster school teachers playing house together had raised any eyebrows then, people had gotten used to the idea over time.

Miss Cahill had died of cervical cancer a year before. My mother had clipped the story. Miss Cahill had rated a paragraph which carried no mention of family or friends, no mention of Mary Cornish. She had left Miss Cornish to live in the little house alone except for three famously ratty-looking Yorkshire terriers.

There wasn't even time to park before Rosey was headed back down Center, then south to Cosgood, and three stop signs to Sutton.

I hung back as she made a left onto Dean and parked across the street from the old frame house where she used to live. I parked too, a few houses up on the opposite side of the street, because there wasn't a doubt that Rosalee Paschen was the woman I'd seen Friday morning and I wondered why she'd lied, and because I didn't like secrets, and because I was waiting to talk to her. But mostly because even though it was spying, I couldn't stop.

Rosey stepped out of her car over the sooty snow piled in the gutter onto the walk and climbed the front porch stairs. As she stood there, the wind blew her hair off her forehead and then whipped it around in the opposite direction like a thick yellow cap pulled down to her cheeks.

I knew from the times I'd rung the doorbell waiting to give Rosey a ride to a softball game or a practice, the times I'd rung it on any slim desperate excuse to see her outside of practice or class, that it was mounted on the right in the white wood siding between the door and the front windows, below the mailbox. But Rosey didn't ring it. Instead she beat against the door with her fist as if she were swinging a heavy hammer. The door opened suddenly and widely, and behind it was the same older woman from the morning before with the white grey hair, this time styled in loose thin curls all around her head. I saw her for just a second and then the door began to swing closed again hard and fast. Rosey caught the door with her hand, and there were words again from Rosey or maybe from the older woman who I took now to be her mother. But the words were so jumbled up in the wind that they were mostly sound and fragments.

The driver's side window of my car was fogging up in the cold. I rolled it down and could hear much better but their conversation still didn't make a lot of sense to me.

Rosey was screaming into the empty space beyond the doorway. "Liar!" She was pushing her way inside the house and shouting, "Son of a bitch! You can't hide behind her anymore!" And the old woman was ducking and dancing in the threshold of the door like some bony marionette as if she could block the words with her body.

The old woman's voice was shrill. "You're the liar!" She had slipped back into the house pulling the door closed while Rosey tried to stop the motion with her hand.

"How can you talk to me this way?" Rosey slumped as if the exchange had somehow weakened her. "I'm your daughter."

The old woman's voice was as cold as the wind blowing through my open window. "I don't have any daughter. I don't have any daughter anymore only a stranger telling lies and I don't know who you are." The words came out in a hard fast spray like buckshot from the barrel of a bird gun and the force of them seemed to push Rosey back from the doorway.

The old woman said, "Whoever you are I wish you were dead."

Rosey's hand dropped away and when the door

slammed, it shook the little house. The sound of wood on metal weatherstripping hung in the wind for what seemed like a long time and I watched Rosalee stand on the porch just waiting, as if the noise had made her stupid and punch-drunk, staring at the heavy white door as if she thought it might open again. Finally she shook her head and walked slowly down the porch stairs, back over the snow in the gutter, and across the street to her red rental car.

I watched that too and the scene seemed to move in slow motion, leaving time enough for me to consider the craziness of my sitting in a car outside her house and watching her like some made-for-television stalker-psychopath, when I was a grown woman with a responsible job and a mortgage and a promise to my friend, Sandra, that I needed to keep.

Rosey sat with her head bent over the steering wheel of her car for a long time before I decided to do the sensible adult thing. I got out and crossed the street, walking towards Rosey's car so I could say my piece for Sandra. I would have sworn that our eyes met for a minute as I was looking into her passenger window, before she turned her key in the ignition and drove away.

She pulled off going south on Dean and this time following her I felt more like chasing her because I couldn't shake the feeling that Rosalee was avoiding me. I stayed behind the red Ford for the twenty miles to the Southtown Valley Mall. Then I trailed her on foot through four department stores, buying things I didn't need: a scarf for my mother two counters down from the costume jewelry where Rosey was browsing; a tie for my father in men's wear where she was looking at sweaters; and some stale popcorn from a man in a clown suit while Rosey used the public toilets. I wasn't sure how I was going to talk to someone who didn't want to talk to me. I kept looking for that perfect conversational opening that might make it possible to pretend that our meeting was some trick of chance. Rosalee finally spun around outside of Tower Records and faced me.

"Why are you following me, Virginia?"

If I'd known maybe I could have told her. But standing in the middle of the mall I was sheepish and she was beautiful. Her trendy haircut had fallen from the wind into unruly clumps that hung in her eyes. She was the messy unkempt Rosey Paschen I'd adored in a grey athletic sweatpants and the same hightop Chuck Taylors I remembered from ages ago. I liked the way her full lips moved even as they said, "What the hell is wrong with you?"

The mall was lit up in one giant orgy of red and green commercialism and "What Child Is This" was roaring out from the loudspeaker system in lieu of the usual Muzak. "Nothing," I said. "I'm doing the Christmas thing, you know. I'm fine. How's it going?" I thought we might sit by the plants and the waterfall in the middle of the mall and talk. I thought we might go shopping. I thought we might go to bed.

"Look," she said. "This is weird, Virginia. I know you've been following me since I pulled away from the White Horse Saloon and I've got trouble enough without having to see your face every time I turn around. I've seen your face more today than Santa's."

She stuck out her lower lip in a way I found especially appealing. "What exactly do you want?"

"I thought you might want to talk." She was making me mad. I said, "I thought you might have something to say about why you needed me to come to this fucking reunion so badly. That's all. You wanted me here. Now I'm here and I thought you might want to talk about it."

When she sat down on the bench by the waterfall and the tropical plants, I told her, "You know, I've been in love with you for years." It had worked for Spike; I thought it might work for me. In the distance down the center walkway I could see a nativity scene with live animals as a kind of petting zoo. "I thought maybe it might be a mutual interest, you know, after all these years, and I was wondering if that's what you wanted to tell me when you called." In some mirrors by the wall I could see myself duck my head as I talked to her in a sweet, stupid sentimental kind of way that I couldn't help. I hoped she would find it endearing.

"This is too weird, Virginia." She laughed and it felt like a punch in the stomach. "You're ten years late. I'm all over that."

I watched our reflections in the mirror by the wall.

"It's funny," she said, "to be saying something like that to a girl."

"Not so funny." It wasn't funny to me. I asked her if she was saying she never cared. "Look, what has changed here?" I said. "What about all the things you said to me? How can you decide to be over me when you didn't even give us a chance?" I asked why she'd bothered to call me in September.

She was pulling the skin off her lips with her teeth. "Not for this." Her reflection rolled its eyes and pouted some more.

"Which means what?" Down at the end of the mall by Sears, a harried-looking mother was yanking her son's arm so hard I thought she might dislocate his shoulder. On the bench beside us a teenage father who looked too young to shave was smacking his toddler upside the head. "Look, I saw you today with that woman on Dean Street. I know it was you on Friday just the same as you know I've been following you. You looked me straight in the eye before you drove away just now." The girl-child on the bench beside us was still wailing. I said, "You saw I was coming over to your car and you didn't stop. So, why don't you tell me what's going on?"

Rosey sighed some more and pushed the hair out of her eyes. "Well, that's complicated, and this really isn't the place. This just isn't working out the way I expected."

This meeting with Rosalee was reminding me unhappily of a woman who I had loved and loved, and who said she was straight and so couldn't love me back. She had called me up one evening after I was over it asking if we could go together to a women's bar. I thought of the sound of my voice when I didn't want her. I heard my own laughing voice coming out of Rosey's mouth at me, and the satisfaction to have moved beyond the things you thought you couldn't live without.

"This just isn't the place." She sighed. "And you don't even know me anymore, Virginia. I'm not sure you ever did." Her eyes looked tired and watery and I thought for a moment she was going to cry, but she didn't. "Listen to me, Ginny. You're not who you were, and I'm not who I was. I'm sorry, but I can't stop time for you. Whatever it is you're looking for, you can't get back."

She was right. I was looking back at that graduation party ten years ago when I thought she loved me. It seemed to me in a lifetime of moments as numerous as snowflakes there must be some that recur, there must be one or two that are exactly the same. The waterfall rained down on the floral arrangement in the center of the mall. The air still smelled like popcorn and fast food; it still sounded like Perry Como. In ten years the mall hadn't changed at all.

Rosalee stood up and crossed her arms over her chest. "Goodbye," she said. "Look, no harm, no foul. If it's any consolation, I've learned everybody needs to hold onto their version of history." She ran her hand through her hair and said, "I think it was a mistake for me to want you to come, but it was nice to see you." She said it as if we were ending a luncheon meeting of the Junior League. "It really was." And her politeness stung me like a paper cut. "I just wanted you to know, however I behaved ten years ago, it wasn't really about you. Do you understand?"

I was nodding even though I didn't and Rosey kept talking, encouraged by the magic of active listening.

She was saying, "Because I just want to be clear with everybody about where my head was then. People don't understand sometimes sex can be so —" She stopped, looking hard for the word she wanted. When she found it, it was kind of a disappointment.

She said, "Sex can be situational. And what I really wanted was to feel in control of something."

I nodded some more. Control was what I wanted too.

"Does that make any sense at all?" Rosey was talking to the dirty white floor tiles near my feet. "Do you understand?" she asked the floor.

"Sure. Okay," I said, although it wasn't really. Sometimes what people do to you is far less hurtful than what they fail to do, especially when you're all tuned up for it. "Listen, Rosey, I'm sorry about your life. I'm sorry about following you today," I said. "I'm sorry about that thing with your mother on the porch this afternoon." I didn't know for sure that they were related, but from Rosey's embarrassed expression my guess was right. If that was how Rosey was going to age, maybe it was best that she was rejecting me now. I told her, "Sometimes I get into it with my mother too and if you want to, you're welcome to have Christmas with us." I didn't know how my folks were going to react given their worries about what they referred to as my "lifestyle," but I invited her anyway because I wondered how her attraction to me could have simply evaporated, leaving, it seemed, not even warm regard. Mine for her hadn't gone anywhere. "It won't be anything really formal." I was talking fast like a second-rate salesman trying to make quota. It surprised me how much her acceptance could mean when she was right that I barely even knew her anymore, but old feelings are like ghosts; they don't rest easy. I said, "It's not going to be anything formal but we're having some single people from my Dad's office and

Harry Hobart too since he doesn't have any place to go."

Rosalee took a deep breath and blew it out. "Thanks," she said, "but no thanks." She had let her face go completely blank; and what had been there before, the frustration with what she couldn't seem to explain to me, had been replaced by a face you put on for strangers. "I'm going back to Manhattan on Monday," she told me. "Christmas Day some friends are coming into town and I'll spend the holiday with them."

I wondered if the friends included Andre Rutherford who I knew was flying to New York the afternoon of the twenty-fifth. It was the question I had promised to answer for Sandra, but I didn't have the heart to ask it just then.

"Goodbye, Virginia." Rosey took a shopping bag in either hand. "Merry Christmas."

She walked off into Macy's and I waited all afternoon for her, sitting in my father's old beat-up car with the engine running and the radio playing Christmas carols on some AM station. I wasn't through talking even if Rosey was. There was the question of Andre's infidelity which I'd botched for starters. There was still her unexplained phone call to me in September and her note and her demand that I come to this reunion. But as sure as I felt that there was more to say, I needed time to collect my thoughts, and the Southtown Valley Mall seemed as good a place as any. A better place than say the Johnny Appleseed since I didn't know if Rosey was planning another visit to Mary Cornish's or her parents before she went back to her room. The parking lot of the Southtown Valley Mall turned out to be a surprisingly tranquil place even in the middle of the Christmas rush and by the end of the afternoon I knew all the words to "Oh Little Town of Bethlehem" by heart.

It was dark when Rosey finally left the mall. I turned off the radio and kept waiting there until she'd backed out of her space and turned down the aisle, until I was sure she couldn't see me. Then I followed her all the way back to town from two cars behind. The bad news was: Rosey didn't go back to the Johnny Appleseed Inn. The good news was: from what I saw, my friend Sandra Rutherford's troubles seemed to be over.

Rosalee drove from the mall to Harry Hobart's house, six miles outside of the city limits. The little ranch house sat back from the road down a long gravel lane. Behind it was nothing but farmland and scraggly brambles and old weeds; somebody had planted hedge fences before there were cars and highways. I cut my lights and pulled over to the side of the road near the entrance to Hobart's driveway, then hiked down the snowy gravel lane to the front of the house. The soles of my shoes squeaked along in the old frozen show, and I was happy for the sound of a car in the lane to cover the noise — until the car almost hit me.

In the floodlight at the bend in Hobart's lane, I caught a glimpse of a little blonde babydoll face before I jumped out of the way. It was stained with tears and running makeup she was way too young to need. The car squealed around the bend and I picked myself up out of the hedge bushes in time to see its red taillights in the dark, glowing brighter when the driver hit the brakes at the end of the lane. They were gone as the car turned away down the two-lane highway.

The car was a dark blue Saab. The plates had said "PAGE 16." Page Crawford, I guessed, Hobart's little tutee. Her father owned Crawford's European Motors off old Route 45. My recollection of Addie's baby-sitting days made Page twelve years younger than me, sixteen or maybe seventeen. She'd been in diapers when Addie had taken care of her and the memory made me feel old.

My feet had gotten wet from the snow in the time I had spent watching the Saab. I kept walking until I could see the lights of Hobart's house. There were two figures in the window, a woman and a man, both wearing glasses. I couldn't hear their voices but in the shadows they made on the blinds, I saw him put both arms on her shoulders and pull her close to him.

My toes were beginning to seize up as the melted snow froze around my tennis shoes; and it seemed then that it was time to go. I took out the cheap little watch I'd found earlier in the pocket of my ski vest, wound and set it at a quarter to eight o'clock by my own, then stuck it under the rear wheel of Rosey's rental car like Jack Nicholson did in the movie *Chinatown* so I would know what time she left. Not that it mattered, but I couldn't stand not knowing if she'd spent the night. Then I tightened my little wool plaid scarf around my chin and began the long walk back down the drive, making up the story I was going to tell my folks about missing dinner.

The wind seemed even colder and I felt pretty happy to see my dad's old beater by the side of the road. I was happier still when after much complaining and flickering of the battery light, it finally turned over and I could head down the road towards home. I was about four miles from Hobart's house, out in the very middle of nowhere, when the engine started threatening death. My gas gauge had registered one quarter full before I'd followed Rosey to the mall, but when I checked it in light of my sputtering engine, it was sitting just south of empty.

Years ago in my prime, I'd taken this old car right down to the wire. Miles on empty, defying the laws of physics, passing gas stations and daring it to stop on me as if those stolen miles were like found money, but I'd lost my nerve somehow.

The first thing I did was to turn off the engine and coast down every hill from old 235 to Jekell Road, driving slowly when I had to drive, with the heater off and the car in low gear. There was three feet of snow blown up against the fences along the road, and I was still a good two miles from home in a hatless condition and a sleeveless fake-down vest that wasn't made for hiking up the ominous hill by the broken-down farm where Brad Johnson Sr. kept his harness rigs and his saddle horses, and where Rosalee had first kissed me. It was nine-thirty by the dying clock on the dashboard when I finally shut off my headlights, praying I could get home on fumes. But things weren't looking very good and at the top of Johnson's hill I floored it, hoping the momentum would take me back up the other side like a roller coaster. It did, but not much further, and I rolled to a dejected stop at the intersection of Jekell Road and Route 45.

But hiking home down the Interstate was no more of a disappointment than the news that Rosey could prefer men, any men, to me. I thought of her under Harry Hobart's ham-handed embraces and couldn't get warm again.

That night Spike's apartment came between me and hypothermia. After the first half-mile, I was elated and relieved to discover her address in the pocket of my jeans and that her place was on the way home. Spike didn't ask any questions when she found me on her doorstep and I was pretty happy about that too. Warm and happy enough to find myself, in short order, lying sideways on her blue tweedy sectional couch with Spike's hands inside my shirt. After a while she spread herself on top of me and we both came from her weight in that old adolescent surprise of friction that used to leave me with a sense of vague chagrin and the nagging question as to whether I had really made love. That night somehow Spike managed to make me think I had. Out of breath and smiling above me in the dim light from the ceramic jug lamp on her end table, she closed her green eyes and gave me a chain of quick little kisses on the mouth; afterwards she was nice enough to drive me back to where I'd left the car with a can full of gas.

"Come by again for a cup of good cheer before

you leave," Spike said as I opened the door to let myself out of her car. Then she reached across the seat and pulled me back in for a goodbye kiss. "Rosalee Paschen is nothing but trouble," Spike said while she had me close, as if a word to the wise was, in fact, sufficient.

Maybe it wasn't. Or maybe I wasn't as smart as I looked.

It was nearly midnight by the time I poured the gas in my tank and got back over to Hobart's place. I drove down his driveway this time, without my lights. The windows were dark and Rosey's car was gone, but my watch was there by the tire tracks and the oil stain in the frozen gravel, by the floodlights near his stoop. The crystal was cracked in too many places to count. It was stopped at ten minutes before nine.

I kept my headlights out all the way down the lane to the highway. I made the left back to town and was following the broken yellow lines the way I'd come towards the lights of Blue River, such as they were, when I noticed another set of flashing blue lights in my rear view mirror and I knew it was the end of a perfect day.

When I was a kid, I knew all the cops in Blue River by name, sight, and reputation. Which ones sat out at the edge of town looking for out-of-state license plates to make their ticket quotas, which ones would chat you up in front of the Whore and then pull you over for driving under the influence on your way home. Which ones would bust you for breaking curfew, which ones got their jollies from cruising the side streets shining their high beams on the half-naked couples making out in parked cars. I remembered Officer Kidder as all of the above and more.

Officer Kidder barked at me through the open window, "All right young lady, let's get out of the car." His baton was slapping out an even, threatening rhythm against his palm and what was worse, in the closed car I could still smell the sex on my clothes from my roll around Spike's living room.

I remembered the Ohio State co-eds my mother said had been found sliced up in these woods, and another story Sandra had told me years ago about this same red-necked Officer Kidder hauling her out of the car half-naked when he'd caught her parked with Reggie Moore one night by Waller State Park. She said Kidder didn't even have the decency to look away while she put on her clothes.

He was a wiry red-faced man with a greying crewcut and beady eyes, all muscle and sinew, his face made redder by the cold. He shifted his weight back and forth on the balls of his feet and he played with his baton as if his hands were itchy. They were as red as his face, chapped and broken from the cold.

"Out of the car, young lady, you heard me." Kidder took my license and grunted at the picture. But when I gave him my registration, I saw Kidder's ugly face crack a smile.

He said, "Oh, you're one of the Kelly girls," as if he liked my Dad or he'd dated my sister. "All grown up, then are you?"

"Yeah," I said.

"Yeah?" He looked me up and down before he handed me back my license. "I guess you are." He rubbed his hands together. "You can get back in the car, honey. I'm going to let you off this time. So, thank me." His laughter sounded like a hacking cough. Then he narrowed his eyes. "But you do yourself a favor and slow down, hear? Because, you'll live longer."

I nodded and he kept babbling like he was lonely for company. "Lots of accidents on this road. Last year some poor bastard hit some black ice down on Route 45 and just slid right into a tree. Last February. Seems like a long time ago. Before those dyke feminist women's crisis center bitches talked my wife into walking out." He was leaning on the car with his head halfway in my open window. "Things sure are changing around here." His ears were red along with everything else and his breath smelled like he'd been burping up polish sausage from years ago. "Damn faggot yuppie bastards moving in, driving up housing prices and drinking fancy coffee like they own the fucking world." He slid his baton back into the loop at his belt. "Hell, you can't even get a hamburger in this town unless you want some goddamn chinese lettuce on the side. You know, I miss her sometimes, my wife, when it's cold like this." Kidder gave me a smile that made my skin crawl. "You tell your old man Kidder told him hi, and you just remember, little lady, you got off easy."

I told him that I didn't doubt it. I waited until the lights of his squad car were faint little specks of red in the distance before I headed home.

VIII

That night I could barely sleep for wondering what Page Crawford was doing leaving her English teacher's house at eight o'clock on a Saturday night, or more importantly, what Rosey could have been doing there for an hour that she wouldn't have wanted to keep doing all night long. I wondered when it was that Rosey and Hobart had gotten together, and whether Marge had known and why Hobart had put on the show for me Friday morning when he'd given me the ride home, pretending he hadn't heard from Rosalee in years. I wondered why Rosey was having Christmas dinner in Manhattan and Hobart was having Christmas dinner at my house. Mostly, I wondered what Rosey had told Harry Hobart about our talk at the Mall, and if her version of our discussion gave me any cause for future embarrassment. All the wondering was giving me a stomach ache and putting crows' feet under my eyes. So, by morning I'd resolved to go over to the Johnny Appleseed and get the story from the horse's mouth. But Sandra called early and made me an offer I couldn't refuse.

"Why don't you come to brunch," she said. "Sid's here. He's dying to see you." Then Sandra whispered into the receiver, "And he's got a new wife." That made the invitation nearly irresistible. Sid was Sandra's father.

When I was growing up, Sid wasn't like the other fathers on our block. For one thing, he was a member of the magic circle; he pulled rabbits from hats and flowers from canes, and scarves that went on forever out of the sleeves of his suit jackets. Sid was a plumbing contractor who didn't work nine-to-five and he always had time in the middle of the day to spend with us. When his name was mentioned in our house, my mother looked stern and my father would laugh like he'd been told a very dirty joke. My father called him "the magic dachshund," when my mother couldn't hear. If Sid had a new wife I figured it had to be number three at least, if you were only counting the ones he married.

In 1969, when divorce was a rare and sordid thing, the disintegration of the Crabs' marriage was the biggest scandal of my parents' set. I remember hearing them whisper the details of Kathy's complaints and Sid's infidelities over coffee at night when they thought my sister and I were asleep, my father muttering weary assent to my mother's provincial braying horror. Over the years, Sid went on to other improprieties — multiple white women, a vasectomy — and then he retired from his plumbing business to spend from Labor Day to April Fools' in Clearwater, Florida. Since Andre's closing in New York stretched from the crack of dawn on the day after Christmas to at least the twenty-seventh, Sid had agreed to bring his new wife for a family Christmas such as it was.

Other adults in my life were Mr. or Mrs., sometimes Miss, occasionally Ms., but Sid was just Sid for as long as I could remember and it never felt strange to call him that. Maybe because the way my parents talked about him, Sid always sounded like a naughty boy. According to Sandra, Sid and his wife had flown in very late the night before and I decided that if Rosalee Paschen had waited ten years she might as well wait a little while longer. Besides, I'd never gotten around to talking to Sandra. After what I'd seen that night at Hobart's I figured I could put her mind to rest.

"I'm going to Sandra's for brunch," I told my mother. "Sid's got a new wife." I let it drop as casually as I could and waited for her eyes to light up, and then I promised, "I'll tell you all about it when I get back." I figured I owed my mother a little happiness.

Sandra's house was a red brick ranch just up the street. The drapes in the picture windows were open and I could see a big metallic tree beside the fireplace. Sid came out on the porch to meet me, saying "You look fabulous, dear, really fabulous," and his eyes creased and crinkled with their old mischief.

Sid Crab was about the same age and size as my own father, but somehow he wore it better. His girth had managed to stay around his chest instead of his waist. He had all his hair and his skin still looked as soft and smooth as Italian leather. The gold around his hairy chest was cold on my cheek as he bent down, grunting, to give me a bear hug.

When I came out of it I noticed an Alfred Hitchcock-style blonde in a tight red suit at his elbow — one of his famous icy blondes pushing fifty with a good nip and tuck doctor. She took my hand in a limp handshake.

"This is Betty." Sid chuckled slightly to himself. "The third time's the charm."

If the remark was tasteless (and I thought it was), Betty didn't seem to notice. My acquaintance with Sandra and Sid had survived Thelma, Lola,

Elaina, Louise and Cheryl after Sandra's mother, Kathy, so I suppose Sid felt he had to say something.

To Betty I said, "Pleased to meet you." To Sid, I whispered, "Yes, I certainly hope so." He winked while he held open the door for Betty and me.

The dining room table was set for five, with an enormous white pine cone centerpiece, gold sparkles glued to its base and sprigs of holly all around it. "Betty likes to do some arts and crafts," Sid said as if this were a major source of her attraction. I made the appropriate polite and appreciative sounds about the centerpiece, then the three of us sat on Sid's long leather sofa, Sid in the middle with Betty and me on either side. Sandra and Andre were in the kitchen.

Sid crossed his long Italian loafers over his knee and spread his arms across the back of the couch. "You married yet, Virginia?" Sid asked. "Any prospects?"

I shook my head and told him I was too young to get tied down. Betty made a clucking sound.

Sid rubbed his chin. "Fine-looking girl like you. Well, I couldn't tell you what's wrong with these young men today." He frowned as if he were thinking hard. "When I was your age, Kathy and I were having Sandra."

"Well, you were too young too, Sid." I laughed and Betty laughed too. The sound was soft and pleasant.

"Ah well, honey," Sid said. "Don't mind an old man." His hand slipped off the back of the couch onto Betty's knee. "Did I say the young folks were in the kitchen?" His hand was working its friendly way

128

north up her well-preserved thigh and I took it as my cue to fade.

In the kitchen Sandra was burning a Texas omelet. She had one hand on her hip and a red plastic spatula pointed at Andre, poking him in the chest. The spatula was leaving grease lines on his Ralph Lauren oxford button-down and he didn't look too terribly happy about it.

"You go on to New York and work on that closing," she said. "But Andy, baby, you are going to be one sorry bastard if I ever find out you're lying to me."

"Don't you think this is something better left for another time?" Andre looked at me and then back at the door with his eyebrows raised in a manner he must have thought was discreet. "I'm sure Virginia doesn't want to hear all this." He was using his best client consultation voice and it may have worked on clients but it didn't work on Sandra.

She was waving her spatula around. "I'm going on the record and I'll tell you one thing, my college-football-playing, big shot, ass-kissing, negro lawyer man. If I ever catch you fucking around on me like you did to Jocelyn, I'll kill you and your little side thing too." Sandra had her neck weaving back and forth again in that don't-you-fuck-around-with-the-sisters way, but her voice was low and sweet as pie. "Black women are over that old go-on-down-the-block-and-make-yourself-a-second-family bull-shit. And I don't care if it did give birth to Jesse Jackson."

"Are you through?" Andre said. He looked at me as if he thought I ought to leave.

Sandra flipped the omelet. "Honey," she said, "I

am too through." She up-turned the whole pan of mess into the sink. Then she dropped the skillet in on top of it and let the cold water run over the grease.

Andre put his hands in his pants pockets. "If you're through then I think I'm going out." The water hissed on the hot pan. Andre snatched his coat and scarf off the back of the kitchen chair and glared at me on his way through the doorway. "I'm out of here."

"Be my guest, Mister Big Shot," Sandra was shouting after him.

I heard the front door slam and a car engine turn over before Sid started yelling for Sandra from the living room. Sandra didn't answer. She was beating some new eggs in a bowl as if she had something against them.

"Rosey called this morning bold as brass and I'm going to tell you something," Sandra said to me. "You know, I've given you little pointers as long as we've known each other and from the way you've turned out it doesn't seem like you've taken most of them to heart."

I gritted my teeth and let that pass. Sandra said, "You'd better listen to this one before you go chasing after that Rosalee Paschen: White women are the only people in this life who have it easy and they will fuck you over to keep having it easy, hear?"

What I wondered was if Betty could hear, and I wished that Sandra would keep her voice down. But Sandra loved talking shit, and trying to stop her when she was on her African-American nationalist soap box was a little like standing in front of a downhill freight train.

I told her, "You know, if Rosey's fucking anybody, she's fucking Harry Hobart. I followed her last night to Hobart's house and saw them." It made me miserable all over again to hear the words, but I thought some good ought to come out of it. "Andre loves you a lot." It was nice to be able to keep two promises in one breath.

"He'd better." She pursed her lips at me.

I said, "I mean it. You know he does."

"Well. If he doesn't, girlfriend, I'm taking every cent he has." Sandra poked her belly out and rubbed the top of it with her open palm. "He's going to do right by me. This baby is going to Harvard right after he gets out of Chicago Latin and don't think that's going to come cheap." Sandra winked at me and I knew everything was going to be okay.

"Sandra?" Sid was shouting again from the living room, "Sandra, what is wrong with your husband. Jesus, he nearly knocked Betty down flying out of here."

Sandra looked at me and laughed. She wrinkled up her nose and her belly jumped up and down. We both laughed because whatever else changed, Sid would always be Sid.

She mixed up some onion with her eggs and shouted back, "Andy's just mad because I sent his lazy butt to the store for some more green pepper." She turned up the gas until the oil in her skillet started to crackle. "I'm telling you, Virginia, sometimes I think you have the right idea. I say,

131

Men: you can't live with them; you can't shoot them all." She pushed an empty glass at me from the counter, still chuckling. "Will you pour me some orange juice, girlfriend? This baby and I could use a drink."

We had worked our way through fruit salad, omelets and french toast without Andre. At one o'clock, when I was hugging Sid goodbye and wishing Betty a long and happy tenure, he was still nowhere to be found. If Sandra was worried, she didn't look it and I hugged her too before I headed off to the Johnny Appleseed.

I took the long way down Jekell Road to route 45, past Crawford European Motors. That's where I saw little Page Crawford in the Saab again pulling out of the showroom driveway. Page made a rather tentative left out in front of my old beater and I hadn't meant to be following her, but as it turned out we were going to the same place. In fact I might have thought we were going to a party because when I pulled into the Johnny Appleseed behind Page's Saab, Andre's Volvo was pulling out of the parking lot. If he saw me, he didn't wave and I thought maybe there were one or two little things Sandra and I were missing.

IX

Page Crawford had sat in the blue Saab for the better part of ten minutes while I watched. Twice I thought she was going to get out, but she just dabbed at her sweet little face with a paper tissue. In the end she just blew her nose, drove away and left me to my own agenda.

That morning, I'd dressed carefully as if the right combination of clothing could make Rosey change her mind about not wanting me.

What did I really expect? To say goodbye with a little dignity, to close a chapter in my fantasy life. This is what I would have told my sometime lover, Em, if she had cared, but the truth was I hadn't decided. I wanted everything and nothing. I wanted to go back in time for a little while, to meet Rosey again for the first time knowing what I knew now. I wanted to know what it would have been like if I'd said yes to her that night ten years before.

I looked at myself in the mirror in the faded dirty hall on the way to her rented room, making sure my face was perfect even though my throat felt like I'd been drinking stomach acid. It didn't help my digestion when Rosey answered the door without a robe like she was expecting someone else. She was wearing black cotton bikini panties with the name of a men's brief manufacturer stitched around the waistband. Her breasts were still full and high and the nipples were pushing against the lace of her thin black brassiere while I was looking down stupidly at the floor, at the walls, at the dirty wall paper in the bathroom and the rickety furniture, at her plane ticket in the blue United folder, anywhere but at her body.

My face was burning up. "I don't have any clothes on," I said when I meant to say nothing. "I mean you don't have any clothes on," I said.

"Jesus, Virginia." Rosalee laughed, it seemed, at me. She let me in and then went back into the bathroom to comb her wet hair while I followed her and stood in the doorway watching. "What does it matter? I don't expect I've got anything you haven't seen before, Virginia. You know, we're both girls."

"Yeah and I think we should talk about that," I said. "Now that you've brought it up."

"So, talk if you need to." Rosey closed the toilet and sat down on the lid. "I'm listening."

And I started: "Well, it's not just some sexual thing. I've really been in love with you for years." I had rehearsed this little flattery, on its face the honest truth, but underneath a sleazy line for where I was hoping it would get me. "You were the first person I ever loved and I've never really gotten over you." I had practiced this little play to death, but the grey and blue airline ticket folder on the dresser had made me panicky that I might not get to finish the second act.

"That's quite an announcement." Rosey ran her hands over her hair like a comb. "But I don't know what to say that I haven't said already."

"I mean it," I said. "You don't have to say anything. I guess I just wanted you to know." I laughed but the sound came out like coughing. I followed her the few steps from the washroom back over to the bed and sat down. "The thing is, I need to know if you ever loved me too, just for my peace of mind."

What makes disappointment is not any single act or omission. Rather it is the gulf between expectation and reality, crushed hopes. I was making a proposal. What did I expect? I suppose a counteroffer that would take us to a middle ground — not her hopes, not mine, but something that was livable for me when I had nothing. A negotiation, as if my feelings counted in the way that she chose to live her life.

Rosey sat down next to me on the edge of the bed. She put her hand on my shoulder as if she meant to be kind. Her palm felt hot. "That's not what this is about which is what I've been trying to explain." She puffed out her cheeks and sighed and stood up again. She walked across the room and back. "I was trying to explain at the mall that it's really not about you. That thing with us in high school was just sort of a symptom of some other problems I was having." She was sitting now on the edge of the bed, looking at the floor between her knees, playing with a little flat religious charm she wore, twisting the chain around in her fingers and I was standing by the bed. She said, "I'm not like you," without looking up.

"You used to be. How about it?" I walked towards her with my sad little proposal and knelt and put my arms around her pale white waist. "How about it? It sounds like you need somebody." I was telling her I needed somebody too and maybe we could try again.

Outside the snow was starting up and I could

hear the wind against the windows. She was saying, "You can't get it back, Virginia. Things are more complicated than that." She pulled the medal away from her neck so that it came between our faces blocking out my view of her lips. "You know my mother gave me this a long time ago. It's called miraculous. Miraculous. That was when she thought I was something special. She said it would keep me safe if I wore it. I never took it off and shit still happened. She was wrong and you can't get it back."

"You can try," I told her. My hands slid up her body in a way I had imagined a hundred times before, up her sides and along the bones of her ribs, then around to her breasts with open palms, until she pushed them away.

"What's wrong with you?" Rosey stood and picked up a shirt from her dresser, then pulled it over her head. "What do you think this is?"

"I don't know." Through the curtains I could see the sky getting dark. I said, "You know, everybody needs somebody."

"What's wrong with you," she said again.

I shrugged and couldn't say. "I have a moon in Scorpio. I guess that explains it all." It was a stupid answer and she looked like she thought so too.

"What?" she said. "What all does that explain?"

I said, "Everything, whatever it is you don't like. I had my natal chart done once on a lark, but I thought what it said was true."

Rosey was alternately running her fingers through her hair, fluffing out the frosted ends, and then smoothing them down again with her palm. She closed her eyes and took a breath before she spoke again. "When I was a kid, my stepfather used to pick us up, me and my sister, by our chins." She was telling me this story of abuse in a voice that sounded like numb recitation, without intimacy and as a shield against my demands, my objectification of her. I had heard this story before in pieces, years ago, more contemporaneously, but dismissed it then as an eccentricity of her family, abuse being so far from my own experience that I couldn't even imagine it happening to others. She was talking slowly, as if to a very stupid child, adding new detail now.

"He used to get drunk and come into our room at night and put his hand over our mouths to keep us quiet. He hit us if we cried. That's when my older sister ran away and my mother made us act as if she had never existed. We moved and then he came to me at night. We moved again and then it stopped and we pretended that nothing had ever happened. But there were other men for me after that, older men who seemed kind when somewhere in the back of my mind I thought I needed a daddy because I didn't have one. Not the kind you're supposed to have, anyway." Her voice sounded angry and used to disbelief. "So, what do you think all that explains?"

"I'm sorry," I said, and truly was.

She looked at me blankly and told me matter-of-factly, "Things are hard and I'm over it now. That's what I wanted to tell you. I wanted to tell everybody, my parents and everyone else that I remember what happened to me and I'm surviving. I'm over it." There were tears in her eyes.

Over it. "I'm still sorry, you know?" I stood up and put an arm around her shoulder and hated myself for mistrusting my intentions.

"Sure, thanks." Rosey wiped her face with the back of her hand. "You'd better go." She showed me to the door and held it open. Not out of any courtesy; it was an escort out of her life. She was over it. Over her hardships, grown past me.

I stood in the hall just looking at the metal door to her room for a while before I knocked again. When Rosey answered it this time she wore a big expensive-looking white terry cloth robe, and a broken expression.

"I am sorry," I said, "but, you know, I just can't leave it this way."

Inside the room was dark, darker than I remembered it a few minutes before. It held a closed sweet smell and behind her I watched the sun set low through a crack in the dirty drapes. Her bottom lip fell open as if she were going to ask me a question and I'd kissed her when I hadn't intended it, before I knew what happened, eyes open. Her breath went in and out and her lip tasted sweet like a full ripe grape with a tough skin.

Before I'd had enough she pushed me away. "Look, Virginia, I'm sorry. I have been with women but I can't do this now," she said. "I can't with you."

"You have with everyone else," I said. "You did with Hobart, and you did with Andre." It was a nasty, mean-spirited guess.

"Whatever." Her voice was sadder than it had been before. "Sure, you just think whatever you want. Whatever anybody wants to think about me. Why not?"

The shadows were mating on the wall behind her. It was something I would regret. But what was done was done.

Rosey shrugged; and I kissed her again half because I was sorry and half because I knew she'd let me. But her tongue in my mouth felt like old habits. She sighed when she pressed her body onto mine like the air pushing out of a slack balloon and I had the feeling Rosey had been through the motions before, and not happily. As we made love, I could have sworn there were hot tears falling over my legs and thighs.

The ghosts on the ceiling whispered how funny that I might have died for this in different circumstances; Emery and I might have changed places. Leaving him in the warm close air of this dingy motel room, with this girl who I knew less and less despite our sudden cheap familiarity, and me in some dark cold place beyond both love and family. I was looking for what? A connection. I could hear him rolling up to the windows with the winter fog, in the wind behind the dirty drapes, coaching me to fuck her again — and better this time — to wipe myself of her indifference. But I laid my head on her chest, instead, and listened to her heart as fondly as if it were my own. It was calming like the sound of the ocean inside a sea shell, and it didn't take long at all to fall asleep.

When I woke up some hours later, Rosalee was gone and the sheets were all over the floor beside the bed. There was no sign that she had ever been there; and when I checked the cheap press-board dresser drawers, they were empty of her things. All that was left was a piece of paper in the waste basket by the phone, a piece of Johnny Appleseed stationery, a strapping pie-faced youth with a backwards baseball cap and a shoulder bag the official logo. In the center of the paper was a phone number — Sandra Crab's. Or rather, Andre Rutherford's, considering who had called it.

I sat on the bed with the little piece of paper in my hand for a long time. The complete emptiness of the room in general gave me a panicky feeling in the pit of my stomach. Then I got mad — at Rosey for vanishing, at me for having put myself there in the first place, at the situation for leaving me with such a profound sense of embarrassment.

It seemed to me that if she hadn't wanted to then she shouldn't have. And if she'd wanted to then I couldn't see what the problem was. What frosted me especially was sitting all by myself in an empty motel room feeling like warmed-over manure because Rosey Paschen didn't know how to end an evening with a handshake. My first thought was to find her and give her a piece of my mind, but I didn't have any idea where she'd gone.

Downstairs at the check-out, the bill had already been paid. In cash. I made my nicest face for the clerk lounging behind the desk with his feet up showing off the patch job at the bottoms of his cheap dress shoes. He wore a textured button-down shirt, fraying badly at the cuffs, open at the neck above the tie, and his undershirt was showing. I was hoping he'd let a little more information drop my way, but he'd topped off his outfit with a kind of self-important smirk that required his lips to remain closed.

"I made a call to Columbus," I said when just cheesing at him didn't get me any dope. "I want to make sure it's on the bill so that we're square.

Could you let me see the phone log for room two-sixteen? I wouldn't want to see you get stiffed."

I figured a place like this kept a pretty tight audit trail for shortfalls, otherwise the staff and their pals were sure to get all kinds of freebies.

"Do you think there might be a discrepancy?" The muscles at the sides of his mouth got twitchy.

"Well, I don't know." I smiled some more. "But why don't you let me see?"

Now we were talking money, and that angle he was buying, retail. He showed me a short little computer printout with phone numbers on it, some of them repeats. A long distance call to New York I recognized from the 212 area code. The rest were local. One was to Sandra's at about ten-thirty that morning, a little before the fight I'd seen between Sandra and Andre. There was one to a local number I didn't recognize at about eleven at night on Saturday after Rosey had left Hobart's, and another to the same number at about five o'clock which she must have made while I was dead asleep in the bed next to her. There were two others on Saturday morning before noon, some others less than two minutes that I figured for carry-out food orders, but those were the high points.

The clerk looked at me expectantly until I told him, "I'm sorry but you don't have a record of the Columbus call." I folded up the phone log, put it in my pocket and pushed twenty dollars at him across the desk. "But I'm sure this will take care of it."

He stared down at the money lying on the top of the wood, and smiled as if he took my meaning.

"Why don't I just sign the guest register and

then I'll be on my way." I leafed through the pages slowly from front to back without even picking up the black plastic pen that was tethered to the binding, but the clerk didn't seem to notice. He was keeping a close eye on the twenty as if he were worried it might walk away. So, I took my time and read the names of the people in the book.

There were no Paschens. The Johnny Appleseed appeared to be visited mostly by Smiths, Joneses, and Browns. I signed my name Kathy Johnson just to stay in the spirit of things. If Rosey had registered, she hadn't done it under her own name. No forwarding address. No phone number. The news was bad, and getting worse.

"Virginia Kelly." The desk clerk looked up from his money long enough to slap his forehead as if he'd just placed me from somewhere in the recesses of his long-term memory. He thumped his chest with an index finger. "Bill Brach, class of 'eighty," and smiled with bad teeth and what I could only imagine to be the worst of intentions. His acne scars were still the size of the craters on the moon and he didn't look like he had managed to integrate many green vegetables into his diet.

"Billy Brach," I said. "This is an unexpected pleasure." I was lying. Blue River was still small enough that it was a sure bet some version of my afternoon activities was going to get back to my folks now. And that promised to make it one hell of a Christmas.

Knowing better, Billy asked me if I needed any help with my bags. Then, he picked up the bill from the desk and snapped it taut a couple times with an end in either fist. When I turned away towards the exit sign at the side of dingy lobby, Billy Brach, class of 1980, was still grinning at Andrew Jackson with true love in his eyes. I could feel him smiling at my back all the way past the threadbare couch and out the glass doors.

After I left the lobby and before I pulled my father's car back out of the gravel lot, I took care of a few things. Sometimes anger can clear your head and sharpen your thinking like a cold shower after a bad drunk. That evening I was thinking clearly enough to save myself the quarter and call the phone company on an 800 number from the cold, lonely pay phone by the side of Winthrop Road.

After I'd explained rather frantically that I was staying at the Johnny Appleseed and some calls I didn't recognize had appeared on my room bill, I read the nice lady in customer service the list of numbers from Rosey's phone log and she told me to whom they belonged. She drew the line when I asked for the addresses, but overall, it was the nicest interaction I'd ever had with the phone company before or since — one full of friendly service and cooperation. Aside from Andre, Rosey had called Harry Hobart once on Saturday morning and her parents three times. She had called the Crawford household once on Sunday, presumably to talk to Page, but from what I saw in the parking lot at the Johnny Appleseed they hadn't connected. There was a call at six o'clock that night to Motel 8 on Route 45. There were two other calls at ten-thirty Saturday night and five o'clock that evening to the Blue River Women's Center Crisis Line. I called the New York number myself on my calling card and found out it was an answering service, but I had no idea of whether it was hers or somebody else's.

I had to use my own money for the next few inquiries, but I figured Rosey still rated a least a buck and there were four quarters jingling around in the pocket of my coat, keeping my fingers company. I took them out and punched up Motel 8. The keys were so cold my index finger stuck to every metal number.

The woman on the phone cracked her gum in my ear and told me Rosey Paschen had a reservation, but she hadn't showed.

"You a friend of hers?" the woman asked. "Because, I'm telling you, she doesn't show by nine o'clock we got to cancel her without a credit card. This place fills up at Christmas time, people passing through, need some nice clean place to sleep for not too expensive. If she don't show, we can't hold it."

It had been about eight o'clock when I left Rosey's motel room. I left a message for her. It was shorter than what I would have said to her in person and a good deal friendlier.

Outside the wind rattled the rickety glass door of the phone booth like an impatient caller waiting its turn. Fishing another quarter out of my coat pocket, I let my hands linger there before I called Avis Car Rental. Then I talked through my nose at the rental agent on the other end of the line, looking out at the cracks in the asphalt and the weeds peeking up from the frozen snow. "Excuse me, dear, I'm Mr. Krantz' secretary, of Krantz, Katz, and Cutler. Miss Paschen has a meeting at our offices tomorrow morning." I said that Mr. Krantz was expecting Ms.

Paschen for a dinner meeting that evening, but she hadn't arrived and the airline wouldn't tell us if she was on the plane. I was hoping I sounded marginally hysterical, but I could hear the rental agent breathing patiently into the phone as if either there were rules for this kind of situation or he was just prodigiously stupid. "Mr Krantz is very upset that Ms. Paschen hasn't arrived. He's called me at home, because you see I was in charge of the arrangements and I thought if we knew whether Miss Paschen had turned in her car at least we could backtrack from our end." I finished up with a heavy sigh and added, "Newark can be such a frightening place at night."

"Oh, I think I can do that, ma'am," the clerk piped up, and I told him he was making points in heaven. What he told me was that Miss Paschen had yet to return her rental car. That meant Rosey wasn't holed up at Motel 8 and she hadn't hopped on an earlier flight back to New York if her car hadn't been returned to Columbus. The former made me especially happy. If Rosey wasn't at Motel 8, I wouldn't feel compelled to go looking for her there. I'd had about all I could stand of fleabag motels for one night.

I made one last call to the Blue River Women's Center Crisis line which was answered by an officious sounding woman who panted, "Crisis line," into the phone after twelve long plaintive rings. I was glad I just needed information instead of emotional support.

As it was, I would have appreciated some express service. My hands stuck down in my pockets to get them warm again after the last call, I was holding the phone with my shoulder. The metal receiver was stuck to my chin and the air was so cold it hurt to breathe. The weather conditions gave the shaking in my voice an air of authenticity as I said, "I talked to someone at your service at about ten-thirty on Saturday night and then again tonight at five o'clock. She really helped me, and I'd like to talk to her again if she's there."

There was a pause and then a loud shuffling of papers. "You talked to two different people if your times are right." The officious woman seemed to imply that they weren't and I thought her bedside manner left a little to be desired. "Ten-thirty Saturday was Lana's shift, and five o'clock today was Spike's. Spike's gone for the day, but I'm Carol." She took a breath as if she were going to say something else, but the wind was whistling through the trees by the side of the road like a locomotive, whistling straight through the cracks in the phone booth, through my scarf, and down both breasts of the grey double-breasted wool coat that the woman at Bonwit Teller had sworn could keep me toasty in the Arctic, and I hung up before I heard what it was.

X

On the way to Rosey's parents' house, my mind was working like a well-oiled Rube Goldberg machine with a lot of motion but not too much in the way of results. I was turning the pieces over in my head, but I just couldn't see the connections. Rosey and Andre. Rosey and Hobart. Rosey and Spike and the Women's Crisis Line. Rosey and me. The last connection was the one that bothered me the most because I still didn't know what might have prompted her to take the trouble, after ten years, to find me, to phone me and beg me to come to our reunion, just to tell me she didn't want me.

As for Rosey and Andre, I had that down as cheap dirty thrills: Andre said no and Rosey said yes — assuming that I wasn't just putting words in her mouth at the Johnny Appleseed. I knew what his reasons might be for lying, but I thought that maybe she had some too. And even if Rosey and Hobart looked like more of the same when I'd followed her on Saturday night, the truth was I had been upset, and Harry Hobart had hugged me too when he'd given me a ride home from Ewing's Friday morning. The truth was I hadn't stuck around long enough to be sure of what had really happened between them, but I knew from my broken watch and the phone call Rosey had placed from her room to the Women's Crisis Line at 10:30 that same night, that she hadn't stayed at Hobart's very long. As for the Women's Crisis Line and Rosey and Spike, I didn't have a clue, but I was sure Spike would tell me if I took off my clothes and said, "Pretty please."

That was a pleasant thought, as I was beginning to develop a soft spot for Spike the way people who are nice enough can make you like them even if you're not initially inclined. The thought of charming that information out of her was such a lovely one, I didn't even mind that the roads were icy and the heater wasn't working very well. The car seemed to know the way to Rosey Paschen's old house and the ride didn't seem to take too long at all.

Rosey's house was on the right side of Dean Street with a willow tree in the front and flower beds that somebody had dug up for the winter on either side of a cracking cement walk. It gave me an eerie sense of deja vu, but the street was empty and quiet except for a bad board in the porch stairs that complained about my weight and another beside the front door. I wiped my shoes on a rubber mat that said *Welcome Friends* and I read the glittery red and green cardboard letters strung up in the front windows. They spelled things like: *Noel, Season's Greetings,* and *Joy to the World.* There was a single light on in an upstairs room, so I rang the buzzer under the rusty mailbox. When I buzzed a second time, the light upstairs went off and another downstairs came on.

It occurred to me then that Rosalee and I had never been close in the way most people think of friends. We were acquaintances, really, drawn together at least on my part by softball and an odd kind of sexual energy that had been new to me. In the hierarchy of Blue River society, there were pronounced differences in our situations beyond race which I didn't have the words to describe when I knew her. The differences took Rosalee Paschen decidedly out of my set. That people knew my father, and that I could look back on shared history from first grade with boys who wouldn't give me the time of day, counted for something in a town where families were proud to have farmed the same tacky little piece of land for a hundred years. Longevity in this little town mattered, the same way that being pretty or smart counted, or if you had nice clothes, a big house, or if you were a boy how far you could throw, kick or bat a ball. But Rosey was a girl, beautiful in her dirty jeans and tennis shoes only to me, living as she was with the taint of an outsider on her, in a rented house some real Blue River family owned.

I'd never actually been inside her house, she'd never been to mine, and ten years ago our interaction had been limited mostly to intramural flirtation and innuendo at slumber parties of mutual girlfriends, and my long, pathetic glances from the bench across the softball infield. It begged the question as to whether I had taken a simple crush driven by the forbidden charm of her otherness and turned it through loneliness and nostalgia into the powerful sense of entitlement that had brought me to the Johnny Appleseed that afternoon. The question took the edge off my anger, and got me thinking maybe I had stepped across some line of decency in my craziness without knowing it was there.

I gave some serious consideration to the prospect that I, not Rosey, might be at fault for the awful way I was feeling, while I stood on the porch and waited for the door to open. By the time it did, I'd come around to the opinion that I might be owing Rosey an apology instead of the other way around. Somehow that made me feel even worse.

The man who came to the door opened it about a hand's width and then stared me down as if he thought I was selling something. He was older than my father, I would have guessed about sixty five, thicker around the middle, stiffer in the face, and white. His eyes were blue and beady with deep cracking lines and bags around them. Most of his hair was growing out of the top of his nose. If he'd ever had any on his head, it had been replaced with peach fuzz and liver spots some time ago.

"I'm here for Rosalee." It was my best, most respectable voice — the one I used for client presentations and answering the phone at work, and I was glad to be wearing my wool banker's coat. If it wasn't keeping out the cold, I thought, at least it added credibility over my jeans and loafers. "I need to talk to her, please."

The old man opened the door a little wider, presumably to get a better look at me, and, it seemed, he didn't much like what he saw. "May I, please, speak with Rosey Paschen," I said again.

"She's not here." The old guy's long thin lips didn't look like they were used to smiling. From what I could see, our conversation wasn't giving him much in the way of practice either, but I went ahead and asked when he thought Rosalee might be returning.

The old man stiffened at that and he squared-up his sagging shoulders. Maybe he had been a brute when he was younger, but his body was shrunken and stooped over now, as if whatever vitality was left had vested itself in his blotchy red face. The face was plump and hairless and its watery eyes looked scared. "She's not coming back here anymore, Miss."

"I thought you might know where she was," I said. "Are you her father?"

"Who are you?" His eyes narrowed some more

until they were just little points and he puffed himself up in the doorway.

"Virginia Kelly." I stuck out my hand, and he frowned at it until I put it down again. "Rosalee and I went to high school together. I'm on the reunion committee," I lied cheerfully. "We thought we'd check who was staying in town for the holidays to see if we might plan some extra alumni festivities. Cold night isn't it. Are you her father?" I asked again, hoping some polite conversation would warm him up.

Maybe it did, because his face got redder than it had been before. "I used to be a long time ago," he said, "but I don't have any daughters anymore." His face was screwed up tight with some complicated emotion, but I wasn't ready to take any bets as to what it was. "Who did you say you were again?"

A woman came up behind him. Her face was caved in on itself like an old piece of fruit drying up from the inside. She said, "What does she want with us?"

The mother was a frail, tentative-looking thing, not merely old like her husband but shriveled and wizened with powder-white hair and thin bony ankles. They stuck out from under the lace at the bottom of her housecoat, and the wind from the door tossed the fabric around her legs.

When the old man turned to her, I could see into the room behind them. It looked warm and homey with a coat tree in the corner and a round coiled wool rug over clean wood floors. Two heavy upholstered chairs sat in front of an old maple console television set. I took my hands out of my pockets and warmed them in the heat coming through the door. I told him again that I was from the high school reunion committee.

"She's looking for Rosey, Mama," he whispered and he put a thick arm across the old woman's shoulders. Her skin was grey and it hung around her cheeks and neck in folds. "We don't know where she is," the woman said to him as if I wasn't even there.

"I'm a friend," I stammered along rather unimpressively. "Well, I used to be her friend and I thought you might have an address where I could reach her."

The old man began to close the door. "We don't know where Rosalee is," he said again.

"Papa, tell her to go away," the old woman was saying. "Tell her we don't want any trouble."

I slipped my loafer against the frame to catch the door before he could close it. "Didn't she come back home to see you, ma'am?" I was fishing. The old man seemed jumpy enough to bite, so I jiggled the line. "She came here to see you, didn't she? That's what she said she was going to do. She came Friday and Saturday. I saw you fighting."

The old man's face looked blank and stupid. "We haven't heard from Rosey in three years, Miss."

"She has," I said and the old woman's head began to tremble on her neck. "Didn't your wife tell you Rose was here to see you, Mr. Paschen?"

The old man shook his head. It was a slow sad movement as if his head were heavy on his neck.

"What did she tell you?" The old woman's face had turned red and she was shouting at me, "What did she say about us?"

"Now, Mama." The old man pulled her closer to him. "This all is going to be okay." He stepped back further from the door saying, "Why don't you just go, Miss, to wherever your home is. Leave us to ours."

The old woman's body was shaking like a thin stray dog. "Rose is a liar whatever it was she said to you." Then, her face lit up with recognition. "You." The old woman pointed a crooked trembling finger as if she were going to plant a curse. "I recognize you." She raised her fist as if she meant to use the thin collection of fingers she had closed around her palm, but then her mouth went slack and her arm dropped to her side. Her voice was a hiss of cold north wind. "I've seen you sneaking and spying on us for her. You tell Rose she's no daughter of mine, and her friends aren't welcome here. You leave or you'll be sorry."

The slim space that was left between the door and its frame got slimmer, until I couldn't see the coat tree or the old woman anymore. She'd slipped away, I imagined to go call the police. I could hear her slippers shuffling along the floor of the warm-looking room with the television set and the heavy chairs. In the doorway, there was only the bald bent man, puffing out what there was of his chest and glaring. I trotted off the Paschen's front porch, back out onto public property. From my vantage point on the curb, I could see the curtains pulled back from the parlor window and replaced by two old grey shapes wishing me good riddance.

I got in the car and took one last look across the seat, out the passenger window at the little white house with the big willow tree in front, but the lights were already out — all but the first one I'd seen upstairs when I'd come. Behind the shades two shadows were fighting.

XI

I pulled my car out into the empty street, the snow in the gutters so deep that my U-turn required turning, backing up, and turning again. The blue numbers on the dashboard clock glowed ten minutes after ten o'clock, a little late to go calling by the genteel standards to which my mother had raised me, but I didn't feel much like standing on ceremony.

What I felt was hurt and guilty and confused; and if Rosalee wasn't at her parents, and she wasn't at Motel 8, I decided she might be at Harry Hobart's. Even if she wasn't there, I thought Hobart might be able to at least give her a message.

I needed the long walk down Hobart's dark, gravel drive to get my head together. I took along the pocket flashlight my father kept in the glove compartment. The broken pieces of my watch crystal were still on the ground where Rosey's car had been the night before, a couple of feet from a fresh oil spot.

When I knocked, Hobart came to the door in mule-style slippers and a short black silk kimono that looked like it might have a dragon embroidered on the back. The brown curly hair that peeked out of the top of his robe was long and thick enough to braid.

"Mr. Hobart," I said. "Hi."

Hobart only opened the door a crack and he didn't make much in the way of friendly faces; he didn't even make an excuse for not inviting me in. "What can I do for you, Virginia." He looked down at his wrist, but no watch was there. So he looked back up at me again. His eyes were red and tired. He said, "You know, it's rather late." But I could see the soft light from the room behind him and I could hear Diane Schuur, the blind blonde jazz singer, loafing away at some Duke Ellington standard in an after-hours voice.

"I'm looking for Rosey," I told him and the words made me feel a little crazy; they even sounded a little crazy when I got them out of my mouth. "She's left her motel and I don't know where she's gone."

In the room behind Hobart a drummer tapped his brush on the high hat cymbals like the sound of gently falling rain and "Sophisticated Lady" was seeping through the door like a slow plumbing leak. The voice gasped discreetly in that breathy sexy jazz singer way, and began another line.

For a moment I thought Hobart might have had Rosey with him there inside, but no rental car sat in the drive nor out on the highway. They might have hidden it somewhere to throw me off, but I chalked that theory up to paranoia.

"So, do you know where she is?" I was hoping he would ask me in and I started a little tap dance of jogging in place and rubbing my hands together, hoping it might encourage him. It didn't.

"Maybe home." Hobart opened the door a little

wider and the music spilled out around him, the stuff of romance and candlelight dinners, but I couldn't see beyond Harry Hobart's barrel chest. His body seemed to expand to fill the doorway. "I've no idea where Rosey is," he said. "Maybe she's gone back to where she came from."

"You wouldn't happen to know where that is, Mr. Hobart?" I asked. "Because I need to talk to her." I was begging and it was embarrassing, but I kept on anyway. "It's really important."

Hobart stepped back from the door and pulled it slightly more closed. "I'm sorry, Virginia." He smiled as if I had some terminal disease. "I haven't seen Rosalee since the night of the reunion party." He was pulling the door more closed by inches, saying, "It's very late, and you'll have to excuse me. I have some appointments in the morning."

Hobart was lying for sure about Friday night because I'd followed Rosey to his house on Saturday. What I didn't know was why.

"Let me know about Christmas dinner." Hobart covered his mouth to stifle a yawn while Ms. Schuur ended the song on a long falling note and some impressive vocal pyrotechnics. Hobart closed his door.

"Goodnight, Mr. Hobart," I said to the painted white wood. But I couldn't help but wonder if they were huddled inside together laughing at me. Or worse, if Rosey was crying on his shoulder, my having become some odd curiosity, some cautionary tale in the annals of lesbian fatal attraction.

Half an hour later, I was confessing most of this

to Sandra — my surveillance of Rosey, the fight with her mother, the ugly sex in her motel room, with just a few prudent editorial omissions (mostly regarding my running into Andre at the Johnny Appleseed, because I hadn't quite decided what I wanted to do with that information). Sandra was shoveling bridge mix candy into her mouth while she made some sympathetic sounds, but mostly she ate. Occasionally, she'd offer me the bag, but not as if she really wanted to share it, which was okay with me; that evening's drama had pretty much killed my appetite.

"I need to find Rosalee and apologize," I said, "I think I made her feel like she had to have sex with me when she didn't want it."

Chewing and swallowing seemed to be taking most of Sandra's concentration. But she looked up from her bridge mix as if my troubles had the shock appeal of say the *National Enquirer* headline: Lesbian Acquaintance Rape.

"I didn't force her or anything," I said quickly. "Things just got out of hand, you know?"

Sandra took another malted milkball. It made a lump in her cheek and I could see it when she opened her mouth. "Well, actually, no, to tell you the truth I don't." She was crunching the candy with her back teeth as she talked. "What could you possibly say to some woman you haven't seen in ten years to make her feel obligated to sleep with you?"

"I don't know," I lied for the sake of simplicity. "But somehow I managed to get into this thing with Spike as well."

Sandra stopped chewing. "Who?"

I said, "Spike, Mary Ellen McMann." I could hear

the plastic bag of candy rustling as Sandra rummaged for her particular favorites.

"Let me get this straight." She looked at me and then back down into her candy again and shook the bag so that the milkballs would come to the top. "You were kicking it with Mary Ellen McMann too?"

I said "straight" didn't seem to have a whole lot to do with it. I figured it might as well all come out. "Spike and I sort of groped around in her car at the reunion and then on Saturday I stopped by her house after I ran out of gas on the way back from Hobart's." I didn't like the way the story was making me sound.

"You've been home for three days and you slept with Rosalee Paschen and with Mary Ellen — twice." Sandra shook her head. "Did she want to sleep with you?"

"Of course." Sandra's tone was making me feel a little defensive. "She started it." And why had I finished it? I didn't know exactly except that maybe Spike was growing on me, in the way that honest pursuit is always refreshing. Maybe I just needed to feel wanted. Maybe I was just plain easy. "Of course, *Spike* wanted to," I said.

"But Rosey didn't?" Sandra's mouth was full, again.

"Well sort of but not exactly." I told Sandra the story of Johnson's farm and the phone call and the letter. I said, "We were in her motel room chatting about her childhood and then we weren't. Then we were horizontal." I thought it was a close facsimile of the truth which was better than nothing.

"So, how do you know Rosey didn't want to? Virginia you're really out of control." Sandra was chiding me from the sofa with her feet up on the coffee table. "You followed some woman you hadn't seen or heard from for ten years like a psycho stalker all afternoon and then you're surprised when she's weird about it."

I tried to remind her that she was the one who had wanted me to find out what Rosalee was up to, but Sandra raised her voice and drowned me out. "I mean you followed her like that woman the police keep dragging out of David Letterman's house. Let me tell you, Ginny, you are way out of control." Sandra stopped to scratch her head. "And there's a part of this I'm really not getting — either you're not telling me or I'm missing it. After Rosey told you no way in the middle of the Southtown Valley Mall, what did you expect to get from following her after that?"

Sandra seemed to have completely forgotten that she had specifically asked me to find out whether Andre was meeting Rosalee while they were in Blue River, but when I thought about it, even I had to admit maybe I'd gone beyond the call of duty and I felt my face get hot again.

"What could you have possibly expected when you went over to her room?" Sandra asked.

"I don't know," I said. "Some kind of explanation about why she'd asked me to come to the reunion, maybe. Maybe I wanted her to tell me why she'd come on to me in high school." I thought, *Or to say that caring for me ten years ago had changed her life as much as it had changed mine.* I said, "Maybe I was just curious about why she'd knocked her mother down in the snow on Friday and then lied about it."

159

Sandra shrugged. "If I'd knocked my mother down in the snow, I'd lie about it too." She patted her belly fondly. "If this boy grows up to think he can raise his hand to me, I hope he has the good sense not to let anybody know it."

Sandra had a point and it didn't say much good about Rosalee, but it was hard to know when you stopped owing your parents obedience and harder still to know if there was ever an instance where you stopped owing them respect. It was the stuff of which critical essays on sociology are made and it was too bad I wasn't a critical thinker. It was too bad I had bigger fish to fry. I rubbed my forehead with the palm of my hand. "Whatever." I thought it was odd that those were exactly the words Rosalee had said to me when I'd accused her of an affair with Andre, but it pretty much summed up my overwhelming sense of hopelessness at the whole ugly mess. I wondered what Andre had been doing in the Johnny Appleseed parking lot before I'd arrived, but then decided it was better not to think about it. "Like I said," I told Sandra in answer to a different question than the one she'd asked, "damned if I know."

"And what did you get?" Sandra was jawing away cheerfully on another malted milk ball.

"Bad sex. Nothing." The truth was maybe I'd gotten what I wanted, the evening with Rosalee Paschen I'd turned down ten years ago and had regretted ever since, the sexual act I thought that would define me. But when I'd gotten it, it wasn't what I'd thought it would be. Either I or the circumstance was different. Maybe I had never really wanted it at all. I said, "Things are complicated."

160

"Yeah, I'll bet," said Sandra. "And sometimes, girlfriend, I do not believe you."

I told her, "Yeah but seriously, I'm a little worried about Rosey. She checked out of the Johnny Appleseed while I was sleeping. Harry Hobart says he hasn't seen her since Friday night but I know he's lying." I told Sandra that Rosey's parents claimed they didn't know where she was, and didn't care, but I thought they could be lying too.

Sandra was picking pieces of chocolate out of her molars. "You're paranoid. Why on earth would Hobart lie?"

"Well, Rosey's straight." It was the part of the story I was hoping to avoid along with the part about seeing Andre in the parking lot of the Johnny Appleseed, but I thought: half a loaf... I said, "We got into this thing where I think I kind of talked Rosey into sex." I put my face in my hands and rubbed my palms back and forth over my cheeks. "I swear she didn't used to be straight, but I guess she is now. Like I said: it's complicated. It's cold and the roads are really snowy; I think it could be my fault if anything happens to her." This thought had just occurred to me and the more I considered it the more guilty and upset I felt. "She called the Women's Crisis Line while I was sleeping and then she disappeared from the motel room. When I woke up, she'd checked out."

"You've got to be kidding." I couldn't help but notice Sandra was laughing, not discreetly with a dainty covered mouth, but a whooping laugh that gave me a better view of her tonsils and the chocolate on her tongue than I would have liked if I'd had the choice. There were tears in her eyes.

"I'm sorry Virginia," she said, but she didn't stop laughing. "God knows before I found Andre, I'd had some dates from hell, but I never needed emergency therapy to get through them."

"I'll give you a hint," I said, "this is not funny."

Sandra was still laughing though, so hard I thought she might miscarry from the shaking. "It will be when you get some perspective," she said. "So, maybe Hobart is lying and maybe Rosey is hiding from you. If you'd coerced me into sex, I might hide from you too. Maybe she told her parents, and even if they'd disowned her they might still be interested in protecting her from wild-eyed, negro lesbians, come banging on their door past polite Sunday calling hours."

I let Sandra know she was really making my day.

"Come on. We're in the heartland here," said Sandra, and I asked where Andre was just to change the subject.

"He went out to get me a double anchovy pizza." Sandra had stopped chuckling expressly in order to treat me to another of her full-belly Mona Lisa smiles and I didn't know which I disliked more. "I had a craving," she said. "And listen, Virginia, I'm sorry about that little spat you had to overhear in the kitchen, we've talked it through now. Andy was a very good boy all the rest of the day. He cleaned the whole house. Top to bottom and he even vacuumed. When Sid and I got home from Christmas shopping he was making a pot of gumbo."

"Yeah?" I wanted to be wrong about Andre and Rosey.

She put her face close to mine. "Andy told me he

couldn't go on if I left him." But I wondered if he'd made any other confessions.

I could have asked her, but I figured that was just buying trouble. Instead, I listened to the list of Christmas presents she'd bought and for whom. I was tired and the big silver tree blinking on and off in the corner was lulling me into a sleepy passivity. Pretty soon Andre came back with a large greasy pizza box. He set it down on the coffee table and then bent to give Sandra a noisy smack on the lips. When she opened up the box the whole room smelled like anchovies.

"Guess what," Sandra announced when she'd gotten her mouth full of pizza. "Virginia's been sleeping with Rosey Paschen *and* Mary Ellen McMann. And Rosey's been sleeping with Harry Hobart."

I reminded Sandra that some wise soul had once remarked that discretion was the better part of valor, but she waved her hand at me. And the light from the floor lamp caught the glitter of her enormous boulder of a diamond.

"Listen, Virginia. How long have I known you?" She took one last bite of her pizza. "We're all family here." She was still chewing as she closed the box and wiped her mouth with a paper carry-out napkin from the stack Andre had left on the coffee table. Sandra told him, "Virginia went over to Rosalee Paschen's room at the Johnny Appleseed motel this afternoon and when she woke up Rosalee had cleared out. Everything, no forwarding address, no nothing." While Sandra was talking she looked straight at Andre as if there might be answers to Rosey's whereabouts in his face.

"Is that so?" Andre gave me the same practiced legal nod that my other lawyer friend, Naomi Wolf, reserved for hearing bad news and I wondered if it was something they specifically taught in law school, the grave detached face for other people's grief. Then he got up, went into the kitchen and made himself a drink. He made one for me too without my asking, and set it down on the coffee table on his way back to the couch without much more in the way of conversation. It was scotch in a short heavy glass over three ice cubes. Andre took a sip of his and stuck out his lower lip in a way my mother used to suggest was courting bird droppings.

I asked him, "You wouldn't happen to know what firm Rosey's with now?" It wasn't my first choice of how to contact her, but I was fast running out of options and Andre's little visit to the Johnny Appleseed made me think he might know more that he was telling.

"How would I know?" He fired me a nasty look that I don't think he meant for Sandra to see. If Andre knew anything, he didn't like me asking. "If Rosalee's not with Brealy & Myers anymore then how would I know what firm she's with?" And there was a silence long enough to be awkward before he suggested, "Why don't you just call the New York Bar." Andre stared uncomfortably into his highball glass for a while more before he cleared his throat. "Well, I told you, Rosey Paschen is a stone freak." He had put on a big brother voice for this public service announcement as if we'd discussed her at length in relation to me when all I could remember from our talk at the Whore was a recitation of his complaints. "What did you expect," said Andre.

"Whatever." I wondered if I qualified too, on the basis of my recent adventures, as a sexual freak, as a bad girl. I tasted the scotch, didn't like it, and drank it down anyway since it was there.

Sandra came over and put a hand on either shoulder and leaned down to me. "You know, you need to get over this thing you have with Rosalee Paschen." She looked at me hard as if that might help her understand whatever it was she was missing. For a moment I thought she was going to kiss me, but instead she just shook her head again. "You know, Virginia, I haven't said this before but I think you could benefit from a little therapy."

We both laughed hard when she sat back down on the couch beside me even though she wasn't joking. What I needed you couldn't buy by the hour. I'd proven that in Rosey's motel room. What I was looking for was what Sandra thought she had: somebody who loved me, somebody to grow old with.

I looked over at Andre swilling his liquor and wondered if Sandra had really found it either.

"What are you going to name your kid?" I asked.

"Taylor, whether it's a girl or a boy." She grinned at the thought and when I looked at him again, Andre was smiling too. "It's an all-purpose name. Andy thinks it will look good on a resumé."

It figured.

"And it's very East Coast," Andre said as if geography had intrinsic value.

I said, "Do you think my little tryst with Rosey will get back to my folks? Billy Brach is the night clerk over at the Johnny Appleseed. I was asking some questions and he recognized me on my way out."

"Yeah, probably." Sandra had opened her pizza box again and she was picking the anchovies off the top of a slice and eating them by themselves. "But the good news is they'll be too embarrassed to say anything to you about it." She stood up and then bent down to hug me. "Get some sleep, Virginia," Sandra said.

I took it to mean she was tired and thought I ought to be leaving. So, I collected my coat from the chair by the window and Sandra opened the door for me while Andre grunted his goodbyes. It was nearly midnight, but I wasn't ready to go home to my parents if it was true that I'd become Blue River's latest sex scandal.

XII

Spike McMann's apartment near the center of town was a colonial-looking brick and wrought iron affair circa 1972. Inside it was full of neutral-colored, wall-to-wall carpeting, teak furniture, and the smell of nouvelle cuisine recipes Spike was trying out for her restaurant. I would like to say that I didn't know why I went to see Spike that evening, that it had nothing to do with Rosey's call to her at the Crisis Center. That I couldn't think of any place else to go for company so late at night and the smell of food can be comforting when you're feeling a little lost. That Spike's place wasn't far and I thought she might be happy to see me and with the quality of my day that had counted for a lot. In the back of my mind I'm sure those are all the reasons why I dropped by, but in the forefront of my consciousness was only the obsessive question of Rosey Paschen and where she had gone.

"Well, hi there." Spike opened the door wide, as if she was glad I'd come but didn't know exactly what had brought me. She wore a ragged pair of sweat pants underneath a short pink bathrobe, and the little shy tilted smile she had before she'd seduced me in the parking lot. After she put my coat away, Spike led me by the hand over to the couch. When I sat down, she sat beside me and kissed me with her tongue.

"This isn't exactly the way I meant for things to go," I said. "I was just really looking for a friendly shoulder to cry on, you know?"

"Don't talk," said Spike. "You'll ruin it." Her hands were in my shirt again and she whispered, "Relax."

So I did; and when we were finished, she gave me a back rub. I told her that Rosalee had disappeared from the Johnny Appleseed and Hobart was sleeping with her and lying about it, that Rosey had said she and Andre had been lovers, and that her parents claimed they didn't know where she was. I skillfully omitted the part about my roll in the hay with Rosy, my tailing her, or my buying the phone log for twenty bucks from Bill Brach at the Johnny Appleseed. Still, it seemed like Rosalee Paschen's was the last name that Spike wanted to hear.

"I'd have thought you'd have gotten that out of your system," Spike said. "Wasn't this nice? I don't know why we have to spoil it by talking about Rosalee Paschen."

"She's gone," I said.

"So what." Spike kissed my shoulders. "So big fucking deal, Virginia."

"Well it sort of is." The air in Spike's apartment smelled like stir fry and sesame oil and something else I couldn't quite place. "You know, she might be in trouble." Trouble was a kind of ambiguous, panicky word, but I didn't have a better one. I'd been thinking a lot about the co-eds sliced up in the woods since my run-in with Officer Kidder who seemed to me a very likely candidate for a closet serial killer. "Rosey told me she'd talked to you and somebody named Lana at the Women's Crisis line."

Spike looked surprised and I hoped the shock would make her more talkative. It didn't; she just stopped kissing my neck.

"So, look, was it business or personal?" I asked.

"Everything at a Women's Crisis line is personal." Spike sat up on one elbow and started rubbing my back with her free hand. "I'm sorry, Virginia, but I can't tell you what Rosey and I discussed. I have a duty of confidentiality."

"Just nod your head." I guessed, "Business? Parents? Andre? Hobart?" I was going to go on until I hit it.

Spike stopped me with her hand on my back. "I'm not going to play these games."

"All right," I said. "But what if you just gave me Rosey's phone number and address from the reunion committee files?"

Sometimes things come out of your mouth and you wish you could take them back right away. The chilly silence from Spike's side of the bed made me pretty sure this was one of those times.

"Virginia, I wouldn't have the slightest idea how to get in touch with Rosey again. She contacted Jane Campbell, the class treasurer, ages before the reunion date was set to ask about it. I forwarded her information as directed to a post office box in New York City. That was the end of it. I could give you the P.O. box, but I really hope that's not why you're here tonight." Spike said, "Listen, Ginny, all this talk is really making me tired. What do you want to make me tired like this for?" She kissed my neck again, but I wasn't in the mood.

"I've got to go," I said. It was three o'clock in the morning according to the digital clock on her nightstand.

"Go then or stay if you want to, but I'm not hearing any more about Rosalee Paschen. It just makes me feel too shitty. All right?" Spike's eyes were wet and veiny and her nose was red. She said, "Sometimes I don't have the slightest idea why I like you."

It made me feel even worse that I couldn't think of one solid reason myself. It seemed a sudden mystery why Rosalee Paschen had moved me to such disappointment, while Spike in her fumbling red-faced pursuit had moved me not at all; and I hadn't meant to hurt her any more than anybody ever means to hurt anybody else. So, I let her put her tongue back in my mouth and stayed with her until it got light the next morning. That night I dreamed that Emery wasn't really dead. It had all been an elaborate practical joke and everybody knew but me.

At thirteen minutes after eight o'clock the next morning, I kissed Spike on her sleeping forehead and slipped out of bed. I pulled the front door closed very gently. On the kitchen table I'd left her a very sweet little note all full of hearts and compliments written out on a paper towel from the roll by the toaster, and I'd washed up all the dishes in the sink. Outside it was a bright clear morning, cold and nearly windless.

XIII

When I got back to my parents' house, I picked up the paper from the porch and dug out a spare key, but the door was already open. So, I stomped the snow off my loafers on the mat in the hall, and let the dog sniff the great outdoors on my pants legs.

"Nice of you to stop by, Virginia," my father said. "Big night?" He was sitting in his chair by the window with the paper up in front of his face again and he didn't wait for an answer. My lifestyle decisions were not letting my father age peacefully.

I helped myself to a turtle from the

box of expensive chocolates my Dad bought every Christmas for my mother, and picked the caramel out of my teeth with my pinky nail.

"Uh huh." My father grunted back into his paper and I went to the kitchen to dial Avis again, sitting on the counter eating Christmas cookies from the covered tins where my mother stored them. Rosalee hadn't returned her rental car yet, so, figuring I had a pretty good chance to maybe make things right was cheering me up a little when my mother came down the stairs her in her bathrobe.

"We missed you at dinner," she said. "Where'd you eat?" What she meant was where did you spend the night? "You could have called."

She was right. "I didn't eat," I said.

She looked at me and then at the cookie in my hand like I was a naughty child. "I can't believe you're eating junk for breakfast to make up for it, Virginia."

Beside the window above the sink someone had framed a sampler I hadn't seen before. It had one of those little naked pot-belly-style children in black face cross-stitched on it. Underneath it read: *God Bless this House.* I wondered if the love of kitsch was another unfortunate inherited tendency. While I thought about it, I had another cookie.

Only half of it was left when my mother snatched it away. "Give me that, Virginia," she said. "You're just disgusting." Her reflexes were still as good as when I was seven. My mother threw the cookie into the sink, leaving me to listen with a stupid expression while the garbage disposal belched and gurgled its enjoyment. "I won't have you eating junk for breakfast," my mother was saying. "And while you're in this house, I won't have you come rolling in at all hours. There are other people living here too, Virginia. You'd best remember that." She poked at the roaring hole in the sink with the end of a wooden spoon. "And if you don't have friends you can ask in, maybe they aren't the kinds of friends you ought to have. I think you owe your father and me some respect. We have to live in this town."

I wondered since when did the hours I kept give her such a heartache and I took another cookie from the tin on the counter while I thought about that. "Get over it, Mom," was my conclusion. "I'm a big girl now. I think that's one thing you're forgetting." I tried to put the cookie in my mouth, but she was faster again.

"Jesus Christ." I was looking at the empty space left between my thumb and fingers.

"Call on somebody you know," my mother hissed. Her eyes were narrow little cracks in her face and her pale yellow skin had turned red in her cheeks. "You're our daughter and people are going to think somehow we must be responsible."

"Responsible for what, exactly." I was shouting to hear myself above the roar of the disposal and the water running in the sink. "What? People are going to think you're responsible for my stinking diet?"

"Don't raise your voice to me." My mother's voice was an even, threatening whisper that was worse than yelling. In my house as a kid, I knew it meant trouble when my parents got quiet. Her voice was hoarse. "You know what I mean. While you stay in our house, I won't have you going around all night with *girls*."

It was hard given my past couple days not to register some small internal embarrassment that I had to wonder exactly who were the particular girls of which my mother was speaking. But this was the closest she'd ever come to calling a spade a spade. And if I hadn't been so angry, I might have been pleased.

"Yeah?" I said, "And I won't have you telling me what I can and cannot do." My mother's yellow chest was red all down the open collar of her bathrobe. Her hands were clenched at her hips. I thought she might hit me then, not with the flat of her hand but with her fist like Rosalee's mother had tried to do to Rosalee. I wondered if I would be fast enough to stop her fist when I hadn't even been able to stop her hand. It came across my face like the old-time figures on the automatic cast iron banks that take a penny from the slot so fast you can only tell it's gone — but my mother didn't hit me. Instead she caught the cookie I held poised in front of my lips and threw that one at the garbage disposal too. I watched the cookie crumble under the water in the sink while my mother was chanting sing-song: "Not this. Not that. Not here in my house," like some kind of crazy fascist mantra.

Each time I took a cookie from the open tin on the counter my mother snatched it and threw that one in the sink too. Took that one, and the one after that, and the one after that. She was formidable even at years past fifty. She knew it and she wanted me to know it too. She wanted me to know she still had the reflexes to stop a child dead with the snatch of an arm just below the shoulder, to swat a running buttock, and put an ugly bite in the words, "Don't let me catch you."

She was scraping at the debris in the sink with her wooden spoon. The porcelain bottom was thick and brown with broken cookies and the water was backing up in the disposal. "You owe us some respect," my mother was saying, "your father and I, for what we've given you girls. Respect." My mother's voice was broken up with indignation. "You owe us respect and decency." What she meant was: You owe us your obedience. You owe us your life vicariously.

I didn't think so and I upended the rest of the cookies out of her metal tin with the poinsettias on the top of it into the brown mess of raisins and nuts at the bottom of the sink. The kitchen was quiet for a while except for the rush of running water and the straining sound of the garbage disposal choking. The cookie pieces floated on the rising water and I reached over to turn off the faucet. "Get off my back, Mom," I said, "will you? That's all you need to remember, all right?"

What I remembered was the flashing vacancy sign at the Johnny Appleseed. I figured I could stand it there until I could get a flight back to Chicago.

My mother put her hands on her hips and she set her chin. "If you don't like the way we live here, then you can leave. We have standards of behavior," she said. "You decide."

The garbage disposal was running down and shrugged, because as tough as it sounded, this

174

confrontation with my mother was a long-running show that was as much a part of Christmas over the years as presents and pine trees and party lights.

I went upstairs to pack my things and I was nearly finished when my father knocked on my bedroom door.

"You don't have to leave." My father sat down on the bed beside me. I was putting my socks in the front pouch of my luggage. I didn't look up so he said it again. "We don't want you to leave. You don't have to leave, Virginia."

"Yeah. I really do. I'm sorry, Dad," I said. "Because I'm twenty-nine years old and I can't let her order me around as if I were a child." I could feel the tears beginning in the corners of my eyes. "I'm not a child anymore, you know?"

I thought there were tears in my father's eyes too, but when he blinked they were gone and I wondered if I'd seen them at all. "We just want you to be happy. You seem so angry, Virginia." He asked me, "Why are you so angry?" He was asking what had gone wrong in my socialization. "We've tried to give you everything." He was asking me to tell him whatever it was hadn't been his fault and it was odd to hear the request for absolution in my father's voice.

"I can't help it." My parents had told me stories of the nineteen-fifties, bus boycotts and protest marches, water hoses and attack dogs, the way other kids grew up on the grim morality of Mother Goose, when all we had was a bourgeois savior who liked his women white and wore silk pajamas just like Hugh Hefner. "How angry were you in the fifties?" I asked him.

He said, "Your mother's sorry for what she said to you." He laughed as if he were clearing his throat. "I just wish you were happier, Ginny. We both just want you to be happy." Then my father stood up to leave and closed the door to my room behind him and I cried some more by myself after he had left.

Later when my mother knocked at the door her face was dry. She said, "We have got to find a way to get along, Virginia. In this world all we've got to depend on is each other. All there really is is family." She hugged me hard around the shoulders as though I would slip away if she let me go. Her body shook and she was crying again. We were crying together. "I love you very much." She kissed my forehead hard. "Always remember that we both love you, Ginny."

"I love you too," I said and meant it unconditionally.

Then, she wiped her eyes on the sleeve of her robe and her face brightened up a little bit. "You know, Virginia, you might still find somebody you like, some nice man. I've lived long enough to believe anything can happen. You could even adopt a child yourself." My mother said, "You make enough money to have a child by yourself."

One thing my mother had was hope and resiliency. I looked at her high yellow skin and her wavy brown hair and chalked it up to one more thing that I hadn't inherited.

Ellen Borgia once told me, "You know, you're too

young to be so jaded." A colleague of mine at Whytebread, Ellen Borgia was as hard as twenty years of corporate abuse can make a woman, but I was beginning to think she was right. The last ten years had been the depletion of my innocence, leached away like top soil dissolving in the rain, and the person I had become was stone. I would not have believed I was the girl I'd been, but my mother had kept the photographs. The hold that Rosalee Paschen had on me was the hold of those old pictures. She was another connection with that kinder, gentler time.

Ellen Borgia had run her hand over her head and stopped at the black cloth barrette that anchored her pony tail. Her hair was dyed reminiscently yellow. She held her own disappointment in the lines on her face. "You really need to get over it, Virginia. I mean who can blame me if I'm hard?" she asked. "I'm pushing forty and there aren't any decent single men."

She said: "The eighties were the decade we figured out money wasn't everything. But it's just such a drag to have to find another scam."

As I wiped my face in the mirror above the bathroom sink, the woman who looked back at me was worn out and chipped at the edges. But I was way too tired to care much anymore and I didn't have the time to read *Learned Optimism*.

Ellen was right. Things change just when you've gotten used to them. I had just gotten used to Emily when she'd left me two years ago and I had gotten used to missing her when she came back. I had just gotten used to living on my own and now singleness was suddenly out of vogue. My old friends were dead or married to women — or sleeping with men. Even the lesbian couples I knew were expecting "turkey baster" babies.

It's awfully hard to gauge your location when the ground is moving under you, not minutely like the steady turning of the earth taking you easily along, but by leaps and bounds, bringing about enormous changes when you least expect them.

"A single woman here in our church just adopted twins. You never know," was what my mother had said.

"You're right," I said to the reflection in my parents' bathroom mirror. "You're right. You never know."

I'd decided to look Rosalee up in the New York Bar to write my apology, but I called Avis anyway on the off-chance they'd give me her home address. They wouldn't, but what they did have to say was nearly as interesting. It seemed that at thirty minutes past twelve o'clock, two days before Christmas, Miss Paschen hadn't turned in her rental car yet. I was starting to think that something funnier than Rosey's affair with Hobart and my own little sexual misadventures was going on.

I didn't know what it was yet, but I knew that if Rosey's car wasn't at Avis Rental, then she couldn't have left Blue River. I called Motel 8 again, but she wasn't there either. Just in case, I called the Johnny Appleseed. She hadn't checked back in, but Billy Brach kept me on the phone for fifteen minutes asking after my folks.

At the kitchen table, I sat down and made a list of the things I knew and the things I didn't on opposite sides of a piece of notebook paper. It was a way I organized my thoughts and in the past it had worked pretty well. What I knew was that Rosey was gone from the Johnny Appleseed; what I didn't know was where, but I knew somebody in town had to be able to tell me. I knew Hobart was lying, but I didn't know why. I knew Andre had seen Rosey Sunday at her motel room and either one or the other was lying about what had happened between them, but I didn't know which. I knew Spike had talked to Rosey Sunday night before Rosey checked out and while I was sleeping, but I didn't know what had been said, because Spike was pissed and wasn't telling. I knew Rosey had phoned Page Crawford but my guess was that it was to ask her to keep quiet about Hobart and Rosey which was information I already had. The last thing I knew was that Rosey didn't like her parents and they didn't like her, but with the drama I'd had myself that morning I could see how that might happen.

When the list was finished, it filled up the page, but the things I knew seemed much fewer than the things I didn't and I felt like I'd run out of places to look for Rosey until I remembered her visit to Mary Cornish's house on Saturday afternoon and the note she'd left in the door when I'd followed her. Mary Cornish seemed like a place to start.

Miss Cornish was a heavyset woman in her late fifties. I remembered her wardrobe of flannel shirts and earth-mother-style, calf-length blue jean skirts that made her look like she could have outfitted a revival of the sixties. Cornish kept three Yorkshire terriers the size of big city rats with long shaggy hair and vestigial tails. Her dogs started yapping the minute I rang the bell. They jumped up and pushed their faces at the glass in the storm door before she let me in, and ran all around my legs on the porch sniffing and growling, backing up and tucking their shaggy rat tails when I tried to pet their heads.

"Don't mind the dogs," Miss Cornish said, but I couldn't help it. She was still in her bathrobe at one o'clock in the afternoon, a dirty knee-length number in crushed velvet that was starting to pill, and her hair was the way she always wore it, knotted up at the nape of her neck in a frosty grey bun. "Curly, Larry, Moe," she shouted at the dogs and they scampered off snuffling and yelping to some other part of her house. Then she put her arms around me and invited me to sit down, pointing to the couch where her dogs had magically reappeared. They made room for me grudgingly, and snarled and curled their little rat tails whenever I moved too quickly. Miss Cornish would chide them half-heartedly until they were quiet again.

"To what do I owe this unexpected pleasure?" Miss Cornish gave me a big open smile that made me think she meant it. Her house smelled like hot toddy and stale tobacco, but not in any unpleasant way, and *Wheel of Fortune* was playing on her TV set, as Pat Sajek was encouraging contestants to guess the first four words of an old adage.

"Just in the neighborhood." I was lying and she could tell.

Miss Cornish turned down the TV volume with her remote control and knitted up her thick greying eyebrows. "Now, I hardly believe you've stopped by just for your health, not that I'm sorry you came, dear. I've always been fond of you, lying aside." She let out a heavy breath. "I don't see as many old students as I'd like."

"Seen much of Rosey Paschen?" I said.

Miss Cornish smiled, a tight inscrutable smile, and I thought she might have been quite a charmer when she was young. She very well might have been queen of the ball at the old dykes' home even now.

"Rosey Paschen? I can't say I have. Would you like some tea?" She got up and headed toward the kitchen. "Some coffee? I was just about to make myself some more."

I followed her and the dogs followed me. "Some tea," I said.

Miss Cornish nodded. She found a tea bag in a checkered metal box on her counter, took the pot off the stove and poured. "Why would you think I'd seen Rosey Paschen?"

I wondered who was lying now. "It's just a hunch. She said she was going to get in touch with you."

Her face was as blank and pleasant as ever but I could tell inside she was laughing so hard that the saucer was jiggling in her hand as we walked back to the living room. On *Wheel of Fortune* a retired shoemaker from Port Washington Wisconsin had guessed correctly: A stitch in time saves nine.

"Come on, Miss Cornish," I said.

She took a seat on her couch and the dog hair and dust flew up at me in a soft friendly cloud. "Come where, dear?" I thought maybe she wasn't getting enough jollies from daytime television, but if she was playing with me, I didn't see much choice but to play along.

I bought a vowel. "All right. I saw Rosey yesterday afternoon and we had a kind of fight. The day before I followed her here. We had a fight about that too."

"I'm not surprised to hear it." Miss Cornish took a demure sip of her coffee as Vanna White was nice enough to show the shoemaker what he'd won.

I wondered if Mary Cornish was a poker player. I wondered what else she'd heard and whether she was going to tell me.

She patted the couch cushion beside her. "Sit down, dear or you'll spill that tea."

"We had a fight because she called me months ago and begged me to come to this reunion. I was trying to ask her what she wanted," I said, "and then she freaked. Now Rosey's gone and I don't know where. I thought she might have told you something about her plans or left an address or phone number." I told Miss Cornish that I'd been everywhere and nobody knew where Rosey had gone.

"The thing is I'm starting to worry. I've even been to see her folks."

Miss Cornish made a show of wincing. "Oh dear, perhaps you shouldn't have gone there. Rosalee has been battling some demons lately, dear, in the person of her father and perhaps she just needs a little space. Maybe they all need a little space." Miss Cornish patted my knee. Her eyes were cloudy and blue. "Virginia, sometimes we like people in different ways than they like us."

She had a voice as low and soothing as a warm bath. It was tempting to tell her the whole story, top to bottom. Everything. About the phone call, the letter, the intimations, the mall and the very disappointing roll in the hay at the Johnny Appleseed, because I thought somehow she would understand. Not just my story but about Hobart and Andre and the Women's Crisis Line, because something in her voice said you can tell me anything and I won't think you're crazy. It was a nice feeling and it was warming me up all over — either that or the tea. But I wasn't so sure about not being crazy.

Miss Cornish got up and turned off her television set. Then she massaged my knee some more in a motherly way while she shared a little parable with me. "When I was a girl in Wisconsin, I had a best friend. Her name was Ann. I thought there was something special between us." She was watching my face while she spoke with her eyebrows knitted together again. "Do you understand? I thought we had something other people didn't have. In the movies we would hold hands like schoolgirls sometimes do. I couldn't call it a crush at the time, but of course, that's what it was. I was very shy and I hadn't had much experience with crushes."

All three nasty dogs had come and sat in the bowl that Miss Cornish's bathrobe made between her knees and she paused in her story to pet their heads one by one until they were all quiet as if they were listening too. She said, "One evening when we were walking home from a Kate Hepburn film, I kissed Ann. It was a mistake. Do you know what I'm saying, Virginia?"

I knew and I was touched that ten years after high school graduation I was having tea on my old guidance counselor's beat up couch while she massaged my knee and treated me to her coming out story.

"I want to tell you how sorry I am about Peggy," I said. "I was going to send a card when I heard, but the time got away from me."

"Why thank you, dear." Miss Cornish's eyes got misty all of a sudden and I pretended not to notice. She said, "Time gets away from us all."

I said, "Miss Cornish, I really need to know what was going on with Rosey when she came to talk to you."

She lifted her coffee cup again and sighed before she took another drink. "Well, I suppose she was going to tell you anyway, so I wouldn't truly be betraying a confidence." I thought she was talking herself into it; so, I just held my breath and let her talk.

She'd made her voice stern, but I could hear a kind of warmth behind it, a dyke camaraderie that made me feel all chummy too. "Virginia," she said, "please be aware that in thirty-five years of teaching and counseling I have never betrayed a student confidence."

"I know, Miss Cornish, but please just tell me about Rosey," I said.

Miss Cornish said, "Dear, maybe what you'd really like is a little drink?" I thought it was an inspired suggestion.

As it was, Miss Cornish looked like she could use one herself. "Well it's after one o'clock," Miss Cornish said. When she came back from the kitchen she had five fingers of a nice rosy sherry in two clear Flintstone jelly glasses.

I thought she got an A for effort and a C for presentation. "Those are pretty healthy servings," I said.

She looked down into her glass and took a swallow. "Do you think so, dear. This is what Peggy always used to give me when I had trouble sleeping." Miss Cornish closed her eyes.

"To Peggy." I clinked the rim of my jelly glass against hers. It was one very nice sherry and we sipped it for a while in a comfortable silence.

"I am relying on your discretion," Miss Cornish told me finally.

"Cross my heart," I said, "and hope to die." But she had another sip of sherry before she began to tell me what I'd come to hear.

"Rosalee was a troubled young girl when I knew her," Miss Cornish began. "Shortly after she'd transferred to Blue River, she talked to me a lot after school about different things, growing pains mostly. In Rose's case, I suspected abuse, but ten, fifteen years ago I didn't have much latitude." The alcohol made legs as thick as turpentine in the glass and she swirled it before she gulped and swallowed again. "Well, people didn't want to believe that kind of thing went on in middle-class homes," Miss Cornish said. "I tried to help her as much as I could, but she was closed up and in the little time we spent together, I couldn't get her to open up. And I couldn't make those kinds of allegations without any foundation, you understand."

Miss Cornish told me that on Saturday morning Rosey came by and confided that her step-father had sexually abused both Rosey and her sister on and off from the time she was six until about the time she was nine or ten. That was when her older sister ran away. Miss Cornish's dogs were tucked so deep into the folds of her robe all I could see was their wet black noses. Every once in a while one would growl softly in my direction.

"Rose said she didn't know why he stopped, but he stopped all of a sudden and then she wasn't even sure if it had really happened." Miss Cornish stroked a shaggy head. "Rosalee had a lot of anger over the situation. She said she wanted to tell me about it when she was in high school, but her memories weren't clear. She felt she'd acted out in some ways that were inappropriate with regard to you and that you might have been confused by it. She was sorry for it. One of the things she was going to do as part of her therapy was to confront her parents and explain to other people in her past why she had behaved in ways she thought were wrong or manipulative."

"Like kissing me," I said, "graduation night at Johnson's farm." It was odd to think ten years of fantasy had simply been a misunderstanding. "And that was what she had to tell me?" I was addressing the carpet on the floor between my feet and there was a knot in the bottom of my stomach that wouldn't go away.

Miss Cornish shrugged. "Well, that's my guess, dear."

"She's isn't gay at all, is she?" I said. "You know, I thought she was going to say she was still in love with me." I had to laugh to keep from crying. "So, that's why she came to see you too. I'm an idiot," I said.

Miss Cornish smiled. "Well, maybe not an idiot." She patted the back of my hand and her fingers were cool and dry. "Incest can damage one's sense of boundaries and trust. Incest, like most violent crimes, Virginia, is about control. I think Rose understands that intellectually, even if she's having trouble getting past her own emotions. She came to see me because she was very interested in my being on the lookout for that pattern in other girls. But sexual abuse has been so over-hyped, dear. People are looking for it in even the most innocent circumstances and I told her about a case of mistaken accusation I'd seen quite recently."

Miss Cornish took another sip of her sherry and pursed her lips behind the taste. "One of the mothers up at the High School received an anonymous note. If I remember, it said something like, 'Your new husband likes little girls. Watch your daughter.'" She waved her hand dismissively and took another drink of her sherry. "Well, something like that anyway. Of course, the mother came to me distraught. She wanted me to talk to the daughter and I did, discreetly. Over the years I've seen children, both boys and girls, who've suffered abuse, Virginia. But this simply wasn't one of those children. If I hadn't been careful it could have been a very great tragedy for a family that has had more than its share of tragedy already."

"I mentioned this to Rose, as a word of caution, but she didn't want to hear it. Everything but. She said maybe the daughter was afraid. Maybe the stepfather had threatened her. She simply wouldn't stop projecting the idea of abuse that in my professional opinion wasn't there. And she walked out of here in a terrible huff. I asked her to stop in again before she left. The note on the door was an apology, nothing more cryptic, I'm sorry to say, and I haven't seen her since. That's all I know about it." Miss Cornish paused for a second and bit her lower lip. "Oh, and there was the little problem with this man, Andre Rutherford."

"What about Andre," I said. "He's married to Sandra Crab."

"Well, yes." Miss Cornish sighed. "Apparently that's so."

"So what," I said.

"Apparently Rose hadn't expected to run into Andre Rutherford again, and that, coupled with confronting her parents, was a little more than she was prepared to take on in a weekend. Her mother appears to be in tremendous denial. She's shielding Rosalee's step-father and Rosey was unable to talk to him as she planned. As if the parental situation isn't difficult enough, it seems that she and Mr. Rutherford had some complicated history as well, and of course, the holidays are hard for us all."

Miss Cornish didn't know the half of it and I

could already hear a shakiness beginning in my voice. "Andre swore to me there was nothing between him and Rosey. Sandra was jealous and he swore to me that there wasn't any reason for it."

Miss Cornish shrugged again. "Rosalee told me they had an affair and there was a child. I only say this to you, Virginia so that you can perhaps understand the strain she's been under."

I couldn't say anything for a long time.

Miss Cornish said, "Dear, I really don't think this is about you."

And when I could breathe normally again, I asked her, "Do you think Rosey could be lying about Andre?"

Miss Cornish tossed back the end of her drink. "I don't think so." She set the empty cup on the arm of the couch. "But of course that's just an opinion."

It was shaping up to be one hell of a bad day. "I've got to go, Miss Cornish," I said, getting up.

The little dogs growled at me some more from the safety of her lap, and Miss Cornish poured the rest of the sherry from my jelly glass back into hers. "Certainly, dear. Pity to let this go to waste." She squeezed my hand. "Do come again. And I don't think you ought to blame yourself too much about Rosalee, dear. I suspect she's simply taken some space. Sometimes people don't give very good cues in this society. I don't know, if I were you and twenty years younger, maybe I would have mistaken her intentions too. My unsolicited advice is that you find a nice girlfriend back in Chicago. And if you want to be happy don't look for perfection." She winked. "Remember, just someone nice."

I thanked her for the DYKE-founding-chapter

words of wisdom. Miss Cornish shooed the dogs off her lap so she could stand and hug me goodbye. Then she picked up the remote control from her coffee table and turned the television set back on.

XIV

I didn't know what I was going to do if Sandra was home, because it seemed to me what I had to discuss with Andre was better done in private so I could really haul his ass.

When he came to the door, he was wearing baggy grey sweat pants with a draw-string waist, and rubbing sleep out of his eyes. "What can I do for you, Virginia," he said, and I told him there was quite a bit.

"Where's Sandra?" I asked. The house was too dark to see behind him into the front room and there was only the big shiny Christmas tree. Every so often a string of colored lights would blink.

Andre's pupils were closed against the light from the door and it made his eyes look mean. He turned around and squinted into the dark room as if he were checking behind him for the answer, then he said, "Sandra's not here. Sid and Betty took her shopping again." He laughed and I didn't like his tone. I didn't like his dimples; I didn't like his face. Not anymore. He said, "With the baby coming, they're buying up the whole damn store this year and I'm getting some sleep so I can work hard enough to pay for it all." He let out another big nervous belly laugh, but I stared him down until the chuckles died out.

"I think you ought to wake up and invite me in," I said. Behind him all the red lights had blinked on again. "And why don't you get yourself a drink," I told him, "because I think you're probably going to need it."

Andre creased his eyes up again and looked at me sideways, but he did what I told him and he left the door standing open while he went to the kitchen. He came back with one for me too and I closed the door and dropped my coat in a pile on the arm of the couch. Then we sat down, him on the couch and me in the straight-back chair near the door, squinting our eyes at each other.

"What's going on?" he said.

"That's what I ought to be asking you," I said. "You remember how you wanted me to talk to Sandra for you about Rosalee?"

Andre gulped his drink and grimaced. "Yeah, thanks," he said. "Things are better."

"Not for me." I could feel my face getting hot. The metallic tree blinked on and off behind him and through the entryway to the dining room I could see Betty's pine cone center piece in the middle of the tablecloth. I said, "Things are worse for me since you set me up."

All the muscles between Andre's nose and chin went limp and his mouth hung open before he managed to ask me what I was talking about.

"Well, for starters," I said, "you lied about sleeping with Rosey Paschen. You fucked her, you knocked her up and then you dumped her." It hurt all over again to say the words, maybe because someone had discarded something I had wanted so badly. Or maybe with what I'd found out about her since the Johnny Appleseed, I'd personalized a little piece of her pain and the words were like picking at those open wounds. "Any way you cut it," I was saying, "you used her." In the room I could hear my own voice and below it the sound of the heater coming on and the pendulum clock in the corner swinging back and forth. There was nothing else. I said, "You used Rosalee and you used me."

And I realized that my outrage was more over the latter complaint than the former which I had already suspected, even in some ways understood when I put it in the context of my own struggles with fidelity and relationships. It was embarrassing that I, even insulated by my lesbianism, could be sucked in just like Rosey, betrayed and compromised by a man with a line and a pretty black face.

Andre was staring pop-eyed and blank as a deer looking into a set of high beams. But sometimes when they're caught in the light on a country road, the big ones will just come running down the yellow lines back at you like they're going to take your car apart.

Andre swallowed hard. Then his face got a stiff and not so very pleasant expression. His voice was hoarse. It was almost a whisper. "Look, Rosalee is a freak. You ought to know that. She got pregnant on purpose and let's get real now, because you didn't say too damn much to Sandra. You were too busy chasing Rosey Paschen through the streets to keep many promises to me, Virginia. I had to dig myself out of that hole with Sandra on my own steam." His mouth stayed open when he'd run out of words like he was thinking up more to say but I got my two cents in before he could get them out.

"So, what happened to the kid? Your first kid," I said. "Or is that ancient history like your first wife?"

Andre's eyes were dark little holes in his face. "I don't know." He answered quietly, as if he thought it might be a trick question and then his voice began to rise. "Why don't you ask Rosalee since you've gotten so close. I paid for an abortion, and she told me she had one." He rolled his eyes. "But what can I do? The woman lies."

"Yeah, who lies?" Andre was making me sick. When I said so, I could tell he didn't like it.

"Let's not talk about sick," he said. "You're an expert on sick."

I said I didn't think I liked his inference.

He was standing by the couch, looking bigger than he had on Saturday at the Whore and his voice was hoarse and quiet and angry. "Rosalee got pregnant to trap me into staying with her when she knew I was getting married to someone else. That's what women want — traps and manipulation."

I said, "You could teach a graduate course on manipulation."

"Women want to cut off your balls," he said, and looked down at me in the chair as if he hated me. "Some women."

"Maybe so." I looked back at him just the same way. "But I think you'd better tell Sandra. Because if you don't, I will." It wasn't meant exactly as a threat, only as an ultimatum, but he took hold of my forearm above the wrist like he wasn't crazy about the choices I'd left him.

"I mean it," I said, but he didn't let go.

"Mean what." Andre maneuvered me up out of the chair until I was standing with my arm twisted behind me, and my elbow pinned against my back.

"Cut it out." I tried to get control of my arm, but he was bigger and heavier.

I could smell his breath, like day-old left-over anchovy pizza, and he was whispering at me deliberately, "Nobody is going to threaten my family. Nobody. Not you. Not Rosalee Paschen. Do you understand?" He jerked my arm until it hurt too much not to nod and then one more time for good measure. He said, "You better understand it, Virginia, because I swear to God, I will make you sorry if you fuck with me."

I felt as if my arm was coming out of its socket and for a minute it seemed like he was going to really hurt me, but when I thought my arm was about to pop, instead he let me go.

"Don't fuck with me," he said again, lightly, as if it were just friendly advice.

I could still feel where his hand had held my wrist. The place felt hot. There were tears coming up in my eyes and I fought them, screaming at him so I wouldn't cry. "Yeah," I said. "Did you fuck with Rosey, did you make her sorry too, you dick?"

"Fuck you," said Andre.

"And you too, you bastard." I was crying then and couldn't stop. "And don't ever touch me again." The inside of my mouth was dry and I could feel my heart pounding against the sides of my chest. I could hear myself screaming, "You touch me again and I'll fucking kill you." I meant it, but Andre didn't seem like he was very much impressed.

He walked to the door and opened it for me. The cold air felt like a slap in the face. It dried my tears which I thought was at least something.

"I think it's time for you to go." Andre's voice was flat and back under control as he handed me my coat. "It's time to leave."

"Yeah?" I said, "Well, I couldn't agree with you more." And I called him a dick again for the satisfaction of having the last word.

Outside, I knew he was watching me as I walked back down the driveway to my car fighting off a bad case of the shakes. I was okay though, and he hadn't hurt me. It was the only thought I had in my head and I turned it over and over again on the giddy rush of that near-miss-on-the-freeway-accident exhilaration. And I couldn't say how it was that about twenty minutes later I found myself in the center of the Southtown Valley Mall, sitting by a mock up of Santa's workshop.

They say: When the going gets tough the tough go shopping. So, I bought another sweater for my Dad and a scarf for my mother, some new age music for Adeline and, unexpectedly, a little something for Spike.

Williams-Sonoma had some very nice things, and with the help of a very tall man in an apron, I settled on an extra mixing bowl for her KitchenAid industrial mixer and a dozen new metal tips for her pastry gloves, gift-wrapped. The sales clerk wrote, "Thanks — Gerard," on the receipt and it was the first present I'd really enjoyed buying for a woman in years. I couldn't figure out exactly whether that had to do with Spike, or myself, but I decided it didn't much matter.

The light thin snow was spread across the highway like powered sugar, and I was feeling almost Christmasy in spite of everything, as I turned down Main and lucked into a parking space right in front of Spike's Cafe.

Spike's was a noisy kind of fern-bar-looking place crammed with wooden ice cream parlor chairs I thought had been designed to cut down on the loitering time after a meal, and light natural wood trim wherever it was even vaguely appropriate. Spike's was two dining rooms of marble-topped tables with long-stemmed red roses in clear glass bud vases, without tablecloths, and placed too close together. I couldn't say how the locals felt about the decor, but the food must have been all right because Spike's was packing them in and the waiter told me it would be forty-five minutes without a reservation. He was a thin dapper man with an arrogant sneer.

"That's all right," I said. "I'm just here to see Spike."

"Spike's working." The waiter looked at me hard and I couldn't tell whether he didn't like my face on general principles or my reputation had managed to precede me. But I could imagine the klatch of gay men huddled around Spike in the kitchen, all trendy haircuts, aprons and attitude, saying "Fuck her girlfriend; she's trash." It was what Emery would have said to me and I missed him for it. I missed gay men in my life with their easy familiarity and their finger-popping savy when some woman had drop-kicked me, telling me, "Honey, you just ought to forget her cause she's just not good enough for you." All that, even when I still thought she was. "What's your name?" the waiter asked like I'd been a hot topic of conversation in the kitchen.

I told him and he told me, "Wait here. I'll see if she has the time."

I waited in the foyer about another five minutes before he came back and motioned for me to come with him. We walked back down a long hall past the restrooms to the kitchen.

Spike, her sleeves rolled up, was hefting her Calphalon, and shouting at her kitchen staff. She wore a white canvas apron with colorful stains and a short-tempered expression.

I didn't know how Spike was going to feel about seeing me. As she came marching across the kitchen I wasn't sure that she knew either, but when I took the package from behind my back it seemed as though she'd made up her mind.

"I brought you something," I fired off before she could start to chew me out. Then I said, "I'm sorry I had to leave this morning. But I knew you had to work and I didn't want to get in your way."

Spike ran her hand through the front of her stiff moussed hair and pointed out that she was working even as we spoke. But she rattled the present discreetly as if she was pleased before she gave it to the waiter to take away. "So, what do you want anyway?" There was the beginning of smile in the lines around her eyes.

I didn't know. "I talked to Miss Cornish about Rosey," I started, "and I still don't know what's going on." I had gotten out that I thought Harry Hobart knew more than he was telling, before Spike cut me off.

"Look Virginia." Spike linked her arm in mine and steered us to a quiet corner of the kitchen. "What I think is that you need to talk to Hobart — not me — and ask him why he lied about seeing Rosey. Because, no offense, honey, but I'm sick of this." Spike kissed me on the cheek and grinned. "You get five stars in presents and a star and a half in pillow talk. So go put this thing to rest, will you? And when you're finished maybe we can swap recipes." I thought it sounded like a promise with some upside.

"Recipes?" I said

Spike winked. She fished a red rose from the bucket of water on floor by the hall and handed it to me. "I'll be done here at five this evening," she said. "If you come by my place around six o'clock, I might even let you take me to dinner."

I told her I'd make reservations with the desk on the way out and she laughed at me. It was nice to hear and I liked the way the lines around her eyes creased up. "Oh, Jesus, Ginny," Spike said, "couldn't we just go somewhere and get a hamburger? I have to eat this nouvelle shit all the time."

XV

The road to Harry Hobart's house was a two-lane highway that wound past a small Jewish cemetery. I wasn't sure where Rosalee Paschen was but I'd known for years where I could find Emery Arkin, even if I'd never had the heart to drop in before. I decided, that afternoon, I would visit him for Christmas and I brought him the rose that Spike had given me, because it didn't seem right to come empty-handed.

The grounds were frozen in a flat hard glaze of ice on the top of the deep snow like a long pan of high white sheet cake. It crunched and sank as I walked across it. Each step felt like pressing and falling and my feet left marks that were more like holes than footprints in the icy snow.

When I found Emery's memorial it didn't look like much, just a flat granite marker in a field of markers, some bigger, some smaller, with his name and his dates, no other inscription. The grey stone looked new and unsettled and the square carved letters of his name were still deep and crisp. Five years of weather had barely taken the gloss off the smooth clean face and I laid my rose on the ground in front of it, piling some snow in a mound on the stem so the wind wouldn't blow my little offering away. Then I crouched down close so I could talk to Emery — and God, both because wherever Emery was I figured they were there together.

"I'm sorry," I told them. My knees were wet and I could feel the snow melting on my shoes from the heat of my body and the water coming up through the sides of the soles. "I'm sorry that I didn't make the time to say goodbye." The words made me feel better. Words said years too late. They were something at least. "I miss you," I said and the wind caught my words and carried them away to wherever wind goes. I told God and Emery about Rosey and Em and Spike, and Sandra and Andre, telling secrets to the grave, and the wind carried off those words too. It left my ears ringing with only the whistling sound of its breath in the old bald trees as if I'd said nothing at all. I didn't know about God, but I was pretty sure that Emery heard me and I thought I could hear him laughing at my troubles in the wind the way that wintertime seems to be filled with ghosts.

My face was streaked and hot and stinging behind the wool collar of my coat turned up against the cold, and when I looked back across the snowy field at the lonely footprints I had left behind, there was a figure walking towards me. Its long smooth gait across the snow, with the wind blowing at its open coat, made it look like another blue grey ghost dancing sadly in the distance. But as the figure came closer I could tell it was nothing more remarkable than Andre Rutherford — although he didn't look too terribly happy; and I wondered how God and Emery were going to get me out of this one.

Andre was shouting, waving his arms as if he were doing jumping jacks to stay warm in the bitter cold and I stood up beside Emery's marker in the snow watching Andre's figure grow inches by seconds as he came closer, running across the frozen lawn.

When he caught up to me, Andre had his chin buried in his white cashmere scarf and his hands sunk down in his pockets. What he said wasn't much of a surprise, and I wasn't in very much of a mood to hear it. "Look, Virginia," he started, "I'm sorry if we had some words this afternoon."

I told him I thought it was an understatement.

"Maybe so." He was pleading. "I'm sorry — if you

want me to say it again. I'll make it up to you but you can't say anything about Rosey to Sandra. Look, I'm begging you, Virginia," Andre said.

I stopped him before he could say any more, and he didn't like it. His face was brick-red from the cold but his chin was set and frozen into pure attitude. "Come on," he said. "You can't screw things up for me with Sandy."

"You watch me," I said. "You fucked Rosey Paschen the minute you got out of Sandra's sight."

Andre caught hold of my shoulder, and his grip was a little tighter than what I would have liked in a good massage. "Come on, Virginia." He was wheedling. "I didn't know what to do. I thought if I told you Rosey got pregnant, you wouldn't help me." His grip felt like a little more than friendly persuasion.

"Damn skippy." I tossed my body hard, jerking away from him, but Andre caught me by the shoulder again and his hand tightened up like a vise on my collarbone. I thought our talk was starting to feel less like a discussion and more like an assault, and I wondered where the cops were when you really needed them. "Cut it out," I said. But Andre was shaking me so hard by both shoulders that my teeth were starting to feel loose in my head.

His breath was in my face and he was growling, "Nothing, I mean nothing, Virginia, is going to affect my life with Sandra, and you're going to be sorry if you try to mess me up like this." Maybe it was the torque he was putting on my collarbone, but I had to admit the threat had some credibility. He said, "You think about that, girlfriend, before you go making any announcements."

I gave it my sincere consideration before I brought my knee up hard in between his legs. Andre bent over, swearing and groaning and I didn't wait to see if he was going to straighten up. But it was gratifying how quickly his hands loosened up on my shoulders and dropped to his crotch.

While he was hanging onto his balls, I ran as best I could through the snow back towards the parking lot. Even navigating the heavy snow, with the fear of Andre and a good north wind at my back, I made it the hundred yards to my car in nothing flat and I thought maybe I ought to give jogging another try.

Spraying gravel onto the lawn on my way past the wrought iron gates and back onto the road, I made a solemn promise that I was going to find Rosey Paschen and make peace with her. Then we were going to hang that bastard, Andre, out to dry together.

At sixty miles per hour down the frozen highway, Harry Hobart's house was only another five minutes away.

XVI

Water was leaking into my loafers and my socks felt squishy as I stood on Hobart's front stoop swinging the little brass knocker against the wood. My toes were getting numb in the freezing water.

So, I was especially thankful when he came to the door.

"Mr. Hobart," I said. "I'm sorry to bother you. But I really need to talk about Christmas dinner." It was a lie, an entry line when I couldn't take the chance of him turning me away like he had the night before, and I felt a great rush of hopefulness disproportionate in significance to the simple act of his opening a door when he asked me in.

Hobart gathered the shawl of his oversized cardigan sweater around his neck while he held the door and looked me over, frowning. His feet were bare at the ends of his corduroy trouser legs and his toes were big and white and hairy. "Hurry up," he said. "It's cold as hell outside."

Hobart folded my coat over his arm like a gentleman host and took it down the hall to a small shallow closet while I stomped the snow off my shoes on the mat in his entryway. I could see a small front sitting room through the arch of an open doorway off to the side and in front of me down a long dark hall were four closed doors. I had never been further than this hall of Hobart's house and admittedly it hadn't been of much interest before, but I found myself curious about it suddenly, this place he had rented and then bought before his marriage to Marge Arkin. Even insignificant details about a winning rival can hold your attention in the face of an especially embarrassing loss, and it was as if the examination of his house might tell me what appeal Hobart still had for Rosey Paschen after the lapse of the same ten years in which I had seemed to have lost all of my own appeal. It was an odd prickly sense of competition now that the episode at the Johnny Appleseed had put me beyond wanting her, as if someone were poking at the ugly bruise Rosey Paschen had left on my ego. The bruise remained and the ache of sore feelings.

Hobart led me through the doorway of his small sitting room and I let my eyes wander across the empty picture hooks on his walls and the general mess of packing cartons and boxes stacked on up the floor. "Moving soon?" I asked.

"Soon enough," said Hobart. "Have a seat anywhere." But he pointed in particular to one of two dark brown leather loveseats that faced a window and he told me to put my shoes by the fireplace to dry them out. "I'll get us something to warm you up." I was thinking of maybe a hot toddy or another glass of good sherry, before he added, "How about some tea," and went out through a second doorway at the back of the room, off to a big yellow kitchen.

While he was gone, I got up from the loveseat and took a walk around the long rectangular room with its white walls and the half-closed steel blinds through which I'd seen him and Rosey the night I'd followed her. On one side was a small fireplace with a wood mantel shelf that ran the length of the wall, and a hearth where I'd put my shoes and socks to dry. There were two low wood bookshelves beside a small antique-looking roll-top desk. In the hutch of the desk was a plane ticket to Paris, France by way of New York City three days after Christmas, a firm storage quote and order for service from Mayflower Movers one day before the date of the ticket, four colored plastic paper clips, a broken number two pencil and some old red lint. And when I'd sat down again, I thought it was odd there were no pictures, not of Marge or Sarah, or the three of them together, in the house of a man so bereaved that by all accounts he couldn't hold down a job. But that of course was the least of my worries.

Staring down at the rug between my knees on Hobart's chilly leather loveseat that looked like it came from a men's club, trying to think of what I would say to make him tell me where Rosey was, I noticed a little trail of silver chain on the dark red oriental-looking rug beside the heel of my foot. The trail led through the white wool tassels of the rug underneath the sofa and when I pulled the chain, a little silver medallion came along with it. I'd seen the medallion before, the afternoon I'd spent with Rosey at the Johnny Appleseed. Then, it had been around her neck. Now, the chain was broken and the medal was held on at one side by what was left of a thick silver ring clasp. I held it up and looked at the rough square cross intertwined with the letter M on the back of the silvered medal, the raised outline of a woman in long robes flowing out over her open arms, the medal swinging in front of my nose like a charm used by a sideshow hypnotist.

A few minutes later, at the sound of a microwave alarm, Hobart came back with a teacup and saucer in either hand, and I put the medal away in my pocket. Hobart lowered himself down onto the twin to my loveseat and set my tea on the end table between us.

The cup was an oversized porcelain affair with a pattern of pale blue cornflowers that seemed to be the one thing in the house attributable to Marge's tastes. Otherwise the place looked scrubbed of female influences. Hobart was holding the dainty handle with his index finger hooked inside it and his pinky extended, smiling hopefully through the veil of chamomile steam from his tea.

"Now what about Christmas, Virginia?" Hobart asked me. He crossed an ankle over a knee and balanced the saucer on the crook of his knee. "I was looking forward to it."

I told him, "I really didn't come about Christmas, it's about Rosey again."

I could hear the wind roll across the flat dead fields outside, flapping at the loose shingles on his roof. Hobart raised the teacup to his lips again and when he put it down he wasn't smiling anymore.

"Mr. Hobart," I said, "I really need you to tell me where Rosalee is." The charm in my pocket made me remember a vacation I'd had once at a Club Med resort, of all places, where heterosexual couples had sex on the beach so furiously that they lost the little bar beads they wore around their necks in the commotion. I thought of Hobart and Rosalee on the floor by his leather furniture and it gave me an ache of embarrassment in the bottom of my stomach. Through the window the sky looked like someone had spread a grey blanket out across it. I said, "I need you to tell me the last time you saw Rosey Paschen, I mean really?" But my voice sounded small and pitiful even to me and Hobart was staring down his handsome patrician nose while he told me again that the last time was at the reunion on Friday.

"Like I said before, perhaps she went home. I'm sorry, Virginia." He met my eyes and his eyes were clear and open as blue sky, but there was a faint shine on his pink forehead that looked to me like a light glaze of fresh sweat and it gave me heart.

"No offense, Mr. Hobart," I told him, "but I can't help but think you're pulling my leg here." I blew hard into my teacup before I went on and the steam flew up around my face. "Ordinarily I wouldn't mind, but I'm tired and I'm broken down and I think it's only fair to tell you that this has been one hell of a week."

Hobart blinked at me from over his heavy black dream-nerd glasses. "I beg your pardon, Virginia?" he said. His expression hadn't changed, but something in his voice had drawn an emotional line in the sand and I took another drink of chamomile tea to slow down my pulse before I crossed that line.

Then I told him, "I know exactly where Rosey is." I didn't really, of course, but close enough. I knew where she wasn't — and that was New York. I knew where she'd been — from the religious medal in my hand that she'd worn the afternoon she'd disappeared, from the shadows I'd seen on his blinds the night before, from the soft music and his lying about having seen her, from the coy way he'd opened the door when I'd come looking for Rosey the night she'd left, and from the fresh oil spot on his driveway. I knew Hobart knew and he had to tell me so I could make my peace with Rosey. I wanted to forget this crazy, confused little chapter of my life and I wanted to know she'd forgotten it too. So that I could go back to remembering her with the syrupy nostalgia people reserve for old long-ago crushes and dead pets.

"I know where Rosey is, Mr. Hobart," I said

again, "and so do you. You better just tell me everything now because I know what's going on." I repeated myself because an appropriately intoned threat, like the click of a loaded gun, can make all the difference in a potentially adversarial interaction. Then, I pulled the little necklace out of my pocket and held it up for him to see. The fading light from the window caught the silver links and the medal spinning around at the end of its chain.

Hobart's eyebrows were arched all the way up to the wrinkles that were beginning on his pretty forehead. He let them drop back down again after a while in a sad ironic kind of way. "Well, I see," he said as if he were telling me my dog had died. "Yes. indeed. I certainly see that you do. I'm awfully sorry to hear it, Virginia." The way he drew out the sounds of the words was making my skin squirm around on my bones. I had the uneasy feeling that I might be missing something — maybe something really important.

Hobart rubbed the stubble on his chin with his fist. "You know, this certainly changes things." He seemed to be hunting for his words as he strung them together into a sentence that had never in my experience boded much of anything good: "Surely, Virginia, you must see the position you've put me in."

I didn't, but I figured it had to be one hell of a pinch for a high school English teacher to be ending a sentence with a preposition.

Hobart sighed. "Well, in for a penny; in for a pound. So, let's get this over with." He cracked his knuckles as if he were going to do something strenuous with his hands and it occurred to me then that not only had I bluffed when I should have folded, but maybe Hobart and I weren't even playing the same game. His eyes were very sad and they seemed to be looking through me, straight ahead out the grey window or maybe at some private spot on the blank white wall beside it.

All of it made me nervous and I was stammering, "Look, all I really want is to talk to Rosey and I saw her stop at your place on Saturday night, so I knew you were lying when you said you hadn't seen her since the party Friday. When I found her necklace on the floor I knew Rosey had been here yesterday after I'd seen her at her motel." I spread my arms out in kind of a shrug and kind of a motion of surrender the way little dogs will roll over and show their bellies to bigger ones as a kind of preventative measure. "Relax, Mr. Hobart," I said. "Rosey's been sort of avoiding me and I just figured if I let you know I knew you'd seen her you'd have to at least give me her address."

I would have said more about what I wanted except that Hobart started to chuckle from low in his throat. It began as a rumble and a quaking in his shoulders before it broke out into a full-fledged laugh. It was a deep hollow sound that came from his chest, almost as if he were sobbing. When he finally stopped, he said, "Oh dear, Virginia, I think we've had an awful misunderstanding." There was the end of a bitter smile on his face.

It made me remember what Rosey had said at the Johnny Appleseed when she told me about her stepfather — and the other men too. Marge Arkin's drowning accident and the conspicuous absence of her pictures in the house of her grieving husband, my sinking feeling that Rosalee had been writing to Hobart too, the plane tickets to France in the hutch of Hobart's desk and the romantic travel brochures for Italy and Greece piled up in his car. It occurred to me that the shadows I'd seen on the blinds when I'd followed Rosalee back here to Hobart's house might very well have been old news, and all either one of them would have had to do was tell me. But they hadn't. Which could have meant a number of things. But the one that came readily to my suspicious mind was that Hobart and Rosey might have killed his wife in order to be together. If that was so, I thought it was a pretty good idea to leave while Hobart was still smiling.

I was smiling too, weakly, as I got up from the couch and began to mumble my excuses. "You know, if this is an inconvenient time why don't I just leave my address and you can give it to Rosey." I was picking up my shoes from the hearth and putting on my socks as fast as could be considered polite. I'd had the unfortunate knack in the past few years of stumbling into situations of wrongdoing — situations of murder, actually — and I didn't know whether the problem was me or the company I chose to keep. But what I hoped was that in this case I could get away clean. Maybe write a nice long anonymous letter outlining my suspicions to the local police from the comfort and safety of my parents' home and let the cops do the job they get paid for. I clapped my hands on my thighs and showed Hobart the watch-face on my wrist. It said four-thirty. I said, "Golly, will you look at the time."

But when Hobart stood up, I didn't think it was to get my coat. Through the window behind the couch, dusk was rolling down the sky. "Not so fast, Virginia," Hobart said. It was the voice of authority I used to dread, the one that stopped teenagers from running in the halls and handed out week-long detention. Ten years later, if for different reasons, I found it could have the same chilling effect. The way to the door was across the room, through the entryway, through Harry Hobart who was too big for me to move and didn't look much like he was inclined to move himself.

"Finish your tea." He was walking back and forth in front of the window. His broad, square body blocked out what was left of the sun, and cast a long grey shadow on the wall. "You understand," he spoke to me softly as he paced, "I can't let you leave now that you've connected me with Rosalee, the police will know just whom to look for."

He sat down again on the other loveseat by the arm rest nearest mine and bent toward me with his hands crossed on his enormous knees. "You might as well know the whole sordid thing." He put in, "Well, as much as I know," and pushed his hair back off his long forehead. "Who can tell what Rosalee could have been thinking. Actually, it would be kind of a relief to discuss it. You know, Rosey didn't seem to even want to listen. No." He shook his head, looking down towards the baseboard under the window, and went on as if he were talking to himself. "She just wanted to talk and of course I had to put an end to that. She accused me of being some kind of pervert. And of killing Marge." Hobart's eyebrows traveled up his forehead and back down again. He said, "Well, of course, she was right about Marge."

If I could have stopped my mouth from hanging

open I would have, but my jaws didn't seem to be working so I just let my lip hang there closer to my chin for longer than I would have ordinarily thought was becoming. All I could think to say was, "You killed Rosey Paschen too?" Mary Cornish's thick, sweet sherry poured over my breakfast of Christmas cookies was making a heavy sour paste in my gut and I didn't seem to be thinking clearly. Somehow I didn't understand why Harry Hobart would do away with his girlfriend, and I thought my ears might be playing tricks on me, because I couldn't believe what I thought I was hearing. I asked again, "Mr. Hobart, are you telling me you killed Rosey Paschen?"

"Well, yes." Hobart added quickly. "I had to, you understand."

But I didn't.

Hobart sighed. "It was complicated and she just wouldn't listen to reason. In a nutshell, that was the problem with Marge too." He let another deep breath out through his mouth. "Marge had gotten the idea that I was molesting Sarah, her daughter. As if it were anything short of ridiculous to imagine that I would focus any energy at all on that stupid, unimaginative child."

I was beginning to realize, numbly, that there was something important here I was still missing. "Mr. Hobart," I said, "what exactly are you talking about?"

Hobart looked up and straight at me. His blue eyes were magnified through thick lenses. "A gift I have given to some of my special students." He took off his glasses and put them on the end table so he could rub the bridge of his nose. "Rosalee was the first. She seduced me, really, while I was tutoring her. I thought it was shocking at first, then I came to understand that her involvement with me was an experience she needed in order to grow. Of course recently, through some very misguided therapy, she'd claimed that I damaged her and she was blaming me for all of it. I suppose she thought if I'd victimized her then that could somehow extend to Sarah." Hobart snorted. "Well, I've had brighter students, Virginia, you among them."

"That's very flattering, Mr. Hobart," I said. I didn't like the turn the conversation was taking at all. Outside the sun was setting inches by seconds and the room was growing dim. My watch said 5:15 and I wondered if my parents were missing me at dinner. After our fight that morning about my comings and goings, I wondered how long I would have to be missing before they realized something was wrong. Rosey hadn't had anyone to come looking for her — no one but me. I wondered if my family was going to come looking for me in time to make any difference. Hobart kept talking in that same smooth, well-modulated voice he used ten years ago to deliver lectures on the authentic American voice of Walt Whitman.

He was telling me that from what he could piece together of Marge's story, Rosey had made some anonymous phone calls to Marge intimating that he was a pervert, and she'd forwarded a love letter Hobart had written to her when she was a girl. "You know I barely remembered writing it. But what could I do?" Hobart shrugged and smiled just slightly as if he felt sheepish thinking about it. "Marge knew my handwriting so I admitted that years ago as a flattered young man not much older than his

213

students, I'd had a brief affair. I told her the girl was precocious and I was charmed into an error of judgement." Hobart picked up his tea again and tasted it carefully, before he gulped the rest. He cleaned the lenses of his glasses on the front of his shirt before he put them back on. "Who's to say it isn't the truth?"

"What about Rosey?" The sun had faded into an orange glow across the frozen corn fields. I said, "What did she think the truth was, Mr. Hobart?"

He sniffled irritably. "Listen, I'm not a bad man, Virginia, and Rosalee was a damaged, vindictive girl, damaged from things over which I had no control. Things I had in fact done my best to fix. She was claiming in effect that I had raped her, Virginia, that she was too young and too emotionally damaged to be responsible for her actions at seventeen years old." He clicked his tongue on the roof of his mouth. "Think of yourself at seventeen."

But I was considering Page Crawford leaving Hobart's house at eight o'clock on a Saturday night. The thought of that and my unwise choices for breakfast and lunch made my stomach feel like there was a big ragged hole in the bottom of it.

I said, "You were sleeping with Page Crawford too, weren't you?" But I couldn't make it sound like much of a question. I remembered the phone call from Rosey's room to the Crawford house and went on, "That's what Page was doing yesterday afternoon, staking out Rosey's motel in her car."

Hobart looked as if this was news to him. "Was she?" The muscles in his face began to twitch.

"Rosey called her house," I said, "Saturday night after she came here to see you."

Hobart clucked his tongue again and rolled his eyes. "There was a scene when Rosey found Page here. She tried to tell her all kinds of slander about me and I sent Page home so she wouldn't be exposed to it. I suppose it was silly for me to think Rosey could be so easily deterred."

"Maybe not." I told Hobart that I'd seen Page Crawford drive up to the Johnny Appleseed and park. "She just sat in her car for a while crying and then she drove away." I said, "Maybe she didn't want to hear what Rosey had to say."

Ten years ago, Harry Hobart had been the teacher I most admired. I wasn't sure if I would want to hear Rosey either. "Why, Mr. Hobart?" I asked and I found it hard to meet his eyes while I waited for him to answer.

His mouth was soft and his full pink lips were still wet with tea. There was the hint of a day-growth beard on his cheeks, and I had to concede that Harry Hobart had to be a pretty attractive quantity to schoolgirls. But then again, who wasn't.

"It was easy," Hobart smiled, close-mouthed and smug. "Who can resist a subject everybody wants to learn?"

I said, "Call me crazy, Mr. Hobart, but I don't think this is what the school board means when they talk about a well-rounded education."

Hobart relaxed back into his chair and crossed his legs. "Well, isn't it?" He was still whispering gently to me like a lover. "Isn't education really all about growth through experience? They want it too, the girls in my classes. Their smooth little hands that rest too long on your arm. Standing by your desk with their lips just slightly parted and their

215

breathless gushing voices asking for it, 'Oh Mr. Hobart, do you think you could find the time to talk to me about Billy Budd after class?' " Hobart's hoarse falsetto sounded a little like Marilyn Monroe on LSD. He was telling me quietly, "Virginia, every year there's a brand new batch of them, girl-bodies, and breasts that seem to have happened overnight at the fronts of their sweaters, unformed minds hanging on your every word and listening with their hormones and imaginations to a lecture you're not even giving."

He held my eyes. "Do you know what they want? They want experience. What they're asking is for me to make something of them. Ten years ago Rosalee was asking for that too."

"No offense," I told him, "but you sound just a little like the straight man's auxiliary of the Man-Boy Love Association."

"None taken." Hobart laughed. "You know, I'm not talking about sex." He smoothed his hair back off his forehead again carefully with his palm. "God knows they're having sex enough with their little pizza-faced boyfriends, groping amateur encounters in the back seats of cars on dark deserted roads. What they're asking, the occasional mature young woman, is an introduction into adulthood. That's what Rosey wanted, and special students after her over the years." He leaned forward again and poked at the air between us with his index finger. "A very few of them, Virginia, over the years. Granted there aren't many girls with potential and maturity, but the problem with education is that we teach the mediocre and I don't see the point in treating students all as a homogeneous class. What I'm talking about, Virginia, is opening minds."

I told him I expected that Page Crawford's daddy would just as soon keep his daughter's mind closed. It made Hobart frown.

"I knew most people wouldn't understand, but I would have expected more from you, Virginia, as the astute observer of human nature that you clearly are — and as a lesbian." He dropped the word in a smooth cool voice that insinuated somehow we had a shared perversion and my body tensed against the arm of the couch.

"Don't you think Rosey told me all about that," Hobart said.

But I wondered what "that" he meant: the crush I'd had ten years before, or the nasty mistake I'd made the previous afternoon. I couldn't decide which revelation I would find the most embarrassing. I wondered if I was embarrassed by the craziness of my actions regarding Rosey or just by the circumstance of his casually calling out my queerness as if it were common knowledge here in the town where my parents lived and were ashamed.

I said, "Queers and pedophiles are two different things, Mr. Hobart. No matter what the New Right has to say about it." But I didn't like the self-righteous quiver I heard in my voice. And I would have preferred a less subjective moral code than the one my middle class queer rhetoric provided me with to separate his sexual minority status from my own.

As it was, Hobart sneered. "Don't even bother to think that I take an interest in your sexual habits any more than you have a right to take an interest in mine. This is about preferences as well — in the case of my students, one for mature company."

I thought what it was really about was sex and power and their linkage. About manipulation and the seductive quality of authority, gentle twisting of a will to please. To be loved. To be special. And the tragedy was Rosalee Paschen had spent her life rolling over for everyone else's manipulations. For her stepfather, and for Hobart and Andre, and for me that afternoon I was trying to forget. "Mr. Hobart," I said, "wouldn't it have been easier just to run an advanced Melville tutorial?"

Hobart shrugged. "People who live in glass houses, Virginia, but you know the rest." Then, he leaned forward in his chair and remarked rather slyly, "Besides, I'm not the one laughing at you." His voice was easy and confidential. "Don't you think Rosalee told me years ago how you watched her so pathetically in those showers after gym class and how she teased you? Did you know that she was laughing, Virginia? At how you wanted her and you weren't even self-aware enough to know it yet." Hobart was grinning, an expression I didn't think I liked much at all.

I said, "You know, why don't we just forget Christmas dinner at my house."

But he kept grinning and whispering gently in a way that gave me goose bumps. "I just thought you'd like to know what went on before you decided who the real victim was, and quite frankly, I don't think either of us is going to make it to Christmas dinner *chez vous.*"

He was still smiling pleasantly, but his voice had

developed a nasty edge. "Please understand, this is not what I would have wanted Virginia. You should have left well enough alone. Rosalee Paschen never did you any favors, but we make our bed and we lie in it, all of us, don't we? No pun intended." Hobart was standing in front of me, rubbing his hands together as he talked.

"So, now we've come down to the end of it. I really thought it had all blown over with Marge, but Rosalee kept calling anonymously, and apparently Marge kept digging until she found some letters Page left for me this past spring."

I thought, good for Marge. Apparently, the more recent letters had been harder for Hobart to explain away, and Marge wasn't buying the picture of a mature man of thirty-seven sleeping with sixteen-year-old girls.

Hobart said, "I tried to tell her, Virginia, the special bond that happens between teacher and student sometimes. The Greeks understood it — and the romantic poets — but it was a concept completely beyond Marge Arkin. We fought and she was threatening divorce and criminal prosecution. That night Marge put some things in her car and said she was leaving. The next day I looked for her at the lake house. She liked it there and I knew that's where she'd go, so I waited and after a while she went out to the lake for a swim to cool off. There was no one around in the middle of the week. I watched her swim out to the middle and then I went in after her."

He paused for a moment and then he reminded me: "I am not an unathletic man. Before I knew what I had done, I was holding her under the water, just holding her down. After a while she was still. I let go of her neck and swam back to shore. A few hours later I called the police and the next day they found her. I do genuinely miss her." Hobart laid his thick palm over his heart. "It was such a waste. Marge was good for me. And Rosalee," Hobart said, and smiled. "I loved Rosalee because she taught me a great deal about teaching."

I told him I thought that was a subject I'd rather not get into.

Hobart was shaking his head again, thoughtfully. "I loved them all and they loved me for the ways I was helping them grow — grow beyond provincial mothers and monstrous families in this deadly little back water town. Don't believe Rosey didn't love me too even if she'd forgotten it. I did a lot for that girl and there was a time when she could appreciate it."

He made a clucking sound with this tongue. "She knew what she owed me then. Let me tell you, therapy can be an extremely dangerous thing, Virginia." He looked almost indignant and his face had gotten very red. "It can make you forget which side your bread has been buttered on. When she wrote after Marge died and said she was coming to the reunion, I imagined it was to thank me for helping her through a monstrous adolescence and out of that awful family of hers. When she came here accusing me of molesting her, I knew who it was who'd put the bug in Marge's ear. Ungrateful bitch. I should have killed her for that right then, but, no, I tried to calm her down. I tried to comfort her but she pushed me away. All she wanted to do was threaten and accuse me over something that happened too long ago even to remember very well. I offered to resign from Blue River. I was planning on leaving town anyway after the term, but it wasn't good enough, she wanted me to confess to molesting my stepdaughter and all these other fantasy crimes of hers, so that I'd never teach again when teaching is the only thing I love. I told her I'd think about it, hoping she'd calm down. But she came back Sunday night as wild as she'd been before. She stood there —" Hobart pointed at a spot on his carpet, "just screaming at me, calling me names and I put my hands on her shoulders to calm her down. 'Don't touch me,' she said, 'nobody has any right to touch me,' swearing at me like a drunken longshoreman, promising to have me put in jail and I just took hold of her neck."

Hobart brought his hands up in a circle by his chest. "Virginia, did I ever tell you I grew up on a farm? When we used to go out to get chickens we wouldn't even think about it. You'd just take hold of them and squeeze with your eyes closed. After a while you didn't even have to look to know when they were dead."

As he talked it seemed as if his voice was coming from someplace outside of his body. But wherever the voice was coming from I felt like I'd been there, someplace she had taken me. Maybe not all the way over the edge, but close enough to look down, to see the fall and the water breaking over the rocks at the bottom.

"In the end it came down to damage control, you understand. Her or me. It came down to her vision of me as some kind of predatory monster opposed to my sense of humanity.

"Afterwards, I held my hands up to my face and

turned them over. They were the same, of course — human hands, but I looked at them for a long time, standing over her with my legs set apart and her body on the floor between them. My hands looked to me as if they belonged to someone else. Someone capable of violence and I hadn't really meant to hurt her — at least not much, but the scarf was twisted around her neck and then it was all knotted up in my hands. She was really the one who had meant to hurt me for something that was, just like her body lying there on the floor by the sofa, so much dirty water under the bridge. The scarf was caught around her neck and I was pulling it and pressing her windpipe with my thumbs. Her eyes were wide and open and her tongue was reaching out from between her teeth as if it were a fat red snail sending its foot from inside its shell and I could smell the cologne rising up from her neck like dark sweet smoke.

"She seemed to drop slowly when I opened my hands as if she were floating and then suddenly there was a dull thud like the sound of a dampened drum when her head hit the floor. The light from the lamp by the couch made a halo shadow of some dark angel around her head and as I looked at my hands, the skin of my knuckles was chapped and cracked from holding on to the wool.

"When I took the scarf away, I could still see the marks it had left around her neck. The friction from the wool scarf had made a ring around her throat like a red choker necklace and there were two thumb marks at the center of her throat coming up into ugly bruises. Her body looked smaller standing where I was, above it, and more fragile, less threatening. The blood vessels in her eyes were broken and the color had drained out of her face but her skin could have still passed for seventeen years old, no lines, no marks except of course at the neck. Her face was smooth and sweet as cream. Her hair was still as blonde as when she was a girl.

"I drew the front curtains and put the scarf in the pocket of her coat, took her hands and pulled her across the carpet towards the front door. The chain of her necklace must have broken then. I could have tried to carry her. I did try, but her body was heavy and awkward like a big sack of potatoes, flopping over my shoulder. Her arms and legs hung limp against my back and I couldn't bear to feel her cool, dead body next to mine. So, I pulled her by the wrists across the entry hall. Then out the front door to her car. The heels of her shoes made a grating sound against the wood and rumpled up the rugs and she shed her hair in a trail out to the porch as she went. Every few feet her head and neck buckled up, then gave, buckled up then gave as I dragged her along. I put it all in the trunk: her body, her coat, her gloves, her purse, her airline ticket, and drove the car out into the woods. I didn't expect anyone would miss her for a week — maybe two, and with any luck no one would find the car until spring. All that was left after that was to vacuum and rest and reflect on her passing over a nice glass of red wine."

"So, what are you going to do now, Mr. Hobart?" I asked him. "What are you going to do with me?"

His glasses had slid down to the end of his nose and he looked over them as if he'd forgotten I was there.

223

"You should let me go." I had stood up and was beginning to work my way towards the door.

"You know I couldn't do that, Ginny, dear. They'd send me to jail." Hobart sighed. "Of course, I'm going to have to kill you. Don't worry, dear. I'm getting better and better at this and if you don't fight me you'll pass out much sooner. It will be over soon really and best for everyone."

I told him I didn't think it was going to be best for me. I thought the best thing for me was to keep Harry Hobart talking. "I won't make it easy for you," I promised. "And anyway, Mr. Hobart, Rosey called Page Crawford to talk about you." I was trying to skirt around him, looking for a clear path outside, but he was still blocking the door and I didn't think I could run fast enough. I didn't want to make him mad. I said, "Page knew Rosey was here on Saturday night. If you kill me you're going to have to kill her too."

"Maybe so." Hobart's voice was quiet and even. He was moving towards me, crowding me away from the door and back towards the wall by the fireplace. "Maybe so," he said, "but I can take care of little Page anytime. I'm really sorry for this, Virginia."

Hobart kept driving me further back into the room, moving just in front of me as if we were dancing politely and when I got to the wall, it didn't take much for him to overpower me even though I kicked and punched him with my fists. I think I caught his shin, but it didn't slow him. He had me up over his shoulder in short order, saying in a voice I remembered my father using when I was a bad little girl, "You can make this easy or you can make this hard, and I like you Virginia so I'm going to give you a little time to think about it." I bumped my head on the door frame as he threw me into the little room.

I landed on my tailbone which throbbed like it was broken and Hobart shut the door to his den softly as he told me, "Soon you'll get tired and that will just make it easier." I couldn't get up for a long time. But when I did I took an inventory of the room.

It was nearly bare except for a metal desk and its chair, olive green, vaguely army-surplus-store-issue. The shiny insides of its drawers were filled with papers and pens, picture wire, hangers and tacks. I rifled the file drawers for something I could use, but nothing except for the picture hangers and wire seemed very useful. In the closet was an ironing board and a small silver iron.

The next thing I did was to scream without interruption.

Hobart was pacing the hall outside and yelling for me to shut up. He was saying, "Be my guest, Virginia, no one is going to hear you." I thought: no one but him. He said, "Just keep on, it will tire you out," and then, "You'd better be quiet, Virginia. If you're quiet this will all go much better for you. If you're not —" Hobart left it like that as if the end of the sentence was something too ugly to say. But I figured the screaming was getting to him. I figured if he was planning to kill me anyway, pissing him off wasn't going to make the end result any different.

I kept screaming and pretty soon the sound of Hobart's footsteps in the hall was replaced by seventies revival music from his stereo turned up way past mellow listening volume. Neil Young seemed to rock the walls. I could barely hear myself but I kept screaming anyway. I was hoping that even out in the middle of nowhere, if the music got loud enough maybe some passerby would call the cops. I kept screaming and Hobart cranked up the volume until I could feel the bass in my teeth and I wasn't screaming words any more. It was just sound. I kept screaming until he gave up and turned off the music. It was quiet for a while except for my screams and the sound of his heavy feet stomping on the wood steps underneath the house. Then all the lights went out.

That was all right because while I'd been screaming, I'd been working too. I heard the sound of a car ignition outside and that was okay too, because by the time Hobart came back I figured I'd be ready for him. I'd wedged the chair back up under the doorknob and beaten the heads of the picture nails into the wall about an inch above the base board, a distance I measured with the knuckle of my thumb. I used the heel of my loafer as a hammer, and thanked God that I'd had the foresight to buy quality. I'd prayed on my hands and knees, crawling along the wall looking for a stud but finding only dry wall, until the nail resisted against my heel. I hammered on it hoping that my screaming would cover the noise until the picture hook was flush against the wall and then I tied the wire around it with a stubborn knot I'd learned at girl scout camp and was surprised not to have forgotten. The picture wire was stretched along in front of the door at ankle height and anchored with another hanger in the stud at the opposite wall.

I had finished by the time the lights went out so the black, windowless room was a seamless comforting dark where I could not see the bruises on my elbows. But my tail bone was a dull disembodied ache and I crouched in the corner with my automatic shut-off iron while my eyes adjusted. When I could make out size and shadow, I propped up the iron in my good arm with my knee and waited.

I don't know how long he'd been gone when I heard his shoes on the wood in the hall again. It sounded to me as if he'd decided my time was up. His footsteps stopped outside the door and I held my breath while he turned the knob very softly to the right and to the left. I could hear him pushing against the door with his hand, then his forearm, but it wouldn't give until he put his shoulder to it. He came through the hollow door with cracking wood and flying splinters and what seemed like all the noise in the world, head down and running. His feet caught on the wire, I could see him flailing and swearing in the dark.

My father always told me if you hit someone you ought to hurt them; otherwise there was no point. Violence wasn't my long suit, but I bashed the iron down on the back of Hobart's head in a spirit of which I thought my dad would approve. I didn't even wait for Hobart to stumble before I followed it up with a two-handed forearm swing to his pretty boy chin. That one was for Rosalee. He was down on all fours and all I can remember was raising and lowering the iron against the back of his head over and over again. I didn't stop swinging until Mr. Hobart wasn't moving anymore.

I've heard there is supposed to be a primal rush of exhilaration after a good fight. But when I crouched down on my hams to check for Hobart's pulse, all I felt was queasy and tired. I had the iron all ready to hit him again if he moved, although I didn't realistically believe that I had another swing left in me. I couldn't find a pulse in his wrist and his head was enough of a mess that I didn't want to touch his neck. So, it was a good thing in my book when Hobart just kept still on the floor of his den.

After I watched his body for a few minutes, I decided he wasn't going anywhere, but I kicked him hard in the kidneys just to make sure, closed the door to the den, and went to throw up in the bathroom down the hall.

When I finished, I called an ambulance and the police from the yellow wall-phone in the kitchen. Hobart's kitchen was at the end of the hall near the front of the house, a large open room with a speckled linoleum floor and formica counters trimmed in nineteen-fifties-style chrome. There was a window above the sink with a red Christmas cactus blooming on the ledge and beside the toaster an open bottle of Chianti with a red rooster in a black circle on the neck. The cord on the wall phone reached from the refrigerator across the room to a door opening out to the side of the house. The floor was still wet from Hobart's shoes, and through the window in the back door I could see his footprints in the light snow on the walk.

The hospital dispatcher didn't have very many questions for me, just Hobart's address and whether I thought he was dead or not. But Officer Kidder of the Blue River Police Department had a curious mind. He told me it might be best if I didn't make any plans to leave Hobart's house for a while and from the sound of his voice I didn't think he was asking me to a tea party. When I hung up from Officer Kidder, I needed a drink.

Both Hobart's Chianti and his kitchen table looked inviting so I filled up a coffee mug and had a seat. My face was in the mug and my free hand was holding my forehead when I felt something damp on the back of my neck. It occurred to me just then that maybe Hobart hadn't gone down as easy as I'd originally thought.

Before I could figure out anything more, Hobart had turned me around and picked me up out of the chair by my neck, holding my throat and squeezing with both hands as if it was his intention that his palms should meet.

Hobart's pretty face had some very nasty bruises, his nose looked broken and his hair was hanging in his face, matted and sticky with drying blood, but the man still commanded a hell of a grip and the more I tried to scream the less wind I could get until my voice was a squeaking gasp. My fists were pounding in a useless pantomime on his chest, and my feet kicked out and twisted looking for the floor. I felt my windpipe start to give and through the tunnel in my field of vision I could see that Harry Hobart was smiling. The harder he squeezed on my neck, it seemed the bigger was Hobart's smile, and the smaller the hole I was watching him through until all I could see was his bloody lips curled back over his teeth like some grisly Cheshire cat. Just as even that was about to disappear, I felt him drop me.

It was the first time in my life I'd ever been happy to be falling. But my legs didn't work and I hit the floor knees first. I broke the rest of my fall with my face. All around me there seemed to be voices. They sounded jumbled and very far away, but little by little I began to recognize them.

When I opened my eyes I realized that Spike McMann was holding my head in her lap. Chianti was all over her shoes, on the floor, the kitchen walls and up my nose. Spike was wiping my cheeks and forehead with the sleeve of her shirt and staring into my face as if she was worried I might not be all right. It changed my mind for good about not liking her looks.

Andre was standing behind her with a sick-looking expression and a broken Chianti bottle in one hand. He helped me to my feet, and I gave him a hug before I dropped my aching carcass onto a kitchen chair. I had to whisper because my voice was still a choked little sputter and my throat hurt, but I smiled at Andy and managed to get out a heartfelt thank you. In repayment for his saving my life, I decided not to have the little talk I was planning to have with Sandra. When I got my voice back I told him so and the rest of the story about Hobart and his little girls. "Thanks again," I said.

"Hey." Andre shrugged. "Don't mention it."

"Don't mention what?" I said. "You saved my life."

"Oh, that." Andre looked down at Hobart's body as if he'd just noticed it. Hobart had a shiner to go with the bumps coming up on the back of his head. I didn't think he'd be charming any under-aged girls with his looks, but his breath was making bubbles in the blood coming out of his nose, and I figured he was going to pull through okay. Andre looked at me and then down at Hobart again. "You know, Spike's the one who did that." Andre bent to survey the damage and his dark complexion had taken on a slightly ashy cast. "Jesus. Did you have to hit him that hard?" Andre turned to Spike, complaining, "I don't know if he's ever going to come around."

I told Andre I wasn't all that sure I cared. "Andre," I said. "He killed Marge, he killed Rosey and he was going to kill me."

Andre said he guessed I had a point, and I could hear the police sirens screaming in the distance, a day late and a dollar short.

"Anyway, so are we friends again?" Andre asked. I thought it was an odd question at first, but when I thought about it a little longer I guessed that's what we had turned out to be in a roundabout way. When he grinned at me I couldn't help but still like Andre. "So, what do you say?" He put out his hand and I let him know for his future reference that Emily Post and my mother had taught me a nice man would never shake a woman's hand unless and until she extended it. "But then again," I said, "you're not a nice man." I hugged him anyway, reaching up to put my arms around his neck. "Yeah, we're friends, I guess." After everything I'd been through, I didn't imagine that Andre's character flaws much mattered anymore and whatever he said about it I wasn't sure Spike could have overpowered Harry Hobart all by herself.

"How did you know to find me here?" I asked.

Andre shrugged again and pointed at Spike who was busy mopping up the floor with a paper towel. I remembered she'd advised me to talk to Hobart after I'd dropped off her Christmas present earlier.

Spike said, "When you didn't show up for dinner, I knew something had to be wrong. I've never known a woman to buy such a nice present to stand me up."

But what I really suspected was she couldn't bear the thought of being stood up for Rosey any more than I could stand the thought of Rosey preferring Hobart to me. "What were you doing looking for me at Spike's?" I asked Andre. "Just so we can have our stories straight for the police."

He said, "At the cemetery I wanted to explain that I'd cleared everything up with Rosey. I'd gone to see her at her motel. I'd just left when you got there. It was an ugly scene, but she wouldn't listen to me. She just kept saying how I'd used her and how she didn't deserve it." Andre rubbed the back of his neck uncomfortably. "I told her what I'd done I was sorry for, but I had a wife and a child on the way and she agreed to let sleeping dogs lie in exchange for a few professional favors."

"Professional favors?"

Andre shrugged, "Referrals and other things."

"What other things?" I wanted to know.

He looked down at the linoleum and whispered, "My firm Richman & Redding does acquisitions. Get it?"

I was starting to. There was a lot of money to be made in knowing who wanted to buy whom and for how much. I said, "So she wanted you to make her rich with trading tips."

"*Res ipsa loquitur.*" Andre managed a weak little smile at the kitchen floor and then he translated since I told him I hadn't had the benefit of a fancy law degree. "The thing speaks for itself." An agreement to trade client confidences was risking disbarment and he had been willing to risk it to keep Rosey quiet. He said, "I guess she thought I owed her something and she ought to make it hurt. Maybe I did owe her. It was all right if everything with my family was taken care of. The next thing I knew you were telling me how *you* were going to tell Sandra. I figured Rosey had to have gone back on our bargain. So, I was looking for her too. I tried to tell you all that after I followed you from Spike's out to the graveyard, but you kneed me in the groin before I could get the story out. By the time I could straighten up again, you were gone. Sandra told me about your thing with Spike so I decided to look for you at her place. I figured if I waited long enough, you'd turn up or she'd lead me to you."

"Why didn't you warn me about Hobart?" I said to Spike. "Did Rosey tell you any of this stuff when she called on the crisis line?"

Spike hesitated.

"She's dead." Saying it out loud gave me the shivers. I told Spike, "No more confidences to keep."

"It's not that," said Spike. "What Rosey told me was about you. It wasn't very pretty and I didn't think you'd appreciate being reminded."

She was right.

"I didn't know about Hobart, all Rosey told me was that her stepfather raped her and she'd spent the rest of her life in and out of unhealthy relationships. When she had sex with you she felt like it was sort of the last straw. She said she wasn't going to take it anymore. And frankly, I told her she shouldn't have to. That was Sunday night, I guess that's when she came over here and confronted Hobart." Spike pointed generally towards the floor with the toe of her shoe. Hobart groaned. He was coming around. Spike kicked him and he went out again.

When the police finally showed up we gave them the PG-rated version without the professional blackmail and the lesbian sex. They seemed to like it well enough to carry Hobart off in handcuffs. But the red-faced Officer Kidder strongly suggested that nobody ought to leave town. That order made Andre all dimples and smiles. "Well, the good news is: I'll be home for Christmas. This whole mess at least kills my closing in New York tomorrow. Every cloud has a silver lining," he said in a way I thought was just plain unseemly.

I didn't know if he was right about the part about the silver lining, but when the police let us go, I made Spike drive me home the long way, past the cemetery, and Rosey's old house, and Emery's place where he lived with his mother before she and Hobart were married. I was looking for pain, the way you pick at the sides of a scab when you know it's going to hurt. Sometimes a little pain can be sweet relief. It's always better than nothing at all. And what I had was less than nothing — a broken heart, empty hands, and not a very good idea of how it had all come to pass.

Rosey had been talking to me but I hadn't been hearing her, in the same way I hadn't heard Emery when he had said five years ago in oblique hints and subtle language that he was dying. I had listened to Rosalee with the hearing aid of my imagination, the same facility with which my father chose to hear me when I told him the facts of my life about my queerness. I couldn't accept the reality of Rosalee as straight and attraction as circumstantial because it obliterated my own elaborate hologram of our future. One future for which I'd rewritten our past.

I wondered if Rosalee Paschen was ever really the person I thought I loved, or if knowing the answer might have helped me to side-step any of this twisted mess — the mean-looking knot I was going to be wearing like a Sunday going-to-church bonnet on the crown of my head, the black eye that I could feel coming up from where I'd broken my fall in the kitchen with the side of my face, the impending interviews with the Blue River Police Department.

All of which made me think there was a serious talk I needed to have with my father before I got too much older. I thought it was probably way overdue.

A few of the publications of
THE NAIAD PRESS, INC.
P.O. Box 10543 • Tallahassee, Florida 32302
Phone (904) 539-5965
Toll-Free Order Number: 1-800-533-1973
Mail orders welcome. Please include 15% postage.

LONG GOODBYES by Nikki Baker. 256 pp. A Virginia Kelly
mystery. 3rd in a series. ISBN 1-56280-042-6 $9.95

FRIENDS AND LOVERS by Jackie Calhoun. 224 pp. Mid-western
Lesbian lives and loves. ISBN 1-56280-041-8   9.95

THE CAT CAME BACK by Hilary Mullins. 208 pp. Highly praised
Lesbian novel. ISBN 1-56280-040-X   9.95

BEHIND CLOSED DOORS by Robbi Sommers. 192 pp. Hot, erotic
short stories. ISBN 1-56280-039-6   9.95

CLAIRE OF THE MOON by Nicole Conn. 192 pp. See the movie —
read the book! ISBN 1-56280-038-8   10.95

SILENT HEART by Claire McNab. 192 pp. Exotic Lesbian
romance. ISBN 1-56280-036-1   9.95

HAPPY ENDINGS by Kate Brandt. 272 pp. Intimate conversations
with Lesbian authors. ISBN 1-56280-050-7   10.95

THE SPY IN QUESTION by Amanda Kyle Williams. 256 pp. 4th
spy novel featuring Lesbian agent Madison McGuire.
ISBN 1-56280-037-X   9.95

SAVING GRACE by Jennifer Fulton. 240 pp. Adventure and
romantic entanglement. ISBN 1-56280-051-5   9.95

THE YEAR SEVEN by Molleen Zanger. 208 pp. Women surviving
in a new world. ISBN 1-56280-034-5   9.95

CURIOUS WINE by Katherine V. Forrest. 176 pp. Tenth
Anniversary Edition. The most popular contemporary Lesbian
love story. ISBN 1-56280-053-1   9.95

CHAUTAUQUA by Catherine Ennis. 192 pp. Exciting, romantic
adventure. ISBN 1-56280-032-9   9.95

A PROPER BURIAL by Pat Welch. 192 pp. Third in the Helen
Black mystery series. ISBN 1-56280-033-7   9.95

SILVERLAKE HEAT: A Novel of Suspense by Carol Schmidt.
240 pp. Rhonda is as hot as Laney's dreams. ISBN 1-56280-031-0   9.95

LOVE, ZENA BETH by Diane Salvatore. 224 pp. The most talked
about lesbian novel of the nineties! ISBN 1-56280-030-2   9.95

A DOORYARD FULL OF FLOWERS by Isabel Miller. 160 pp.
Stories incl. 2 sequels to *Patience and Sarah.*   ISBN 1-56280-029-9   9.95

MURDER BY TRADITION by Katherine V. Forrest. 288 pp. A
Kate Delafield Mystery. 4th in a series.   ISBN 1-56280-002-7   9.95

THE EROTIC NAIAD edited by Katherine V. Forrest & Barbara Grier.
224 pp. Love stories by Naiad Press authors.   ISBN 1-56280-026-4   12.95

DEAD CERTAIN by Claire McNab. 224 pp. 5th Det. Insp. Carol
Ashton mystery.   ISBN 1-56280-027-2   9.95

CRAZY FOR LOVING by Jaye Maiman. 320 pp. 2nd Robin
Miller mystery.   ISBN 1-56280-025-6   9.95

STONEHURST by Barbara Johnson. 176 pp. Passionate regency
romance.   ISBN 1-56280-024-8   9.95

INTRODUCING AMANDA VALENTINE by Rose Beecham.
256 pp. An Amanda Valentine Mystery — 1st in a series.
        ISBN 1-56280-021-3   9.95

UNCERTAIN COMPANIONS by Robbi Sommers. 204 pp.
Steamy, erotic novel.   ISBN 1-56280-017-5   9.95

A TIGER'S HEART by Lauren W. Douglas. 240 pp. Fourth Caitlin
Reece Mystery.   ISBN 1-56280-018-3   9.95

PAPERBACK ROMANCE by Karin Kallmaker. 256 pp. A
delicious romance.   ISBN 1-56280-019-1   9.95

MORTON RIVER VALLEY by Lee Lynch. 304 pp. Lee Lynch at
her best!   ISBN 1-56280-016-7   9.95

THE LAVENDER HOUSE MURDER by Nikki Baker. 224 pp. A
Virginia Kelly Mystery. Second in a series.   ISBN 1-56280-012-4   9.95

PASSION BAY by Jennifer Fulton. 224 pp. Passionate romance,
virgin beaches, tropical skies.   ISBN 1-56280-028-0   9.95

STICKS AND STONES by Jackie Calhoun. 208 pp. Contemporary
lesbian lives and loves.   ISBN 1-56280-020-5   9.95

DELIA IRONFOOT by Jeane Harris. 192 pp. Adventure for Delia
and Beth in the Utah mountains.   ISBN 1-56280-014-0   9.95

UNDER THE SOUTHERN CROSS by Claire McNab. 192 pp.
Romantic nights Down Under.   ISBN 1-56280-011-6   9.95

RIVERFINGER WOMEN by Elana Nachman/Dykewomon.
208 pp. Classic Lesbian/feminist novel.   ISBN 1-56280-013-2   8.95

A CERTAIN DISCONTENT by Cleve Boutell. 240 pp. A unique
coterie of women.   ISBN 1-56280-009-4   9.95

GRASSY FLATS by Penny Hayes. 256 pp. Lesbian romance in
the '30s.   ISBN 1-56280-010-8   9.95

A SINGULAR SPY by Amanda K. Williams. 192 pp. 3rd spy novel
featuring Lesbian agent Madison McGuire.   ISBN 1-56280-008-6   8.95

LODESTAR by Phyllis Horn. 224 pp. Romantic, fast-moving
adventure.   ISBN 0-941483-83-5   8.95

THE BEVERLY MALIBU by Katherine V. Forrest. 288 pp. A
Kate Delafield Mystery. 3rd in a series.   ISBN 0-941483-48-7   9.95

THAT OLD STUDEBAKER by Lee Lynch. 272 pp. Andy's affair
with Regina and her attachment to her beloved car.
                                              ISBN 0-941483-82-7   9.95

PASSION'S LEGACY by Lori Paige. 224 pp. Sarah is swept into
the arms of Augusta Pym in this delightful historical romance.
                                              ISBN 0-941483-81-9   8.95

THE PROVIDENCE FILE by Amanda Kyle Williams. 256 pp.
Second espionage thriller featuring lesbian agent Madison McGuire
                                              ISBN 0-941483-92-4   8.95

I LEFT MY HEART by Jaye Maiman. 320 pp. A Robin Miller
Mystery. First in a series.   ISBN 0-941483-72-X   9.95

THE PRICE OF SALT by Patricia Highsmith (writing as Claire
Morgan). 288 pp. Classic lesbian novel, first issued in 1952 . . .
acknowledged by its author under her own, very famous, name.
                                              ISBN 1-56280-003-5   9.95

SIDE BY SIDE by Isabel Miller. 256 pp. From beloved author of
Patience and Sarah.   ISBN 0-941483-77-0   9.95

SOUTHBOUND by Sheila Ortiz Taylor. 240 pp. Hilarious sequel
to *Faultline*.   ISBN 0-941483-78-9   8.95

STAYING POWER: LONG TERM LESBIAN COUPLES
by Susan E. Johnson. 352 pp. Joys of coupledom.
                                              ISBN 0-941-483-75-4   12.95

SLICK by Camarin Grae. 304 pp. Exotic, erotic adventure.
                                              ISBN 0-941483-74-6   9.95

NINTH LIFE by Lauren Wright Douglas. 256 pp. A Caitlin
Reece mystery. 2nd in a series.   ISBN 0-941483-50-9   8.95

PLAYERS by Robbi Sommers. 192 pp. Sizzling, erotic novel.
                                              ISBN 0-941483-73-8   9.95

MURDER AT RED ROOK RANCH by Dorothy Tell. 224 pp.
First Poppy Dillworth adventure.   ISBN 0-941483-80-0   8.95

LESBIAN SURVIVAL MANUAL by Rhonda Dicksion.
112 pp. Cartoons!   ISBN 0-941483-71-1   8.95

A ROOM FULL OF WOMEN by Elisabeth Nonas. 256 pp.
Contemporary Lesbian lives.   ISBN 0-941483-69-X   9.95

MURDER IS RELATIVE by Karen Saum. 256 pp. The first
Brigid Donovan mystery.   ISBN 0-941483-70-3   8.95

PRIORITIES by Lynda Lyons 288 pp. Science fiction with
a twist.   ISBN 0-941483-66-5   8.95

THEME FOR DIVERSE INSTRUMENTS by Jane Rule. 208 pp. Powerful romantic lesbian stories. ISBN 0-941483-63-0   8.95

LESBIAN QUERIES by Hertz & Ertman. 112 pp. The questions you were too embarrassed to ask. ISBN 0-941483-67-3   8.95

CLUB 12 by Amanda Kyle Williams. 288 pp. Espionage thriller featuring a lesbian agent! ISBN 0-941483-64-9   8.95

DEATH DOWN UNDER by Claire McNab. 240 pp. 3rd Det. Insp. Carol Ashton mystery. ISBN 0-941483-39-8   9.95

MONTANA FEATHERS by Penny Hayes. 256 pp. Vivian and Elizabeth find love in frontier Montana. ISBN 0-941483-61-4   8.95

CHESAPEAKE PROJECT by Phyllis Horn. 304 pp. Jessie & Meredith in perilous adventure. ISBN 0-941483-58-4   8.95

LIFESTYLES by Jackie Calhoun. 224 pp. Contemporary Lesbian lives and loves. ISBN 0-941483-57-6   9.95

VIRAGO by Karen Marie Christa Minns. 208 pp. Darsen has chosen Ginny. ISBN 0-941483-56-8   8.95

WILDERNESS TREK by Dorothy Tell. 192 pp. Six women on vacation learning "new" skills. ISBN 0-941483-60-6   8.95

MURDER BY THE BOOK by Pat Welch. 256 pp. A Helen Black Mystery. First in a series. ISBN 0-941483-59-2   9.95

BERRIGAN by Vicki P. McConnell. 176 pp. Youthful Lesbian — romantic, idealistic Berrigan. ISBN 0-941483-55-X   8.95

LESBIANS IN GERMANY by Lillian Faderman & B. Eriksson. 128 pp. Fiction, poetry, essays. ISBN 0-941483-62-2   8.95

THERE'S SOMETHING I'VE BEEN MEANING TO TELL YOU Ed. by Loralee MacPike. 288 pp. Gay men and lesbians coming out to their children. ISBN 0-941483-44-4   9.95

LIFTING BELLY by Gertrude Stein. Ed. by Rebecca Mark. 104 pp. Erotic poetry. ISBN 0-941483-51-7   8.95

ROSE PENSKI by Roz Perry. 192 pp. Adult lovers in a long-term relationship. ISBN 0-941483-37-1   8.95

AFTER THE FIRE by Jane Rule. 256 pp. Warm, human novel by this incomparable author. ISBN 0-941483-45-2   8.95

SUE SLATE, PRIVATE EYE by Lee Lynch. 176 pp. The gay folk of Peacock Alley are *all cats*. ISBN 0-941483-52-5   8.95

CHRIS by Randy Salem. 224 pp. Golden oldie. Handsome Chris and her adventures. ISBN 0-941483-42-8   8.95

THREE WOMEN by March Hastings. 232 pp. Golden oldie. A triangle among wealthy sophisticates. ISBN 0-941483-43-6   8.95

RICE AND BEANS by Valeria Taylor. 232 pp. Love and romance on poverty row. ISBN 0-941483-41-X   8.95

PLEASURES by Robbi Sommers. 204 pp. Unprecedented
eroticism.   ISBN 0-941483-49-5   8.95

EDGEWISE by Camarin Grae. 372 pp. Spellbinding
adventure.   ISBN 0-941483-19-3   9.95

FATAL REUNION by Claire McNab. 224 pp. 2nd Det. Inspec.
Carol Ashton mystery.   ISBN 0-941483-40-1   8.95

KEEP TO ME STRANGER by Sarah Aldridge. 372 pp. Romance
set in a department store dynasty.   ISBN 0-941483-38-X   9.95

HEARTSCAPE by Sue Gambill. 204 pp. American lesbian in
Portugal.   ISBN 0-941483-33-9   8.95

IN THE BLOOD by Lauren Wright Douglas. 252 pp. Lesbian
science fiction adventure fantasy   ISBN 0-941483-22-3   8.95

THE BEE'S KISS by Shirley Verel. 216 pp. Delicate, delicious
romance.   ISBN 0-941483-36-3   8.95

RAGING MOTHER MOUNTAIN by Pat Emmerson. 264 pp.
Furosa Firechild's adventures in Wonderland. ISBN 0-941483-35-5   8.95

IN EVERY PORT by Karin Kallmaker. 228 pp. Jessica's sexy,
adventuresome travels.   ISBN 0-941483-37-7   9.95

OF LOVE AND GLORY by Evelyn Kennedy. 192 pp. Exciting
WWII romance.   ISBN 0-941483-32-0   8.95

CLICKING STONES by Nancy Tyler Glenn. 288 pp. Love
transcending time.   ISBN 0-941483-31-2   9.95

SURVIVING SISTERS by Gail Pass. 252 pp. Powerful love
story.   ISBN 0-941483-16-9   8.95

SOUTH OF THE LINE by Catherine Ennis. 216 pp. Civil War
adventure.   ISBN 0-941483-29-0   8.95

WOMAN PLUS WOMAN by Dolores Klaich. 300 pp. Supurb
Lesbian overview.   ISBN 0-941483-28-2   9.95

SLOW DANCING AT MISS POLLY'S by Sheila Ortiz Taylor.
96 pp. Lesbian Poetry   ISBN 0-941483-30-4   7.95

DOUBLE DAUGHTER by Vicki P. McConnell. 216 pp. A Nyla
Wade Mystery, third in the series.   ISBN 0-941483-26-6   8.95

HEAVY GILT by Delores Klaich. 192 pp. Lesbian detective/
disappearing homophobes/upper class gay society.

                                            ISBN 0-941483-25-8   8.95

THE FINER GRAIN by Denise Ohio. 216 pp. Brilliant young
college lesbian novel.   ISBN 0-941483-11-8   8.95

THE AMAZON TRAIL by Lee Lynch. 216 pp. Life, travel & lore
of famous lesbian author.   ISBN 0-941483-27-4   8.95

HIGH CONTRAST by Jessie Lattimore. 264 pp. Women of the
Crystal Palace.   ISBN 0-941483-17-7   8.95

THE PEARLS by Shelley Smith. 176 pp. Passion and fun in
the Caribbean sun.   ISBN 0-930044-93-2   7.95

MAGDALENA by Sarah Aldridge. 352 pp. Epic Lesbian novel
set on three continents.   ISBN 0-930044-99-1   8.95

THE BLACK AND WHITE OF IT by Ann Allen Shockley.
144 pp. Short stories.   ISBN 0-930044-96-7   7.95

SAY JESUS AND COME TO ME by Ann Allen Shockley. 288
pp. Contemporary romance.   ISBN 0-930044-98-3   8.95

LOVING HER by Ann Allen Shockley. 192 pp. Romantic love
story.   ISBN 0-930044-97-5   7.95

MURDER AT THE NIGHTWOOD BAR by Katherine V.
Forrest. 240 pp. A Kate Delafield mystery. Second in a series.
                                             ISBN 0-930044-92-4   9.95

ZOE'S BOOK by Gail Pass. 224 pp. Passionate, obsessive love
story.   ISBN 0-930044-95-9   7.95

WINGED DANCER by Camarin Grae. 228 pp. Erotic Lesbian
adventure story.   ISBN 0-930044-88-6   8.95

PAZ by Camarin Grae. 336 pp. Romantic Lesbian adventurer
with the power to change the world.   ISBN 0-930044-89-4   8.95

SOUL SNATCHER by Camarin Grae. 224 pp. A puzzle, an
adventure, a mystery — Lesbian romance.   ISBN 0-930044-90-8   8.95

THE LOVE OF GOOD WOMEN by Isabel Miller. 224 pp.
Long-awaited new novel by the author of the beloved *Patience
and Sarah*.   ISBN 0-930044-81-9   8.95

THE HOUSE AT PELHAM FALLS by Brenda Weathers. 240
pp. Suspenseful Lesbian ghost story.   ISBN 0-930044-79-7   7.95

HOME IN YOUR HANDS by Lee Lynch. 240 pp. More stories
from the author of *Old Dyke Tales*.   ISBN 0-930044-80-0   7.95

SURPLUS by Sylvia Stevenson. 342 pp. A classic early Lesbian
novel.   ISBN 0-930044-78-9   7.95

PEMBROKE PARK by Michelle Martin. 256 pp. Derring-do
and daring romance in Regency England.   ISBN 0-930044-77-0   7.95

THE LONG TRAIL by Penny Hayes. 248 pp. Vivid adventures
of two women in love in the old west.   ISBN 0-930044-76-2   8.95

AN EMERGENCE OF GREEN by Katherine V. Forrest. 288
pp. Powerful novel of sexual discovery.   ISBN 0-930044-69-X   9.95

THE LESBIAN PERIODICALS INDEX edited by Claire
Potter. 432 pp. Author & subject index.   ISBN 0-930044-74-6   29.95

DESERT OF THE HEART by Jane Rule. 224 pp. A classic;
basis for the movie *Desert Hearts*.   ISBN 0-930044-73-8   9.95

SPRING FORWARD/FALL BACK by Sheila Ortiz Taylor.
288 pp. Literary novel of timeless love.   ISBN 0-930044-70-3   7.95

FOR KEEPS by Elisabeth Nonas. 144 pp. Contemporary novel about losing and finding love. ISBN 0-930044-71-1 7.95

TORCHLIGHT TO VALHALLA by Gale Wilhelm. 128 pp. Classic novel by a great Lesbian writer. ISBN 0-930044-68-1 7.95

LESBIAN NUNS: BREAKING SILENCE edited by Rosemary Curb and Nancy Manahan. 432 pp. Unprecedented autobiographies of religious life. ISBN 0-930044-62-2 9.95

THE SWASHBUCKLER by Lee Lynch. 288 pp. Colorful novel set in Greenwich Village in the sixties. ISBN 0-930044-66-5 8.95

MISFORTUNE'S FRIEND by Sarah Aldridge. 320 pp. Historical Lesbian novel set on two continents. ISBN 0-930044-67-3 7.95

SEX VARIANT WOMEN IN LITERATURE by Jeannette Howard Foster. 448 pp. Literary history. ISBN 0-930044-65-7 8.95

A HOT-EYED MODERATE by Jane Rule. 252 pp. Hard-hitting essays on gay life; writing; art. ISBN 0-930044-57-6 7.95

WE TOO ARE DRIFTING by Gale Wilhelm. 128 pp. Timeless Lesbian novel, a masterpiece. ISBN 0-930044-61-4 6.95

AMATEUR CITY by Katherine V. Forrest. 224 pp. A Kate Delafield mystery. First in a series. ISBN 0-930044-55-X 9.95

THE SOPHIE HOROWITZ STORY by Sarah Schulman. 176 pp. Engaging novel of madcap intrigue. ISBN 0-930044-54-1 7.95

THE YOUNG IN ONE ANOTHER'S ARMS by Jane Rule. 224 pp. Classic Jane Rule. ISBN 0-930044-53-3 9.95

OLD DYKE TALES by Lee Lynch. 224 pp. Extraordinary stories of our diverse Lesbian lives. ISBN 0-930044-51-7 8.95

DAUGHTERS OF A CORAL DAWN by Katherine V. Forrest. 240 pp. Novel set in a Lesbian new world. ISBN 0-930044-50-9 9.95

AGAINST THE SEASON by Jane Rule. 224 pp. Luminous, complex novel of interrelationships. ISBN 0-930044-48-7 8.95

LOVERS IN THE PRESENT AFTERNOON by Kathleen Fleming. 288 pp. A novel about recovery and growth. ISBN 0-930044-46-0 8.95

TOOTHPICK HOUSE by Lee Lynch. 264 pp. Love between two Lesbians of different classes. ISBN 0-930044-45-2 7.95

MADAME AURORA by Sarah Aldridge. 256 pp. Historical novel featuring a charismatic "seer." ISBN 0-930044-44-4 7.95

CONTRACT WITH THE WORLD by Jane Rule. 340 pp. Powerful, panoramic novel of gay life. ISBN 0-930044-28-2 9.95

THE NESTING PLACE by Sarah Aldridge. 224 pp. A three-woman triangle — love conquers all! ISBN 0-930044-26-6 7.95

THIS IS NOT FOR YOU by Jane Rule. 284 pp. A letter to a beloved is also an intricate novel. ISBN 0-930044-25-8 8.95

FAULTLINE by Sheila Ortiz Taylor. 140 pp. Warm, funny,
literate story of a startling family.   ISBN 0-930044-24-X   6.95

ANNA'S COUNTRY by Elizabeth Lang. 208 pp. A woman
finds her Lesbian identity.   ISBN 0-930044-19-3   8.95

PRISM by Valerie Taylor. 158 pp. A love affair between two
women in their sixties.   ISBN 0-930044-18-5   6.95

OUTLANDER by Jane Rule. 207 pp. Short stories and essays
by one of our finest writers.   ISBN 0-930044-17-7   8.95

ALL TRUE LOVERS by Sarah Aldridge. 292 pp. Romantic
novel set in the 1930s and 1940s.   ISBN 0-930044-10-X   8.95

CYTHEREA'S BREATH by Sarah Aldridge. 240 pp. Romantic
novel about women's entrance into medicine.
          ISBN 0-930044-02-9   6.95

TOTTIE by Sarah Aldridge. 181 pp. Lesbian romance in the
turmoil of the sixties.   ISBN 0-930044-01-0   6.95

THE LATECOMER by Sarah Aldridge. 107 pp. A delicate love
story.   ISBN 0-930044-00-2   6.95

ODD GIRL OUT by Ann Bannon.   ISBN 0-930044-83-5   5.95
I AM A WOMAN 84-3; WOMEN IN THE SHADOWS 85-1;   each
JOURNEY TO A WOMAN 86-X; BEEBO BRINKER 87-8. Golden
oldies about life in Greenwich Village.

JOURNEY TO FULFILLMENT, A WORLD WITHOUT MEN, and   3.95
RETURN TO LESBOS. All by Valerie Taylor   each

These are just a few of the many Naiad Press titles — we are the oldest and
largest lesbian/feminist publishing company in the world. Please request a
complete catalog. We offer personal service; we encourage and welcome direct
mail orders from individuals who have limited access to bookstores carrying
our publications.